THE COBBLER'S APPRENTICE

LYNETTE REES

B

Boldwood

First published in Great Britain in 2025 by Boldwood Books Ltd.

Copyright © Lynette Rees, 2025

Cover Design by Colin Thomas

Cover Images: Colin Thomas

A CIP catalogue record for this book is available from the British Library.

Paperback ISBN 978-1-80549-021-0

Large Print ISBN 978-1-80549-020-3

Hardback ISBN 978-1-80549-019-7

Ebook ISBN 978-1-80549-022-7

Kindle ISBN 978-1-80549-023-4

Audio CD ISBN 978-1-80549-014-2

MP3 CD ISBN 978-1-80549-015-9

Digital audio download ISBN 978-1-80549-017-3

This book is printed on certified sustainable paper. Boldwood Books is dedicated to putting sustainability at the heart of our business. For more information please visit https://www.boldwoodbooks.com/about-us/sustainability/

Boldwood Books Ltd, 23 Bowerdean Street, London, SW6 3TN

www.boldwoodbooks.com

This book is dedicated to the memory of my paternal grandfather, Myrddin Evans, who was such an inspiration to me. Like Jimmy in this story, he had to work from a young age, and in his case, supported his widowed mother. In later years, he supported me too – with my love of writing. I have a memory of him typing up one of my stories on a child's typewriter to send off to a writing competition, this was when I was around eleven years old. The story didn't place anywhere, but he had faith in me even at that age that I could tell a good story.

I love you, Dad.

1

MERTHYR TYDFIL 1886

Sixteen-year-old Jimmy Corcoran had grown up a lot lately, particularly since securing employment as a cobbler's apprentice for Mr Baxter on the high street. The old man knew his profession well, his intention being to pass all he had learned on to him, and Jimmy was keen to acquire those newfound skills.

Another reason he'd had to mature fast was because Mags needed his support more than ever now that Elgan was serving time at Cardiff Gaol for handling stolen goods. But overall, life was on the up as things were going well between himself and his sweetheart, Enid. He couldn't wait until they were alone together again, which wasn't that often, but when they did get an opportunity, he found he had to cool his ardour and not get carried away. Enid had become very attractive of late; he'd noticed how men's heads turned in her direction, but that didn't bother him. In fact, it made him proud that she was his girl.

Mags summoned Jimmy, shaking him out of his reverie, as he was about to leave the house. 'Do us a favour will you, lad, before you go out?'

Jimmy, who had already put on his jacket and cap, whipped his head around to face her.

'Aye, what is it? I only have a few minutes, though, as I promised I'd get to the shop early to see Mr Baxter this morning.'

Mags sighed, her hands on her hips. 'Won't take you more than two minutes. I've run out of milk, and I wondered if Martha's got some going spare. I don't like to ask her, but she does owe me some as I gave her a jug of it a few days back, and now there's nothing left even for a cup of tea.'

'Oh, I see,' said Jimmy, nodding as he noted that Mags seemed more on her uppers now that Elgan was inside and if the woman owed her a jug of milk anyhow, what was a little drop for a cup of tea? In any case it might give him a chance to see Enid and arrange another catch-up with her. Maybe they could go for a walk by the river after chapel finished on Sunday.

As he approached the Hardcastle house with a cup in his hand for some milk, he noticed Richards the landlord stood outside puffing on a cigar. He appeared to be waiting for someone.

Two men emerged from the property carrying a table between them.

'Hey, what's going on here?' yelled Jimmy. 'Why are you taking their furniture away?'

Richards shook his bowler-hatted head and laughed. 'That's the least of their problems, son!' And then he pushed him out of the way.

Jimmy gritted his teeth. 'You've caused that family no end of bother, taking the key off them and making them buy it back from you for a higher price!'

'Watch your lip, Jimmy. Or you and Mags will be out on your ears as well!'

Out on their ears? 'H... have you evicted the Hardcastles for good then?'

Richards gave a self-satisfied nod. 'I have at that. That father of theirs wasn't coughing up on time.'

'But where will they have gone to? They have nowhere else,' protested Jimmy as fear flooded his veins.

'That's not my problem!' said Richards, taking a key from his pocket and locking the door behind the men.

It was then Jimmy noticed a cart parked some distance away onto which the furniture was being loaded.

Richards turned to Jimmy. 'I'm taking their furniture as part payment for what they owe me. They won't need it where they're headed anyhow!'

'And where's that?'

'The workhouse of course!'

Jimmy stood there in stunned silence as he watched Richards head towards the cart to give the men some orders and then he entered the pub opposite. It was all right for him. While he was swilling ale down his neck like there was no tomorrow, the Hardcastles were suffering in silence.

He rushed back home to tell Mags what had happened, pushing the empty cup into her hands.

'Well, I never,' she said, shaking her head. 'He's gone and finally done what he's threatened to do for months. Arthur Hardcastle will never get over this.'

'How'd you mean?' asked Jimmy, blinking.

'It's a question of pride, you see. The man's already lost his job at the ironworks, now to lose the roof over his family's head too, it's so demoralising for him. Elgan reckons Arthur has a bit of a gambling problem and that's why there are issues with them paying the rent.'

Jimmy hadn't known that. What would become of them all now? He'd miss seeing Enid most days; she'd only been a few footsteps away.

* * *

A couple of weeks later Mags had some news for Jimmy from Betsan who was at the workhouse herself following some family problems as her father could no longer work. Although Mags had been estranged from Betsan's mother for some time, she had been overjoyed one day to discover the girl had come looking for her, but saddened at the same time to hear the news that her only sister, Gwendolyn, had unfortunately passed away. But since then, Mags and Betsan had become close again to one another and, somehow, it did something to heal the hurt of Mags never having made it up with her sister before her death.

Betsan had said that Enid had been boarded out to a big house owned by the Clarkson family, to work as a maid. It seemed the ideal opportunity to kill two birds with one stone. He decided to visit, offering his services as a cobbler, and would request permission to see Enid while he was there. Luck was on his side as Cook at the house had been particularly welcoming towards him. And not only did he get to see Enid, but he also received a pile of the staff's footwear to repair at the same time.

It was good to see Enid again, though of course he couldn't hold her in his arms and kiss her passionately with the staff around, but they both sneaked a quick kiss when Cook and her helpers were at the far end of the kitchen. The pair had decided to keep their relationship going by writing letters to one another and, on Enid's afternoon off, they planned to meet up. So, for the time being, Jimmy was pacified knowing that whatever it took, he and Enid would never be apart.

2

Jimmy was mystified why Enid hadn't replied to his last couple of letters. Mags had tried to reassure him by indicating that maybe letters were withheld from staff at the house, but he doubted it as Enid had told him they'd been encouraged to write and receive letters to keep their spirits up. What was so strange about it was that the last time they'd met one Sunday afternoon, she'd seemed happy at the house; there were no major problems as far as he could tell. He tried to reassure himself that maybe she was too busy to write to him and that he'd receive a letter any day, so when that didn't happen he began to question things, taking matters into his own hands by calling at the Clarkson house and asking to speak with Cook.

Mrs Shrimpton had been busy that morning and the woman's tone had been as if she was wary of being overheard, which alarmed him somewhat, but she had imparted the information that Enid had been dismissed from her duties at the house the Sunday before last over some sort of misunderstanding on the mistress's part. She could tell him no more than that: only that Enid had done no wrong whatsoever and she had no idea where she was now.

The only thing he could do considering this was to call to the Merthyr workhouse, as surely that was where he'd find her?

He was on his way from the marketplace when he spied a familiar face in the crowd. Wasn't that Betsan there, ordering something from the bakery stall? His heart skipped a beat. Maybe she'd know what had happened to Enid. He realised how close the girls had become. They'd encountered one another that night of a dreadful snowstorm when Betsan had run away from home following a row with her stepmother. Martha Hardcastle had kindly taken the girl in, and she'd shared Enid's bed for the night. Surely Betsan would know something, some whisper at the workhouse, maybe?

After jostling his way through the throng, he managed to draw up beside Betsan as she was being handed what looked like a couple of loaves of bread and a jar of pickles. She was still in her workhouse uniform but around her shoulders was draped a cream fringed shawl that was most definitely not regulation issue. As she became aware of someone watching her, she turned suddenly and smiled to see Jimmy standing there, her cheeks flaming as though embarrassed for him to catch her in her workhouse garb.

'Hello, Jimmy,' she said. Then she turned back towards the stall-holder, who was a large middle-aged woman with a gap in her front teeth and a sprout of facial hair on her chin. The woman dropped some small change into Betsan's hand, and they thanked one another. Then Betsan turned her attention towards Jimmy.

'What have you got there?' he asked, his eyes enlarging.

'Oh, just a few provisions for Cook at the workhouse. She's not best pleased because the guardians are having a last-minute meeting today and she doesn't have time to bake for them, so she sent me to the market.'

He nodded. 'I see. May I carry your basket for you? I'm off to the workhouse anyhow.'

She furrowed her brow. 'Really? Why's that?'

'I need to find out what happened to Enid. I've spoken with Cook from Hillside House, and she explained Enid left very abruptly over something that wasn't her fault. Do you know where she is?'

Betsan's face paled, appearing flustered and distracted as she handed the basket to him. 'All I... I know, Jimmy, is that there was some sort of "unfortunate incident" at that place. I don't know what occurred though;

in fact, no one seems to know. I wasn't even allowed to see her before she was transferred to the Cardiff workhouse.'

'So, that's where she is! I should have guessed.' He let out a breath of relief.

Betsan bit on her bottom lip as if maybe she'd slipped up letting that piece of information out. 'I suppose the only ones who might know – apart from the staff, and they aren't giving anything away – are her parents.'

'That's what I was thinking. I might ask if I can speak with her father.'

A shadow fell across Betsan's face, which troubled him. 'You could try that, but it might be a tricky subject for him to speak about...'

'How'd you mean?'

'I've heard he's not been himself since losing his job. And rumour has it he's been getting hold of alcohol inside the workhouse.'

'Oh, that's not good. A bit like Mags when she hit the bottle.'

Betsan nodded as though understanding.

'Still, it can't hurt to ask to see him, can it?' he said, hopefully, but he could tell by the expression on Betsan's face that he might be asking too much of the man.

When they reached the workhouse, Betsan took her basket from Jimmy's grasp, wishing him good luck as the porter opened the gate for her.

* * *

The porter at the Merthyr workhouse entrance wasn't very forthcoming when Jimmy enquired about Mr Hardcastle, causing him to raise his voice to the man. He seemed very evasive and kept questioning him what business did he have being there in the first place. Then Jimmy had an idea. Was this the same porter that Mags had sweetened up to get in to see Betsan when she'd first entered this place? From the description Mags had given him, he guessed it was. The man had a grey bushy moustache and thick sideburns, just as she'd described.

'It was my auntie who told me you'd help me,' Jimmy explained, his tone a little quieter now. 'She said you were most helpful to her...' He was appealing to the man's better nature, and it seemed to be working as his interest was piqued.

'Oh, did she now? And who is your auntie?'

'Mags.'

'Doesn't ring any bells with me, lad.' He rubbed his chin and then folded his arms, placing his hands beneath his armpits, almost as if he was trying to ward off Jimmy in some way.

Jimmy was beginning to think all was lost when the man dropped his hands to his sides and his eyes narrowed. 'What does this auntie of yours look like?'

'Oh, she has long blonde hair and is very attractive. I say she's my auntie, but she's not really. She's been looking after me. She's not as old as what I might have made out. If you met her, you'd not forget her!'

A lustful gleam illuminated the porter's eyes as a little smile danced across his lips. 'Come to think of it... there is one woman of that description that I remember.' Then he lowered his voice to barely a whisper: 'Right tasty bit o' stuff she was an' all.'

'Er, what's that?' asked Jimmy, knowing full well what the man had said but smiling inside at having taken advantage of the situation.

'Nothing of importance, lad,' said the porter, speaking in a normal tone now. 'Just think I know the woman. She wanted me to visit her sometime, but I don't know where she lives...'

Oh dear, this was going to be awkward. Mags had obviously flattered the bloke, but he knew that she wouldn't be disloyal to Elgan. He was just going to have to tell a fib.

'Well, if you get me in to speak to Arthur Hardcastle in the men's wing or bring him out here to me, I'll give you our address.'

The man smiled broadly and, for a moment, Jimmy wondered if he might be married and was looking for a little adventure on the side. That was probably it. He'd got him in an excitable, expectant state, which he felt bad about, but if it got him to speak to Enid's father with a view to finding out more about Enid, where was the harm in that?

'I'll see what I can do then, lad.' The man winked. 'I'll be back in a tick...'

* * *

Jimmy waited expectantly at the gate while the porter strode off towards the main building's entrance arch. It seemed as though he'd been waiting an age and his heart plummeted to see the man was alone when he returned, but he had a grin on his face. What was going on here?

'Arthur Hardcastle has just been summoned from the vegetable allotment, he'll be along here presently. Now about that address you promised me...'

Thinking on his feet, Jimmy said, 'I'll give it to you after I've spoken to Mr Hardcastle and not before, just in case you're thinking of tricking me!'

The porter's face reddened – so much so that the whites of his eyes seemed to be bulging out of his head. Oh dear! He'd really upset the man by the look of it, but at that point, Mr Hardcastle began striding towards them, making it difficult for the porter to demand that address.

Jimmy's mouth gaped open, shocked at Arthur's appearance. Previously, before entering the workhouse, he'd been a well-built man. Now his workhouse uniform seemed to hang from his frame, like an empty coal sack. His skin looked sallow, and his large eyes appeared sunken in their sockets. This didn't look like the same man at all, yet it was evidently him, Arthur Hardcastle, Enid's father.

'What do you want, son?' He scowled when he saw Jimmy standing there, turning to glance over his shoulder as if someone had either followed him or was watching him.

'I, er, wondered where Enid is?'

The man turned back to face Jimmy and narrowed his gaze. 'And why would you need to know that?'

Jimmy was feeling uncomfortable now, the palms of his hands moist, so he wiped them on his trousers – his mouth had dried up so much that his tongue felt as though it was twice its normal size. 'Because Enid was writing to me, and I haven't heard back from my last letter a couple of weeks ago. I'm concerned something might have happened to her.' He decided it was best not to tell her father what he already knew.

Arthur shook his head. 'It's nobody's bleeding business but ours!'

'B... but is it right she's been sent to the Cardiff workhouse, Mr Hardcastle?'

Arthur hesitated before replying. 'Yes, it is. You keep away from her, sonny. She doesn't want to be bothered by the likes of you.'

'Is that what she told you?'

'Yes!' yelled Arthur, appearing exasperated. 'She told me to tell you she no longer wishes to correspond with you!'

What Jimmy felt in that moment was like a sickening blow from someone's fist to his stomach. It was as if all the wind had been taken out of his sails, his insides emptied out.

With tears in his eyes and a large lump in his throat, he could find no words to say. An overwhelming feeling of sadness engulfed his being. For him, this was worse than when Elgan had been put in gaol. At least then, he knew he'd see the man again someday, but now he wondered if he'd ever catch sight of Enid again.

Without another word, Arthur turned and walked away. In the distance, Jimmy could see the porter head towards him again. He was in no mood to be forced to give out Mags's address, so he turned and ran away from the workhouse as fast as his legs could carry him.

* * *

'I don't believe what Enid's father told you was true for a minute, Jimmy!' Mags said, shaking her head.

It had taken some time for him to calm down after his earlier upset and he'd been so out of breath from running, puffing and panting, distressed too, that it was a good couple of minutes before he could relate the tale to the woman.

'You don't?'

'No, I ruddy well don't. That girl was really sweet on you.'

Jimmy nodded. 'I thought that, and I assumed we'd marry someday, but she never said she agreed to any such thing. She wasn't as lovey-dovey towards me as I was towards her.'

'Maybe that's because she's been brought up to respect herself and keep herself for marriage, that sort of thing. It would look bad if she appeared too willing, shall we say?'

He smiled, realising Mags was probably right. 'But if her father lied to me, why would he need to do so? Doesn't he think I'm good enough for his daughter?'

'I wouldn't think that's got anything to do with it. Nothing at all. Something's happened that he doesn't care to discuss with you.'

Sometimes, Jimmy wondered if Mags had an inkling what had happened to Enid at that big house. Betsan, too, he felt had been a little guarded with him, but he didn't want to force the issue. It was clear that Mags had been in discussion with her niece about Enid, but what had been said, he couldn't be sure.

* * *

There seemed nothing for it other than for Jimmy to throw himself into his work. If he were able to get to Cardiff, and could ask Mr Baxter for a sub on his wages for the train fare, what then? Most probably, as he wasn't family, he wouldn't be allowed to see Enid. And even if she was agreeable to a meeting, the workhouse master and matron might not allow him in anyhow. To them, he might appear as a young man with questionable morals.

No, it was better left this way, he figured. If Enid wanted to see him, she had his address and would be capable of writing a letter to him. It was obvious she wanted no further contact like her father had implied.

The following week, Jimmy sat on the bench outside the parish church watching folk milling past, going about their business. He had a bit of spare time before he was due to deliver a pile of footwear to a large house owned by a doctor nearby. He'd been given strict orders to deliver them at two o'clock. Why then, he had absolutely no idea, but he guessed it might be as the staff were busy before then and someone would be more likely to receive both him and the shoes at that time.

He didn't think he could ever work in a big house. It seemed so constraining to him. He loved being on his own cart and being his own master – in a way. Mr Baxter was allocating him more jobs lately as old age took over. The man wasn't as agile as he'd once been, and his eyesight was failing more each day – Jimmy had noticed the way he screwed up his eyes when he worked on a piece of footwear, and he feared the man might end up hitting one of his fingers with that hammer of his. More than once, he'd asked Jimmy to complete stitching a pair of shoes for him as if he hadn't been able to finish them off. Jimmy, though, had been more than willing to comply. It felt to him as though the old man was passing on his skills before it was too late. The Baxters had no children of their own to take over the business, and Jimmy was the nearest thing they had to a son.

Sighing, he returned to the cart where he passed the outdoor market that sold all manner of things from fresh gingerbread to Welsh flannel petticoats and beautifully knitted shawls.

He tutted as there was a delay: a carriage drawing up outside a hotel on the high street near the marketplace. A top-hatted gentleman alighted. The man waited as the carriage driver helped his female companion down from the coach.

Jimmy's heart began to pound. He watched mesmerised as the young lady, smartly dressed in a fancy gown with a matching bonnet, moved to stand beside the gentleman. She glanced up and down the street. There was something familiar about that young woman that he felt so drawn towards her.

No it couldn't be, could it? She looked like Enid – the same heart-shaped face and expressive eyes – but what convinced him most was the beautiful red hair bouncing on her shoulders. Yet how could it be her? Someone from a poor background, who was supposedly interned at a workhouse, couldn't possibly be arriving in a fancy carriage with a gentleman who was obviously of some means. It must be someone who looked like her.

There was no time to stare any further as the man and young woman disappeared inside the hotel and the flow of traffic surged forward.

3

Mags was becoming increasingly concerned about Jimmy and she well understood why; he was missing Enid so much. It didn't help that she'd been sworn to secrecy by Betsan who knew that something bad had gone on at the big house for the girl. The master's son had been improper with her somehow. It seemed that Enid's version of it all was not to be believed by either the mistress of the house or the powers that be at the workhouse, hence she'd been dismissed to the Cardiff one.

It had occurred to Mags that maybe there might even be a pregnancy involved, so that was her reason for not encouraging the lad to run after her to Cardiff. Heck, she could have given him the train fare to get there, but even if she had, she doubted they'd have let him in to see her as he was not a blood relative and probably any liaison with someone of the opposite sex would be forbidden anyhow, quite naturally of course. And if Enid was pregnant, then the master and matron there might assume that the girl had loose morals.

Mags had decided it was time to speak with Martha, the girl's mother who was still interned at the Merthyr workhouse. She'd need to tread carefully of course, say the right thing. But if things were as bad as she feared then maybe it would be best if Jimmy severed all ties, both for the girl's sake and his own.

Mags washed her face and combed her hair, then donning her best shawl – the brown one with the ribbon threaded through it and the cream fringing – she made off for the workhouse to see Betsan. The visit went quite well. Her niece was hopeful that she might be released soon, so Mags had a proposition to put towards her to ask if she'd like to join her sewing petticoats for Mrs O'Connell's stall. The girl had jumped at the chance as she'd acquired a lot of needlework skills while interned there and wanted to follow in her mother's footsteps as a seamstress.

'Do you think there's any chance of me seeing Martha Hardcastle before I leave here?' she asked the girl, then she chewed on her bottom lip as if wondering if she was doing the right thing.

Betsan's eyes enlarged.

Oh dear, had she said the wrong thing? But then her niece smiled. So, she was just surprised, that was all.

'I can always ask the supervisor if you like? I'm sure if I ask Mrs Parry-Jones nicely, she might consent.'

Mags grinned broadly. 'I'm so proud of how well you're doing here, Betsan. You've grown up such a lot these past few months.'

Mags was allowed a few minutes with Martha before the woman had to attend to her workhouse duties. They were both seated on a bench in the exercise yard.

'I know this might be hard for you, Martha...' she said, taking the woman's roughened, calloused hand in her own. 'Enid's your eldest daughter, the one who you were first to carry in your womb, but Jimmy hasn't a clue what's been going on and he misses Enid dreadfully.'

To Mags's horror the woman began to tremble as her eyes filled with tears. Mags took Martha in her arms as she wept violently. Why, she was only a bag of bones since being interned at this place. Was it the poor diet she'd been forced to eat here or was it something else? And that something else pointed to what had happened to Enid.

'It was dreadful for Enid, simply dreadful,' Martha sobbed as Mags dabbed away at the woman's eyes with a handkerchief.

'What was?' Mags asked, looking into Martha's glassy blue eyes.

'It was after she went to work at that Hillside House. We assumed things were ticking along nicely for her. She even came to visit us here one Sunday to tell me and Arthur how well she was doing at the place. She'd turned into a right young woman. Seemed more capable somehow, if you get my drift?'

Mags nodded, understanding all too well, as hadn't the same thing happened to Betsan? Both girls had been forced to grow up so quick after entering this place.

'Anyway, within a couple of weeks, the next thing we knew was, one Sunday, Enid had been given her marching orders and Mrs Parry-Jones gave us some time with her before sending her off to the Cardiff workhouse. It was simply 'orrible our Enid going in that manner, as if she had something to be ashamed of. Me and her father were shocked by it all.'

'And what exactly happened, if you don't mind telling me?' Mags blinked.

Martha suddenly grabbed Mags's hand as if her life depended on it, pressing so hard that Mags was relieved when she finally let go. 'What I'm about to tell you, you mustn't tell Jimmy being as Enid would be so hurt. Do you promise me?'

Martha fixed her gaze on Mags with such a strong stare that Mags found herself nodding, not wanting to let her or Enid down. 'No, I won't. He already knows something happened at the house and your daughter was sent away in disgrace, but he's no idea what that thing was.'

'It was the master's son, you see. Him who is not fit to be called a gentleman!' To Mags's surprise, Martha spat on the ground, her eyes now filled with hatred. Her voice became full of venom as she continued spitting out the words as though spilling poison from her lips. 'He took our Enid by force, against her will. No, she wasn't willing at all,' she said, shaking her head.

As Martha's words sunk in, Mags gasped in horror. 'You mean he...?'

'Raped her? Yes. And by all accounts it was a violent act at that.'

Mags narrowed her gaze. 'But why wasn't she believed? The man should be behind bars!' She was outraged at what she was hearing.

'Because his mother thinks the sun shines out of his backside, that's why! According to Enid, he can do no wrong.'

'But that's preposterous!' Mags glanced around the exercise yard, noticing that a small group of women were watching them now, backs up against the wall. Although she realised they probably couldn't hear anything, the distance they were away, she lowered her voice nevertheless. 'So, the master and matron here, what did they say about it all?'

'They're in cahoots with the Clarkson family, aren't they? Apparently, they make large donations to this place, so they don't want to lose none of that. Oh, they're crafty so-and-sos, that pair are. It's all about the money to them!'

'Yes, I know all about that. When me and Elgan applied to take on Jimmy as a parish orphan, it was a long time until it was agreed. In fact, Elgan had applied before I came on the scene, and they opposed his application. They won't do the likes of you and I any favours, that's for sure. The Clarksons have them in their pockets!'

Martha nodded, knowing that was the truth.

Mags tilted her head to the side in a display of sympathy. 'So, what will become of Enid now?'

Martha brightened, despite her tears. 'She came to visit me with Mr Clarkson senior just last week.'

Mags startled at hearing that. 'But how was that? If they're so against her.'

'I never said he was – he's a good sort. He visited her at the Cardiff workhouse to find out the truth of what occurred and wishes to make amends following his son's violation of our daughter.'

Mags's mouth popped open as realisation hit home. 'It all makes sense now.' She smiled.

'What does?'

'Jimmy claimed he thought he'd seen Enid all dressed up getting out of a fancy carriage on the high street near the marketplace and that she was accompanied by a posh gentleman.'

'Yes, that was her. She stopped over in a hotel.' Martha narrowed her eyes. 'Please don't tell Jimmy. Let him think it was someone who looked like her. It's best he lets her go. Enid feels she's spoiled for marriage now.'

Mags nodded, understanding why Martha would speak that way. 'I won't say anything to him but please don't underestimate our Jimmy. He's a good 'un and Enid means the world to him.'

Martha groaned. 'I know she does but she thinks it best to leave well alone and would be mortified if he were to know she was raped.'

'I understand,' said Mags, letting out a long sigh. 'I'll not go against your daughter's wishes if that's what she wants.'

On the way back home, Mags mulled things over in her mind, feeling sorry for Jimmy, but her biggest sympathy was with the girl. This would probably wreck the rest of her life. Mags, herself, had been loose with her morals having an affair with Elgan when he was married to Thelma, but Enid had done no wrong whatsoever and lost her virginity in such a brutal fashion it might well mar the rest of her days.

4

Jimmy had promised to meet Betsan, so there was no time to waste. He'd left the horse and cart tethered to a post at the back of the Crown Inn. The landlord had an agreement with Elgan that the horse could be left there from time to time and, fair play to Elgan, the man had given him enough business of the ale-drinking kind. So Jimmy made the short way to the meeting place and waited patiently on the bench outside the parish church.

Betsan had left the workhouse, at long last, after Mags had put forward the idea to her that she could help make petticoats and other garments for Mrs O'Connell's market stall. She also helped on the stall occasionally, so now was able to provide for herself.

Jimmy sat with Betsan on the bench, sharing a poke of peppermints as the girl explained that a man called Joshua Arden, from a nearby clothing factory, had spotted her working at Mrs O'Connell's market stall and enquired who had made the garments sold there. After she'd explained that she and her Auntie Mags made them, he'd been highly impressed by the workmanship, particularly Betsan's embroidery. She'd picked up a lot over the years both watching her mam at work and later at the workhouse in the sewing room, when the seamstress had taken her under her wing. Mr Arden had offered her a job at his factory, she explained to Jimmy. She didn't think she looked smart enough to walk across to the nearby premises and introduce herself to him, but he managed to convince her she looked clean and presentable, and so she decided to go there with a view to finding out more about it.

* * *

Jimmy comforted himself with the thought that although he hadn't heard anything from Enid, she did have his address and knew where he lived. But seeing her get out of that carriage escorted by a gentleman had unnerved him somewhat. Who on earth was he to her?

Might she have married him? Surely not! The man looked old enough to be her father or grandfather, even. Yet sometimes much younger women did marry older gentlemen.

But even if that were the case, what would the circumstances be of such a liaison? How could someone of Enid's background become involved with someone of such standing? It made no sense whatsoever.

A feeling of dread washed over him. Often when a young woman from a poor background became involved with a wealthy gentleman – it meant one thing and one thing only – prostitution was involved, and they had appeared to enter a hotel.

Oh, no!

He tried to quash the thought but for some time it dwelt in the dark recesses of his mind. That dirty, murky place that turned his thoughts into a cesspit of swirling supposition.

He decided to talk to Mags about it again before his mind ended up running riot. Being Mags, she thought it highly unlikely it was Enid in the first place, and even if it had been her, she said the girl would never entertain such a thing; she was far too well brought up for that. She had morals and scruples – that was why.

The thought continued to play on Jimmy's mind though and the only way he could get some semblance of normality was to throw himself into his work, ensuring he took on as much as was humanly possible. As well as the work from Mr Baxter, he also sought extra for himself by knocking on the doors of other posh dwellings in the area to offer his delivery service as a cobbler.

Mags began to complain as he was now a night owl, repairing footwear by candlelight, well into the wee small hours. He'd sleep, then rise early again to clean and polish the footwear before setting out to deliver it.

It was one endless cycle of work and short sleep for him, and that's what helped him through his constant longing for Enid.

* * *

Something Jimmy noticed was that the orders for shoe repairs from Hillside House had finally ceased. He wasn't sure if it was because he was making such a good job of repairing the footwear that they didn't need any more repairs for some time or because someone at the house had declared that they should no longer associate with him due to his involvement with Enid. But who and why? The only people he knew for sure who knew the link were the cook and housekeeper. He couldn't for a moment think it was kindly Cook. That housekeeper though seemed a bit toffee-nosed, but even she wouldn't stoop that low, surely? Unless the order had come from way on high from the mistress herself. All the woman would have to do was enquire about any associations with Enid and she'd have found out about him. It was time to move on.

There was another nearby house, not as large as that one, called 'Mountain View'. He'd received a good reception when he'd called there recently touting for work and was told to collect some footwear for repair this afternoon.

There was no lodge keeper at this house either. The gates were wide open, so he rode the cart up the driveway and parked outside the tradesman's entrance, otherwise known as the back door. He smiled when he thought of that. Some of the staff at these big houses were so full of themselves while looking down at him, yet they could only use the tradesman's entrance themselves. They wouldn't be allowed free rein to walk up to the front of the house on a whim. Yet those sorts had their own pecking order. A right plum in their bleedin' gobs! That's what Mags used to tell him when he complained about them.

There was no one like that at Mountain View though, at least none he'd met so far. He dismounted from the cart and tethered the horse to a post while he knocked on the back door. Presently the door swung open and, just in time, he remembered to remove his flat cap as a sign of respect.

He found himself staring into the dark brown eyes of a member of staff he'd not encountered before. Going by the white mob cap on her head, black dress and white frilled long pinafore, she was obviously a maid of sorts. She appeared to be around his age and had a round face with a pretty smile. Her dark hair had been secured beneath her cap, but curly strands had broken out, framing her attractive features.

'Hello?' She smiled and then she tilted her head, waiting for him to introduce himself.

'Hello, miss. I'm Jimmy Corcoran. I called here a few days ago and was promised a pile of footwear to take away to repair...'

She looked unsure at first as she frowned and then her forehead smoothed out and she smiled broadly at him. 'Oh, I see. Mrs Brogan, the housekeeper, did mention it to the staff but I'd forgotten myself as things have been hectic here of late.'

Oh dear. Jimmy hoped they hadn't all forgotten to gather any footwear. 'I can wait if you have something you'd like repairing, Miss er...?'

'Samuel. It's Carmen Samuel.'

'What a pretty name!' He watched as both her cheeks suffused with heat, turning an alluring shade of pink, which made her appear even more attractive. 'And how did you acquire such an exotic name?'

'It's after the opera, you see. Bizet's *Carmen*. The master here loves that opera, and he started calling me by that name as he said he thinks I look Spanish.'

Jimmy thought that seemed a little odd and was about to ask her real name when he had no need to as a voice summoned her.

'Polly, you're needed in the drawing room!'

Polly? That was a far cry from the exotic-sounding Carmen!

'Coming, Mrs Brogan!' the girl answered as though fearful of getting into trouble, and now he felt guilty for delaying her at the door.

Then a middle-aged woman wearing a high-necked navy dress appeared by her side. 'Ah,' she said as she appraised Jimmy and recognition dawned. 'You're the cobbler's apprentice who turned up here a few days ago. But it's not today is it that you said you'd call back here?'

'I'm afraid it is!' Jimmy was puzzled as he thought he'd made the date and time perfectly clear, as after all, he'd been trying to help the woman choose a suitable time.

The housekeeper's hands flew to her face in shock, then she dropped them, displaying the palms in an open gesture as she huffed out a breath of disappointment with herself. 'I'm terribly sorry,' she said, shaking her head, 'I've been so busy sorting things out here as some important visitors are due to arrive soon that it completely slipped my mind. I did tell the staff though a few days ago. Can you wait while I check to see if anyone has anything for repair? I'm sure they will have. I have a couple of work boots myself. Better still, maybe if you returned in a few days?'

Jimmy, wanting to strike while the iron was hot and not return for an unnecessary journey, calmly reassured the woman. 'Look, I have plenty of time today. Maybe I could have a cup of tea and wait a while for you to ask people to bring out their footwear to me.'

She nodded. 'Yes, of course. I'll do so now.' Then she turned towards Polly. 'Take, er, um, sorry, I've forgotten your name?'

'It's Jimmy.' He grinned.

'Take Jimmy into the kitchen and make him a cup of tea.'

All thoughts of Polly being summoned to the drawing room appeared forgotten for the time being. Polly didn't seem to mind either, a smile dancing upon the young girl's lips.

* * *

Jimmy was grateful for the cup of tea Polly placed before him. They were seated at a long pine table at the far end of the kitchen. In the distance were the sounds of the usual clinking of cutlery and clanging of pots and pans as the kitchen staff worked away. Polly didn't seem bothered by any of that; instead, now, the girl was curious about him and not the other way around.

'So, how long have you been working as a cobbler?' She wanted to know as she sat opposite him, elbows on the table, with her chin resting on both fists.

He took a sip of the strong, sweet brew, then laid his bone china teacup down in its saucer with a little rattle. 'Not so long as all that – just a few months. I'm working for Mr Baxter, the cobbler on the high street. Do you know of the shop?'

'Oh, yes. Of course I do. But why are you providing a collection and delivery service? I'm sure a member of staff could just as easily drop them off to you.'

'You're right: they could, and they can. But think about it. Would you like to lug a load of heavy footwear down to the town?'

The girl shrugged. 'I suppose you're right. Don't expect the master would allow any of us to use his precious coach anyhow so we'd either have to walk or catch a cab there.'

'This is more efficient as I can pick up all the footwear at the same time instead of you dropping them off in dribs and drabs. Also, I polish them up to perfection and sometimes dye them, if necessary, before returning them almost as good as new.'

'I suppose that makes sense though I've not heard of any other cobblers in the area providing that sort of service.'

Jimmy shook his head. 'No, they don't. We're the only one to do so as far as I'm aware.'

'How very resourceful of you!' Polly grinned.

She was a nice girl, and he loved the way her eyes sparkled and shone when she got excited by something. They'd been chatting for some time when Mrs Brogan summoned Polly to the drawing room in a stern voice. It was then he realised that for the first time in ages, he'd been distracted by another young woman, and that made him feel guilty for not thinking of Enid. Still, at least his heart seemed to be on the mend.

* * *

Jimmy left the house with eight pairs of working boots belonging to the staff, some refined-looking shoes worn by the mistress, and the master's stout leather walking shoes. He wasn't about to make a fortune here, but orders such as this one kept things ticking nicely along.

When he returned home, he placed the heavy bags in the corner of the room, and then turned to see Mags was waiting for him with his supper on the table, which that evening happened to be beef stew and dumplings.

'My, something smells good,' said Jimmy as he patted his stomach.

'It should fill you up for all of five minutes,' quipped Mags. 'You seem in a good mood today. What's got into you?'

He debated saying anything and then decided to ask her a question first. 'Did you hear any more about Enid when you visited the work-house? Did you get to speak to Martha?'

'I did, but she couldn't tell me much. Only that Enid was sent under a bit of a cloud to Cardiff.'

'Are you sure that's all she said?' Jimmy persisted, feeling as though the woman was keeping something from him.

Mags heaved out a little sigh. 'Yes. It's frustrating I know, Jimmy, but you must accept that Enid has now left your life and you're unlikely to set eyes on her again.'

'That's not true though, is it, Mags? I saw her getting out of that carriage outside a hotel not so long ago. I'm positive it was her. The only thing that puts doubt in my mind is she was all togged up like a lady.'

'Then it can't have been her, can it?' Mags said sharply. 'You just wanted it to be her, so you imagined it was.'

Jimmy had to admit that maybe Mags was right; his thoughts had overtaken him in recent weeks. 'I suppose,' he reluctantly admitted, feeling as though his imagination might have got the better of him.

'Now then, are you going to tell me what put you in a good mood this afternoon?'

Jimmy cocked her a satisfied grin. 'I met a nice young lady when I went to pick up some footwear. She's a maid working at one of those big houses.'

'Ooh la la!' said Mags as she chuckled. 'She's certainly put a spring in your step today!'

He hated to admit it, but she was right. When he thought of Polly, he found any reflections of Enid slipping further and further from his mind, but he didn't know if that was a good thing or not.

'You'll be returning to that house again soon, I take it?'

He nodded. 'For sure, once I've repaired that lot over there!' He pointed to the two large carpet bags he'd brought into the house with him. 'Why do you ask?'

'Because,' said Mags as a little smile danced upon her lips, 'it will be an opportunity for you to speak to the young lady again and maybe she'd consider coming here for tea one afternoon.'

'Aye, maybe.' The truth of it was, though, that Mags's kind invitation reminded him too much of the time he'd invited Enid for tea. The memory wasn't that far away.

'What's the matter, Jimmy?' Mags frowned. 'Have I said something wrong?'

'It's not that. It just feels too recent since the time Enid came here for tea.'

'Aw, I hadn't considered that. It was thoughtless of me. How about you offer to take her somewhere for afternoon tea then?'

'Possibly. I'll think about it.'

'Don't think too long!' shouted Mags as Jimmy headed for the door to lead Casper the horse and the cart to the stable for the night.

5

Mags thought she'd been trying to be helpful in suggesting the young lady come one afternoon for her tea, but now she realised she'd put her blinking foot in it by reminding Jimmy of Enid and it was better the lad forget all about her. There'd been too much water under the bridge to contend with.

It had been a busy day working making petticoats for Mrs O'Connell's market stall and now she was worn out. She'd been back home for all of a couple of hours but Alys and Aled had needed attention too. They'd been attending the school at St David's Church in the town, but they couldn't stop there all day and all evening, now they needed her. Of course, as it was, they still didn't realise she was their mother. They loved her well enough, but she was 'Aunt Mags' to both little darlings still, but she realised the time had to come soon when she told them who she really was.

But when the time would be right to tell them she wasn't completely sure. It didn't feel right for now, not while Elgan was still in prison. After all, he was their father, and they hadn't even met him yet. No, she decided the best time to tell the poor wee mites was when they were all reunited as a family. This past couple of years hadn't been easy but, somehow, she'd got through it all, especially with Jimmy's help. That lad was a godsend in all sorts of ways. Any young woman would be pleased to have him as a husband someday. It was just a shame that it wasn't going to be Enid. Mags realised that it would break Jimmy's heart if he realised she'd been raped while working at Hillside House. It would throw his world upside down. There was no need for him to ever know.

She was as sure as she could be that Enid wouldn't be returning to Merthyr to live. Apparently, according to the girl's mother, she was now about to start work as a maid at another big house, but this time in Cardiff. With any luck Jimmy's and Enid's paths would never cross again and both would get on with their lives.

* * *

When Jimmy next turned up at Mountain View House, he was taken aback to see Polly. Her eyelids were swollen and red-rimmed as if she'd been crying, something that was far removed from the previous cheery persona he'd encountered a few days ago. He wondered if she'd been ticked off by the housekeeper for some misdemeanour or another.

Not feeling he knew her well enough to comment, he just smiled at her and said, 'I've brought the footwear back all polished and repaired!'

She smiled at him, but he could tell it was forced, making him fear that something quite grim had happened to the girl since his last visit.

'I'll just inform Mrs Brogan,' she sniffed.

'Thank you. Please give her this.' He tapped the top pocket of his jacket and then drew out a sealed envelope. 'I have an invoice here signed by Mr Baxter himself for the cost incurred.'

She nodded, took the envelope from his outstretched hand and left him at the half-open door. It didn't look as if he was even going to be offered a cuppa today. Oh well.

Mrs Brogan appeared promptly at the door with the envelope in her hand, looking at him. He wondered if she'd forgotten about his visit this time too but then she said, 'Thank you, Jimmy. If you follow me to my office, I'll sort the payment out for you.'

He nodded appreciatively and then followed her inside. There was now no sign of Polly and a pang of disappointment hit him, but there was no time to dwell on any of that. He had more big houses to deliver to.

He followed the woman down the long corridor, being mindful to walk behind her and not at her side as this was obviously someone who spelled authority. No doubt she wasn't a bad person as such, just someone who liked others to know she was in charge and had probably recently scolded Polly. In any case, it was none of his business.

Mrs Brogan stopped at a door and then she turned the knob, and he followed her inside. Turning to face him, she said, 'Usually, I'd check out any deliveries most thoroughly, but I'm snowed under today as those guests I mentioned to you the other day have arrived and the house is in uproar.' She smiled a smile that lit up her eyes and, for a moment, she almost seemed human.

Then she slit open the envelope using a pearl-handled knife and, glancing at the invoice, laid it out on her desk. After perusing it for a moment, she unlocked a drawer in her desk and pulled out a tin box. She extracted some coins, then turned and then dropped them into his open hand. 'Here we are,' she said, 'two shillings and sixpence, precisely!'

He grinned at the money in his open palm and then placed the coins in the inside pocket of his jacket for safekeeping. More orders like this he could do with. 'Er, thank you, Mrs Brogan.' He paused for a moment. 'Might I have a word with Polly before I leave?'

'This is most irregular!' Mrs Brogan lifted her chin but then smiled. 'But seeing as it's you, I'll send her to the back door. If you wait there, you can hand over the footwear to her. She's not to be delayed too long, mind you!' She wagged an index finger in his direction. At this, he realised the housekeeper wasn't as stern as she appeared. Maybe she hadn't chastised Polly at all.

A few minutes later as Jimmy was waiting at the closed back door, it swung open, and he saw Polly standing there. Her eyelids didn't look as red-rimmed or swollen now. Maybe she'd washed her face. Her mood had lifted too.

'If I might call and collect the bags in a day or so, please? I need them for more deliveries later this week.'

'Yes, that's fine.'

'If you don't mind me asking you, Polly... Was anything wrong when I arrived here?'

'No, why do you ask?' She seemed taken aback by his question.

'You looked as though you'd been crying.'

'Oh no,' she said brusquely, 'I was peeling onions in the kitchen; that was all.'

Why didn't he believe her? Peeling onions might make her eyes red and watery but the girl had looked upset to him.

'That's all right then as I wouldn't want anything to upset that pretty face of yours.'

She looked down now and that faint blush spread over her cheeks again. Then she glanced up and met his gaze. 'Thank you, Jimmy.' She took the two bags and closed the door behind her.

He didn't know whether she was thanking him for the compliment paid or for the shoes.

* * *

Betsan decided to accept the job offered to her by Mr Arden. She'd been impressed with how the clothing factory was run and by how well the Arden brothers treated their workforce. Mags, though, had been complaining a lot since.

'I dunno how I'm going to finish off all of this!' she whined as she sat at the treadle machine. 'I'll be up all night long.'

Jimmy cast his eye over the mountain of petticoats that needed sewing. 'You don't begrudge Betsan the chance to work in the factory though, do you?'

'No, of course not!' She smiled. 'I think it's going to give her a real opportunity. She has a flair for dressmaking and who knows where it may lead. It's just that she was fast and efficient like her mother was. She could work at a much quicker pace than me.'

'Maybe you could do with another assistant?'

She tapped her chin thoughtfully with her finger. 'Now that's an idea. It would need to be someone I trusted though and a hard worker at that.

They're few and far between around these parts – at least the ones I've encountered are.'

Jimmy knew all too well the sort she was referring to: the women who worked at the wash house in China. It was rumoured that in addition to washing clothes the place doubled as some sort of brothel, but Jimmy wasn't altogether certain that was true. Maybe one or two provided extras and some tended to hit the bottle, so they might not be the best of workers. In any case, Mags had a right front calling those women lazy as she'd been like that herself some time ago when she'd hit the bottle. Totally unreliable she'd been back then. Now since encountering her niece again and having her beloved twins back in her life, she was like a different person. And as the saying went, 'A new broom sweeps clean', or as in Mags's case, a new woman!

He'd given her some food for thought though.

She stood and stretched and then, yawning, rubbed her eyes. 'I suppose I better get our tea ready.'

'You have a sit-down, Mags,' Jimmy said gently. 'I can easily knock something up for us and boil the kettle for a cuppa.'

Thankfully, she nodded and, rubbing the small of her back, made her way to the armchair nearest the hearth, which was Elgan's favourite. It didn't seem right without him in it and for a time both himself and Mags had found it hard to sit in it. She slumped down in the armchair and closed her eyes. Then they flicked open again.

'What about that young lady?' she asked.

'The one who got out of that carriage outside the hotel that day?' Jimmy furrowed his brow.

'No, the one at the big house. Did you ask her out for tea?'

'Er, no.'

Mags blinked several times. 'What? Have you changed your mind or something?'

'No, it's not that. I didn't really get the opportunity. The other day when I arrived to deliver the footwear, it looked as though she'd been crying so it didn't seem appropriate.'

'Oh, I see. Why do you think she was upset?'

'I don't know. She made out she'd been peeling onions...'

'And you didn't believe her?'

'Nope.'

'Maybe she was telling the truth. I know whenever I peel those blessed things, my eyes sting like hell!'

Jimmy sighed. 'It wasn't just that; she looked so unhappy when I arrived. I thought at first that the housekeeper might have been on her back, barking orders at her, but I don't think so now. That lady's not as stern as she first appeared to be.'

'Her bark is worse than her bite then, you mean?'

He nodded. 'I think something else upset her.'

'Or someone,' said Mags thoughtfully. 'Look, invite her to tea one afternoon. As I said it's not got to be here if it's painful for you as you brought Enid here the last time.'

'No, I must get on with things. I was speaking with Betsan the other day and she's lost touch with Enid too. It's obvious she wants to sever all connections with Merthyr and any friends she has here. I think it's time to move on.'

Was that his imagination or did Mags look relieved there as she let out a long, slow breath?

'Yes, it's the best thing to do, lad.' She smiled. 'Sometimes it's better to let things lie.'

* * *

Jimmy was presented with the opportunity to invite Polly out for afternoon tea a couple of days later when he turned up at the house to collect his carpet bags. This time the girl seemed more relaxed, which he put down to the visitors having left the house. No doubt, having them there had caused a lot of stress for the staff as there'd be extra cleaning duties, more food to cook and more elaborate menus employed, as well as a whole host of other things to do like ordering extra rations. No, it couldn't have been easy for any of them. From the employers' point of view though, it had all gone without a hitch.

He was pleased to see the girl appeared a lot happier too as she handed him the empty bags.

'I was thinking, Polly...' he began, 'how would you fancy coming out for tea sometime? Maybe on your afternoon or day off from here?'

For a moment, he thought she was about to decline his invitation but then a small smile spread over her lips.

'I'd like that very much, thank you, Jimmy. In fact, I have a free day this month: next Saturday, if you're free too?'

He nodded appreciatively. He did have some work on that day, but it would only be early morning delivering footwear to a couple of houses. 'I'll be free from midday. Shall I pick you up or meet you somewhere?'

'There's a small tea room on Merthyr high street that's just opened called "The Copper Kettle". I could meet you there about one o'clock, if that suits?'

Jimmy nodded eagerly. It did suit indeed as it would give him time to return home and spruce himself up.

'I know the one. It's a date then,' he said, smiling at her.

She glanced up the corridor and then began to close the door. Someone was obviously coming, and she didn't want to be seen chatting to a young man on the doorstep. He well understood that as she had her reputation to think of.

'Saturday, one o'clock...' she whispered as she closed the door on him.

It was silly, he realised, but he felt like doing a little jig, right there on the doorstep. It was a long time since he'd felt so elated – not since before Enid's departure, but life had to go on and, as Mags had told him, he was unlikely to see Enid ever again. And surely, if she had felt anything for him at all, she'd have kept in touch at least by letter.

* * *

Early Saturday afternoon, Mags had chuckled at Jimmy's attempts to get himself ready. He'd even bought himself a new shirt for the occasion but wasn't happy with the jacket he intended wearing. The tweed garment was riding high on the wrists.

'You must have had a growth spurt lately,' Mags said as she watched him appraise his appearance in the full-length wardrobe mirror. 'You've filled out in the shoulder area too. Look, Elgan's not going to need any of his clobber where he is right now, so you're welcome to borrow his best jacket.'

Jimmy didn't need asking twice. He riffled through Elgan's clothing hanging up in the wardrobe until he found the right garment. The jacket with the black astrakhan collar. He removed the tweed one, tossed it on the bed, slipped Elgan's on and then took another look at himself in the mirror, from the front and then side on. He had to admit the jacket wasn't a bad fit at all and made him appear more mature.

'My, my. It does look smart on you, Jimmy lad!' Mags clasped her hands together. 'It'll probably be too big for Elgan to wear anyhow as he's lost a lot of weight since being in prison.'

Jimmy frowned at her. 'I do feel guilty though wearing it while he's inside.'

'Don't be daft! It suits you and he'd want you to wear it. You know he thinks of you as his eldest son, Jimmy, even though we have the twins. He's looking forward to seeing them when he comes home. Oh, it will be great! We'll be a real family at last!'

Knowing how much it all meant to her, he stooped to place a kiss on her cheek. To be fair, both Elgan and Mags had always treated him like a son, and he was grateful for that.

Mags gave the jacket a vigorous brushing down with a clothes brush before Jimmy left the house and he headed off towards the high street with his head held high, whistling a familiar tune he'd heard Elgan sing sometimes, and it was then he realised he hadn't whistled in ever such a long time.

The tea room was a smart building with a fancy façade and double-fronted bay windows, a big black sign bore the words 'The Copper Kettle' in elaborate gold lettering above the entrance. Jimmy watched various folk passing on by. Most he didn't recognise but there were one or two who seemed familiar to him. Probably either regular customers of Elgan's or Mr Baxter. If he did see someone, he knew then they'd hardly recognise him. He seemed to have suddenly sprung up these past few months; his voice had deepened too. He'd become a young man instead of a lad, though Mags still insisted on referring to him as that as a sign of affection.

As he waited, his hands dug deep into his trouser pockets, he heard a church clock chime the hour in the distance, so he was well on time. He wouldn't like to keep a lady waiting – that would be most rude indeed, but as time ticked away, he wondered why Polly hadn't shown. Had something happened meaning she'd been forced to stay on and work at Mountain View House? Or had she decided not to show after all? He didn't even know how long he'd been waiting for until the same church bell chimed on the half hour.

Half an hour was long enough to wait for anyone. He'd given it a decent amount of time and he was just about to head off back home and remove all his clobber when he heard a voice cry out.

'Jimmy! I'm so sorry!'

Rushing towards him in an agitated state was Polly, her face flushed as she appeared out of puff.

He smiled when he saw her and took both her hands in his to steady her. 'Is everything all right, Polly?'

She shook her head. 'No, not exactly, I'll explain when we get inside,' she said, glancing anxiously at the tea room door.

They stepped over the threshold, a little bell tinkling as they entered, and found the only available seats at the back of the room. Thankfully, though, a waitress showed up to take their order almost immediately, so on Polly's agreement Jimmy ordered a pot of tea and a plate of fancies.

'Now tell me,' said Jimmy, 'what on earth happened? You appear to have been rushing to get here?'

She nodded. 'I was ready to leave early as it's a fair walk down the hill to the town but then I was detained by the master, Mr Goodrich...'

Jimmy raised his brow. 'And what did he want? You have the afternoon off.'

He heard a little sigh escape her lips. 'Oh, it's getting right tiresome now. Whenever his wife isn't around and there are no other staff present, he tries to get me into conversation with him. I don't expect he means any harm but it's so tedious. I can't seem to get away from him. It's almost as though he's trying to impress me.'

'He sounds a flamin' nuisance!' Jimmy scowled.

Polly grimaced. 'I suppose he is. Anyhow, he kept me talking and I tried to explain I needed to be elsewhere, but he wouldn't listen. He even offered me a glass of brandy.'

Jimmy's mouth gaped open. 'Was he drinking in the middle of the day, then?'

'Yes, he often does. Obviously, I declined but he kept wittering on and on. I only managed to get away as there was an unexpected caller at the house who wanted to see him.'

'You had a lucky escape there. Tell me though, are you happy at the house, Polly?'

She shook her head as her eyes filled with tears. 'I was before the master started demanding so much of my attention.'

'I must admit I found it strange him naming you "Carmen" like that. It didn't sit right with me. It seems a bit creepy!'

'At first, I thought it a compliment, but he told me whenever people asked my name to tell them it was "Carmen". The rest of the staff kept ribbing me about it, making out I'm his little pet. It felt silly when I first met you, telling you that was my name.'

He smiled. 'Don't worry. It wasn't long before you gave me your real name anyhow.'

The waitress appeared at the table with a silver tray of tea and a cake stand of fancies.

'I think I have a little business proposition for you, which might suit,' said Jimmy hopefully. He waited until the waitress had laid out the pot of tea, crockery and the cake stand on the table, before continuing. 'Can you sew?'

'Yes, I can,' said Polly, smiling now. 'Do you know of any sewing jobs then?'

'Yes, I do. I live with a lady called Mags Hughes who sews garments for a market stall. She needs to employ a new girl since her niece, Betsan, left to work at the Arden Brothers clothing factory.' He bit his lip. 'The only problem is, though, if you leave the big house, where would you live?'

'My parents live in Georgetown. I could move back home there. They'd be pleased to have me as I can help Mam around the house. What would I need to do to get this sewing job?'

'Don't concern yourself about that. We'll enjoy our tea together then I'll take you to meet Mags. You'll need her approval to start work but she's desperate as she's staying up until all hours to sew garments for the stall and she has young twins to care for, too.'

Polly nodded. 'I quite understand.'

* * *

Mags was surprised to see Jimmy turn up at the house with his new young lady in tow. Alys and Aled, seated at the table, both looked up as they arrived, shovelling spoonfuls of stew into their mouths.

'And who do we have here?' asked Mags, knowing very well who Jimmy's companion was.

'This here, is Miss Polly Samuel,' said Jimmy with a flourish of his hand as he introduced her. 'And this lady here is Mags who I told you about, Polly.'

Both nodded and smiled at one another.

Mags immediately liked the look of the young woman she saw before her as she watched her make her way to the table to speak to Aled and Alys, asking them their names. Both smiled at her. Then she returned to stand beside Jimmy.

'I just adore young children!' she enthused.

Mags nodded. 'They're my own but I've only recently been reunited with them,' she whispered, mindful that the twins might overhear. 'They were brought up by my sister, Gwennie, God rest her soul.'

Polly smiled.

Jimmy fixed his gaze on Mags. 'I brought Polly here, Mags, as you're looking for someone to help you with your sewing business, aren't you?'

'Oh yes! So, you can sew then, can you, Polly?'

'I can indeed. My mother sews bits and pieces for us, so I know how to use her sewing machine. I'm not as experienced as her, mind.' She chuckled.

Mags rubbed her chin in contemplation. 'But what I don't understand is how you could work a lot of hours for me if you're working at a big house too?'

Polly smiled tentatively. 'Jimmy and I were discussing the fact I need to leave there. I'm getting too much attention from the master and it's making me feel uneasy.'

'Yes,' added Jimmy. 'Polly was a half hour late turning up as he kept her talking to him and tried to get her to join him in drinking a glass of brandy!'

'*Duw! Duw!* That's not good,' said Mags, shaking her head. 'I know all about the perils of drink and what it can lead to, believe me. I think you are best off out of that house.' Although it seemed obvious to Mags what the master was probably after, she wasn't so sure it was obvious to Jimmy and Polly. Maybe it was because of what had happened recently to Enid that put the thought in her mind. Still, there was no point in putting the girl at risk, so she asked, 'How soon could you start work here?'

Polly smiled broadly. 'As soon as you like, Mrs Hughes. I could return to the house right now and pack my stuff and leave a letter for Mrs Brogan, the housekeeper. I don't want any fuss when I leave nor anyone trying to persuade me to stay. My mind is made up!'

'That's the spirit, gal!' Mags enthused. 'Jimmy, you'd better go back with her just in case there's any trouble. Take the horse and cart. Of course, after this you might not be welcome at the house any longer, lad. So, you can forget any more orders for shoe repairs there.'

Jimmy sighed. 'I hadn't thought of that! But Polly's safety is more important than losing an order at the house.'

Mags smiled. Jimmy had definitely grown up of late and not just in stature either.

6

It all fitted in nicely with Polly working for Mags. Work production doubled and the girl was also able to help from time to time with the twins.

'The best thing you ever did was bring that girl here,' Mags said to Jimmy with a big smile on her face as she bundled up a pile of petticoats and waistcoats ready for Mrs O'Connell's stall.

'Yes, she's most definitely an asset here,' said Jimmy, smiling at the twins who looked the cleanest and tidiest he'd seen them for a long while. They also appeared calmer too. Performing a juggling act of work and being a mother, along with her husband being in prison, had taken its toll on Mags, but now there appeared to be some light at the end of the tunnel at long last.

'Don't get me wrong,' said Mags, 'I miss our Betsan working here but she's got some great things ahead of her. She's now assisting that Bradbury designer fellow. The one who's a right dandy working for the Arden brothers.'

Jimmy quirked an interested eyebrow. 'Don't think I know of him?'

'Oh, believe me, once seen never forgotten. Betsan introduced him to me one day when I called there to see her. You should see the length of his hair, very bohemian indeed!' She chuckled.

Jimmy found it hard to believe that someone as down to earth as Betsan was now knocking around with his sort and for a moment he wondered what Enid would make of that. No matter how many times he'd mentioned Enid to Betsan, she just batted off any questions, as if it was a closed book. In the end, he'd given up asking. In any case, it didn't seem right him dwelling on what Enid was doing now when he had Polly to think of. He was so glad he'd got her away from Mountain View House. She was a vulnerable young lady who was far safer working in China than at that house. It was odd as folk made out that the China district was so dangerous, and in a way it was, as there were lots of fights and even the police hated attending any incidents here, yet the people who lived here were, for the most part, salt-of-the-earth characters who would give even a stranger their last crust of bread. Yet, those rich sorts were the people who kept crusts of bread out of the reach of the poor while they increased their wealth. Life was so cruel. There were the haves and the have-nots, particularly in Merthyr Tydfil.

"Ere, what you thinking of, lad?' Mags's shrill tone broke into his thoughts.

'I was just thinking I'm glad Polly is working here instead of for that toffee-nosed family!'

'Aw, Jimmy, you're right of course but don't go on thinking all rich people are cut from the same cloth.'

'In my experience, most of them are like that – thinking too highly of themselves and lowly of the poor and unfortunates of this town.' He gritted his teeth. 'I know Mr Hopkins from Georgetown who I boarded with wasn't exactly rich, but he wasn't poor either. Maybe the man was bordering on being middle class, but he was a horrible bastard!'

'Jimmy!' Mags glared at him. 'I know you have particular feelings towards that man and rightly so, but you can't tar all well-off people with the same brush.'

'Hmmm, maybe I can. I am sorry for swearing but anyone who has money who tries to take advantage over someone poor, in my book, deserves to be labelled with that particular swear word!'

She nodded now, as if realising he was doing his best to contain his anger. 'So, I take it you're sweet on Polly still?'

He smiled as his earlier anger began to ebb away. 'Yes, of course. Do you think she likes me as much?'

'I would say so, yes. Particularly as she talks about you an awful lot and praises you up. I think she sees you as her knight in shining armour!'

Jimmy laughed. 'I wouldn't go that far, maybe her rusty old tin can!' he quipped. 'Sorry you mentioned something about Betsan helping that Bradbury fellow earlier. What were you telling me about that? I don't think you'd finished?'

'Betsan told me that he'd viewed some of her sketches and had been listening to her ideas, which he'd tried to incorporate into some garments. I think I've got this right that she's somehow assisting him these days.'

'That sounds great, but I hope she's getting the recognition for her work and he's not taking all the credit for it.'

'Oh, I think they're all pleased with her work at the factory. She has her mother's talent for sure,' said Mags, a twinkle in her eyes.

Jimmy wished he'd got to meet Gwendolyn as so many people spoke highly of the woman and Betsan seemed like a chip off the old block.

* * *

It was a few weeks later that Mags noticed there was something wrong with Polly. The girl seemed to have trouble arriving on time to begin work. When she was twenty minutes late arriving that morning, Mags realised she had to say something as they had a big order to complete. Mrs O'Connell had told her that some toff had arrived at the stall and put in an order for several girls' dresses, petticoats and underwear, along with some boys' waistcoats and britches. Mags hadn't asked any questions at the time but she did think it odd that so many were required of around the same sizes, then she heard that someone in the area was setting up a school for disadvantaged children. Some posh lady with too much time on her hands, no doubt. But to give the woman credit, she was trying to help the poor, which was a far cry from what Jimmy had recently spoken of.

'Polly!' Mags said, looking up from the sewing machine. 'I've kept quiet up until now with your constant late arrivals this past week or so, but this takes the flamin' biscuit today – you're twenty minutes late, *cariad*. Is something wrong?'

She rose from the chair to approach the girl and then, to her horror, Polly's face creased, and she burst into tears.

'There, there,' said Mags gently as she took the girl into her arms. 'Perhaps if you tell me what it is, I can help sort it out for you. Is it trouble at home? Is that it?'

'No! I only wish it was!' Polly wailed, trembling as she sobbed in Mags's arms.

Mags held her at arm's length for a moment, peering into her eyes. 'Then tell me what it is. Look, take a seat near the fire.' She gently guided the girl to Elgan's armchair and made her sit. 'I'll fetch you a cup of tea; there's one still in the pot as I just had one.' Quickly, she poured the tea into a cup, added a splash of milk and a spoonful of sugar, then handed the cup and saucer to Polly. Taking a seat on a nearby stool, she said, 'That'll make you feel better.'

Gratefully, Polly sipped the tea and then looked at Mags through glassy eyes. 'I... think I'm p... pregnant!' she said, and then her face creased again as she began to sob.

Mags took the cup from her hand in case she tipped it and set it down in the fireplace, then returned to the stool. She allowed the girl to cry some more before handing her a handkerchief. 'Here, wipe your eyes and blow your nose. A good cry will make you feel better, my girl.'

Polly did as told and then she picked up her cup and finished her tea before speaking. 'That's why I've been late most mornings; I have very bad sickness.'

'So, you know for sure you're pregnant then? You wait until I have a word with Jimmy when he gets back here!'

'No!' Polly said firmly. 'Jimmy mustn't hear of this.'

'But he has to; after all he must be the father.'

Polly shook her head.

'You mean it's someone else's baby?'

'Yes.'

Mags's mouth gaped open and then she snapped it shut. 'But if it's not

Jimmy's baby, whose baby can it be? You mean to tell me you've been knocking around with some other lad since you've been seeing him?'

'Oh no! I love Jimmy!'

'I don't understand,' said Mags, feeling perplexed now. This just wasn't making any sense whatsoever.

'It's Mr Goodrich's baby I'm carrying. When I said he was often delaying me, I meant he kept getting affectionate and trying to kiss me and things so that's why I'm having his baby.'

Mags understood all too well what that 'and things' meant. In some ways Polly was quite a naïve young woman, not as aware as Betsan or even Enid might be. 'Look, you'll have to tell me in detail what's gone on as you don't seem to know.'

After a little more conversation, it became evident that Polly could not possibly be pregnant from what occurred at the big house; that was if she was telling the truth. The kiss she spoke of was only on the cheek and the 'and things' was him grabbing hold of her and sometimes tickling her. Not completely innocent but not what Polly had implied either.

'Hasn't your mother ever told you about the facts of life, Polly?' Mags asked.

Polly looked at her blankly before shaking her head. 'My parents are very chapel-going sorts and everything is viewed as a sin. I'm too scared to ask such questions.'

Mags smiled sympathetically. 'You can ask me anything. I can't say I have all the answers as I've made a right mess of my own life, but things are sorting out nicely now. Have your courses begun yet?'

Polly tilted her head to one side, frowning. 'Courses? What are they?'

'Your monthly bleeds?'

'Oh? So that's what's been happening to me. I thought I was having pains from being pregnant and I was losing the baby.'

Mags thought briefly what a daft young mare Polly was to have no understanding of how babies were made, but then again, if her mother kept her in the dark, why should she know? Maybe even the maids at the big house didn't discuss such matters.

Mags sat with her a while longer before filling her in on what happened when a young girl had her monthly and how she might become pregnant if she wasn't careful enough to hang on to her virtue. She felt it important to stress everything to the girl just in case she and Jimmy ever became intimate with one another. When satisfied the girl understood what was happening to her body, she said kindly, 'Now, what I think has happened is that you've been feeling unwell due to your first monthly arriving. You're a little later in age than many young girls having your first but we're all different. You need to watch out for your next one and make sure you have plenty of clean rags to line your underwear. But you must be careful that you and Jimmy don't get carried away if you don't wish to become pregnant. And from what you've told me about your parents, they'll be furious with you if you do.'

Polly shook her head. 'But me and Jimmy, we're just like friends, Mrs Hughes. He's never even kissed me on the mouth.'

Mags blinked. In her mind, she'd assumed Jimmy had the same sort of relationship with Polly as he'd had with Enid. How wrong could she be? It was patently obvious now that although the pair spent a lot of time in one another's company, they had taken their relationship no further.

Enid had obviously taken Jimmy's heart with her when she left Merthyr. The question was when would it ever return to him?

7

Betsan explained to her Aunt Mags that Francis Bradbury had been working in Paris for none other than the designer Charles Worth. The Arden brothers would be opening several stores throughout South Wales, the flagship store being in Merthyr, and that soon there would be a fashion show, demonstrating his designs. Betsan would be there of course on both the opening day and for the show as a lot of her work was involved in it.

'Just think, Jimmy,' said Mags with mounting excitement, 'our Betsan is going to be famous someday!'

Jimmy huffed out a breath. 'I flippin' doubt it! What chance does a young girl from Merthyr have of being a famous designer when you've got people like that Bradbury bloke poncing around the place? Thinks he's a cut above, he does!' He sniffed loudly.

'Jimmy Corcoran, I swear you're jealous,' said Mags as she poked him in the chest with her index finger.

He realised deep down that Mags was on to something. He'd always liked Betsan and if he and Enid hadn't been an item at the time, he might have asked the girl out, but these days she seemed under the spell of that Bradbury bloke.

'It's not that.' He sighed softly. 'Well, in a way it is. I just feel like I'm losing Betsan, and she feels like my last connection to Enid.'

Mags shook her head sadly. 'Haven't you got that girl out of your mind yet?'

'Nope. And I don't know that I want to.'

'What about Polly though? I hope you're not stringing her along?'

He held up his palms in defence. 'There's nothing really going on between us. I had thought, when I first met her, we might be sweethearts by now, but to tell you the truth, she's awfully naïve. Doesn't have much nous or anything.'

Mags nodded in understanding. 'I have to agree with you there.'

Why was Mags saying that though? 'You agree?'

'Yes, I won't go into details here but a while ago she didn't even know how babies are made. She's been cushioned from real life. I hate to say it, but she's not the girl for you, lad.'

'I know and I agree, but she'll always be my friend and I like looking out for her.'

'Nothing wrong in that at all. But why do you think you're losing Betsan?'

'Nothing I can pinpoint as such; it's just that she seems so ambitious lately.'

'Is that a bad thing though? She's had it tough with her mother dying and her father still being interned at the workhouse. Maybe throwing herself into her work will turn out to be a good thing?'

'I'm sure you're right. Have you heard any more about her father lately?'

'Only that there's no sign of him being released from the workhouse any time soon. Betsan keeps enquiring but the workhouse doctor says it's best he stays in until his memory is fully recovered. I know I haven't thought that much of his new wife, Elinor, in the past but I feel so sorry for her being pregnant and all, and him acting as though she were a total stranger when he lost his memory after that blow to the head. Though Betsan has said there's been improvement there lately, his memory slowly returning.'

Jimmy remembered that incident where David Morgan had been

injured all too well. Working at the Star Inn as a barman had meant the man encountered all sorts of ruffians. 'Must be hard.' He shrugged, realising that maybe he was being a little unfair to Betsan, and he vowed to try to see her sometime soon.

* * *

The following day, Jimmy called to the shop to see Mr Baxter as he needed more supplies, but there was no sign of anyone in the shop at all. That was odd. The door still had the closed sign on it. Usually it was open by eight thirty on a weekday morning. He rattled the door in case the old man had forgotten to change the sign to 'open', but it was firmly locked.

He rapped on the knocker but there was no reply, so he peered through the window, cupping his hands together to see if there was any sign of life within. He mulled it over in his head for a moment.

Now when did I last see him? It's Tuesday today and I didn't call here yesterday as I was busy on my rounds... The weekend I had no need to call. Was it last Friday or Thursday when I spoke to him? No, it couldn't have been Friday as that day I had a lot of work on. No, it was definitely last Thursday as I called in for some more tacks for the shoes. That means I haven't seen him for five whole days! Has something happened since then?

He was about to turn around and go back home with a view to returning later when he heard a clicking in the door like the sound of someone turning a key in a lock and then the door partially opened. But it wasn't Mr Baxter standing there, but his wife.

Jimmy was shocked by the woman's appearance. Her face looked a deadly shade of puce and her grey hair, which was usually pinned back neatly, had escaped its hairpins and was falling into her face. Her rheumy blue eyes were brimming with unshed tears.

'Jimmy...' was all she said, and he knew something was up. Her very appearance told him so before she even uttered a word. She was still in her nightgown with an old woollen shawl draped around her shoulders, a sorry-looking figure indeed.

'What's up, Mrs Baxter?' He blinked as his heart pumped profusely, causing a faint thudding noise in his ears.

'It's Josiah...' she inclined her head '...he was taken ill yesterday and is confined to bed.'

'Have you got the doctor out to him?' Jimmy asked with some alarm.

Nodding, the woman looked up at him and swallowed hard before speaking almost as though she were forcing herself to keep the tears at bay. He realised how close the couple were to one another.

'And what did he say?'

'That he's too old to be cobbling shoes. His eyesight is failing anyhow and that's why you've had to do so much lately and we're both very grateful for that. But it's more than his eyesight; he's just plain worn out.'

Jimmy realised the old man was a good age now, though he had no idea how old exactly. He reckoned he was around eighty. The doctor was right though; maybe he needed to rest more.

'Is there anything I can do to help?' he asked.

The woman nodded. 'Just carry on with what you're doing and maybe if you could open the shop just mornings during the week and make your collection and deliveries in the afternoons? That would be a great help to us.'

He nodded and smiled at her. 'Of course. May I go up and see him?'

She waved a hand. 'Not right now, Jimmy. He's just gone to sleep but if you wait until this afternoon when he wakes, I'll send you up to see him. I'm sure he'll be pleased to know the shop is in such good hands.'

Jimmy hesitated for a moment. 'Would you like me to come in and open the shop now for you, Mrs Baxter? I'm sure customers must be turning away when they find out it's shut. I could then leave a sign up when I leave this afternoon to say it will be open again in the morning?'

'Yes, that would be so good of you.' She drew the door open wide to allow him access inside.

As he stepped over the threshold, he inhaled the familiar smell of leather and glue. It was an odour he felt comfortable around. In the corner of the room was a shoe last with an upturned leather boot on it. It looked as though maybe Mr Baxter had been in the middle of repairing it before he was taken ill, as on the counter beside it were some scattered tacks and a hammer. The shop seemed sad without Mr Baxter in it. He was so used to seeing the man in his leather apron, shirtsleeves rolled up to the elbows, either hunched over that last or stood at the counter handing over footwear, freshly repaired and polished, to happy and loyal customers.

'I called this morning for more supplies to mend a pile of footwear, but I suppose I could bring them over here now instead and repair them on the premises. I'll stay here for the time being in case any customers show up, and I'll collect the footwear later when it's quiet. How's that suit?'

Mrs Baxter smiled and nodded approvingly. 'Thank you, Jimmy.'

'Now, you look like you need a bit of kip yourself, so go back to bed for an hour while Mr Baxter is in the land of nod.'

'Aye, I think I will; I've been up half the night as Josiah has been so restless.'

He watched the woman leave the workshop area and head towards the Baxters' living quarters. The best thing for both of them now was that they should rest and recuperate.

* * *

Business was steady that morning as customers called to either collect footwear or drop them off for repair. Mr Baxter had a red hard-backed ledger in which he scribbled orders, which made it easier for Jimmy to locate the footwear they were seeking. He also tied labels to pairs saying things like 'Work boots, steel toecaps and segs added – D.G. Giles Croft house farm' or 'Ladies' leather shoes, soled and heeled – Mrs Griffiths, Nightingale Street, Abercanaid'. The labels corresponded with the entries in his ledger, so Jimmy had no problem locating them. The only problem he had was that he wasn't entirely sure of the exact prices to charge customers, but he didn't want to bother Mrs Baxter as she was getting some very hard-earned rest, so he looked at previous entries in the ledger. He had no idea if the man was still charging the same as he did a few months ago or whether it varied on the type of soles employed but it would have to do for now. No customer had complained of the prices yet, so he guessed he must be on the right track, though he hoped he was charging enough.

It was a good three and a half hours later when Mrs Baxter rose from her bed, and now she looked fresh. There was a little sparkle back in her eyes. She was dressed in a smart day dress covered with a white starched pinafore and her hair was neatly pinned in place.

'Thank you so much, Jimmy,' she enthused. 'That rest did me the power of good. I don't know what we'd do without you.'

Smiling, he enquired, 'How is Mr Baxter?'

'He's awake now and rested. I'm just going to warm up a bowl of cawl for him and take it up with a nice piece of bread and then when he's eaten, you can go up to see him. He's relieved you've called in here this morning and to hear that you're now going to open the shop every day. How did you manage with your own repairs? Were you able to complete them while you looked after the shop?'

'Some of them, yes.' He huffed out a breath. 'I was able to pop back home and get them while I had a quiet five minutes, but I still have some to complete, which I'll do at home later. I wasn't too sure though about the prices to charge customers. Mr Baxter usually works it all out for the big houses when I take an invoice there. I had to work out rough prices going by what he charges recorded in the ledger.'

'That's fine, Jimmy. You can take a pencil and paper and ask him later for advice.'

He nodded eagerly.

'Would you like a bowl of cawl, too?' Mrs Baxter's blue eyes shone with kindness.

His stomach had been growling for the past hour or so, so he was more than happy to accept and, quite soon, the most delicious aroma of lamb and onions wafted towards him from the Baxters' living quarters.

Later when he'd eaten, with Mrs Baxter's permission he climbed the stairs to pay a visit to her husband, gently tapping on the bedroom door before entering.

He was pleased to see the old man seemed alert and was sitting up in bed wearing a nightgown, well propped up with pillows. He smiled broadly at Jimmy.

'Don't stand on ceremony, lad! Come over and take a seat.' There was an old wooden chair by the side of the bed so, tentatively, Jimmy sat, unsure what to say for a moment. After an awkward pause, he found his voice. 'How are you feeling today, Mr Baxter?'

'Oh, I'm fine. My wife is fussing around after me, but I'll be right as rain in a few days if I rest up. I'm glad you've called to see me as I have a proposition to put towards you.'

'Oh,' said Jimmy, straightening in his chair. He hadn't been expecting this as, after all, it was only recently that he himself had put a proposition to the old man.

'Yes,' said Mr Baxter, lowering his voice as though not wishing to be overheard by his wife. Though why, Jimmy had no idea, as the woman was still busy pottering around in the kitchen, washing dishes and tidying up.

Jimmy shuffled in his chair so that he was closer to the man to hear what he wanted to say. 'Please go ahead, Mr Baxter; I'm all ears.'

A wistful expression came over the man's face. 'I'm not getting any younger and the doctor has told me I should be resting up more. My eyesight isn't what it was either and lately I've been having problems with intricate work, sewing and gluing, that sort of thing. There was a time when I could work quite easily in the shop from dawn till dusk. I was no stranger to hard work. Indeed, even as a young boy I'd help one of the stallholders at the local market, particularly after my mother was widowed so young...'

Jimmy furrowed his brow, wondering where all this was going. He was beginning to feel a little frustrated as there was footwear that needed delivering to some of the big houses this afternoon and, as he'd been covering at the shop, he was also a little behind on his shoe repairs. Not wanting to stop the man in his tracks though, out of respect, he let him whittle on for a while and then, quite out of the blue, Mr Baxter said what needed to be said.

'You see, son – well, I think of you like a son – when me and the missus pass away, we'd like to leave this shop and shoe business to someone. We have no children of our own or other living descendants, so we'd like to leave it to you after our days.'

Jimmy gulped. He honestly hadn't been expecting that. 'I... I don't know what to say, Mr Baxter. It's a very kind and generous offer but I don't feel ready to run a shop on my own yet; I'm only learning the trade.'

'And you shall learn the trade, every aspect of it,' said Mr Baxter, straightening in the bed. After saying all that, the old man seemed more alert, his eyes shining with enthusiasm. 'My plan is for you to start running the shop now under my guidance and when I'm satisfied all is going well, I'll make you the manager here and you'll be able to take on your own cobbler's apprentice someday yourself. Then when I pass away, if I go before Mrs Baxter, God willing, she'll receive a modest income from this place and be allowed to still live here if she so wishes. Then after her days, all will be yours – the shop itself, the business and all the accommodation that goes with it. What do you say?'

Jimmy opened his mouth, but no words came out. It was hard for him to speak due to the shock of it all. It was some time before he was able to process what the old man had said. 'That's very kind of you, Mr Baxter, but does your wife know of this plan?'

The old man nodded eagerly. 'Yes, indeed she does. She's more than happy for the shop to pass to you after our days. Now what do you say? Are you in agreement?'

A big smile broke out on Jimmy's face and before he knew it, he was shaking the man's hand and thanking him.

'Now that's settled then,' said Mr Baxter. 'That's a load off my mind and as soon as I'm well enough, me and Mrs Baxter will see a solicitor to get a will drawn up where you are the sole beneficiary after our days.'

In amongst all the melee, Jimmy had forgotten about the piece of paper and pencil Mrs Baxter had told him to bring with him.

'Before that,' Jimmy said, 'I need to know more about the prices you charge for repairs. I've some idea, of course, and referred to your ledger to charge customers this morning, but I want to double-check with you in case you've increased any of the prices of late?'

'That's what I like about you, Jimmy, you always use a bit of nous.' Mr Baxter chuckled heartily.

Whatever was ailing him right now, the chat they'd just had seemed to have done him the power of good by easing his mind, and for that Jimmy was most grateful.

* * *

Over the following weeks, Jimmy began to step into Mr Baxter's shoes and although he found it hard going at times, somehow he managed to take on the lion's share of the work, under the man's watchful gaze. It was reassuring having him around. Even if he was in the back room resting, Jimmy could pop in and ask him a question. It was several weeks later before Mr Baxter told him the time had come for him to take on an apprentice of his own. There was a twelve-year-old boy called Harri Howells who called into the shop with his mother now and again who often liked to stay and watch him at work. Harri reminded Jimmy of himself at that age and so the lad was asked how he would like some work.

Harri's duties were mainly helping to fetch and carry items Jimmy needed, sometimes accepting orders across the counter and even receiving money for repairs. Jimmy put a lot of trust into Harri. He thought maybe he was a little too young to go out on the cart on his own yet to drum up business at the big houses as he himself had done. But maybe in a year or so, that might happen.

All appeared to be going well in Jimmy's life, until one afternoon the shop bell tinkled, and the door forcibly swung open, banging against the wall, startling him. He glanced up from where he'd been repairing a boot on the last. Harri had been sent out on an errand, so he was all alone. He'd just finished tapping in a few tacks into the leather-soled boot so was expecting it to be either a customer turning up to pick up a pair of shoes or drop them off.

The man glaring at him had such dark, menacing eyes, seeming to penetrate his soul, that he shivered momentarily.

'C... can I help you?' Jimmy asked.

The man standing before him wore a scruffy old jacket that had seen better days, a flat cap and a muffler around his neck. He wasn't anyone Jimmy recognised as a previous customer and his air of intimidation unnerved him somewhat.

'Maybe you can at that...' he said, stepping forward as he loomed over Jimmy in a threatening manner, smelling of alcohol with a faint whiff of tobacco. 'Grab all the money out of that till and hand it over to me now!'

'W... what?'

'You heard me!' he yelled as his eyes grew large.

'I can't do that. It's not my money, mister, it belongs to Mr Baxter.' His teeth were chattering now, he was that frightened of the man.

'You'll do as I say. That money is my inheritance!'

Puzzled, Jimmy got up from the stool and stood his ground. 'I think you've made a mistake.'

'No mistake at all! Josiah Baxter is my father!'

Jimmy's mouth gaped open. This wasn't making any sense at all. Hadn't Mr Baxter told him that he and his wife had no children? And that's why all their worldly goods would eventually be left to him?

Jimmy wasn't quite sure how to handle the situation. Mrs Baxter was out shopping in the marketplace while Mr Baxter was resting in his living quarters. What should he do? Taking a step forward he said, 'I'm sure you must be mistaken. Mr and Mrs Baxter have no children and never have.'

The man shot him a salacious grin. 'She doesn't but the old fella does!'

Jimmy frowned at him. How could that be? It wasn't making any sense to him at all.

'Are you thick or something?' said the man, growling with anger now as spittle sprayed from his mouth. 'Hand over the takings from that till as it's only what's owed to me after all these bloody years!'

'Over my dead body!' yelled Jimmy as he rushed behind the counter to stand beside the till.

'You want it the hard way, do you?' The man grabbed the knife Jimmy had left on the workbench. It was for cutting pieces of leather, so it was very sharp. The man sliced through the air with it in an aggressive manner as though to prove a point.

Even though Jimmy was shivering now, he still held his ground as he feared more than losing the money should the man break through to the living quarters and attack Mr Baxter, whose health was still in a fragile state.

'Look,' yelled Jimmy, 'the money is not mine. I'm on good terms with the local police constable, Sergeant Cranbourne. If he finds out about this, he'll do you and you'll get a long sentence in Cardiff Gaol. My father is locked up there and he could make things difficult for you.' That was a lie, of course. Elgan wasn't his father and lately was unlikely to make things difficult for anyone as a lot of the fight had gone out of him. But Elgan had a way with folk, so if this man were interned maybe Elgan would only have to put out the word to get the man beaten up.

To Jimmy's surprise, the man dropped the knife with a clatter onto the floor. 'Sergeant Cranbourne, you say?'

'Yes!' said Jimmy. 'Do you know him?'

'I should say I do. I've got a lot of respect for that man and maybe I did do a bad thing today coming here to demand money, but it is my birthright. Josiah Baxter is my father, though I don't know if his wife realises it.'

Jimmy stared at him in shock. 'I don't understand at all,' he said, calmer now.

'He got my mother pregnant out of wedlock years ago. Didn't do the right thing by her and the next thing she knew, he was marrying someone else.'

Jimmy was stunned. He'd always thought well of Mr Baxter, thought him an upright, honest citizen. What this bloke was telling him couldn't possibly be true. 'You're lying!' he shouted.

'Look, lad, I wouldn't lie about something like that. I admit I did come here to rob the till as I've hit upon hard times. I don't even care to see the old man himself; I just want what he owes me. Me and my mother had to struggle for years as there was no breadwinner in the home.'

Jimmy had to admit that the man sounded sincere. He'd gone from a raging beast to a gentle lamb as tears welled up in his eyes.

At that moment, the doorbell jangled. Both their heads turned to see Mrs Baxter enter with a wicker shopping basket over the crook of her arm.

'My, my, 'tis a bit parky and windswept out there today,' she said as she rushed through to the back of the shop with her wares. She'd taken no notice whatsoever of the stranger in her shop. There was no flicker of recognition in her eyes either.

When she was safely out of earshot in the living quarters, Jimmy said, 'Strangely enough, I do believe there might be something in what you're telling me, but you can't just rob the till. You need to speak to your father, that is if Mr Baxter really is your father.'

The man nodded. 'Can you fetch him for me, please?'

Jimmy shook his head. 'No, not right now. He's been unwell and anyhow, if I did, Mrs Baxter might overhear. Give me a day or two to speak to him and I'll see if I can get him to meet with you.'

'Promise?' said the man, his eyes softer and brimming with tears.

'I promise I'll ask, though I can't guarantee he'll see you. But you mustn't try to rob this place again or make any threats against anyone.'

The man stooped to pick up the knife and, for a moment, Jimmy thought he might threaten him again, but instead he placed it on the worktable where he'd found it. Turning towards Jimmy, he said, 'Sorry, lad. I must have frightened you half to death. I don't usually feel this way, but I need the money as my mother is sick.'

Jimmy nodded, now feeling some sympathy for him. When he left the shop, Jimmy let out a breath of relief, bolting the door for the time being until he was certain the man wouldn't return – at least not for now. Trembling all over, he realised how well he'd done to keep the fella at bay. He might have done a lot of damage with that knife and robbed the shop's takings too.

* * *

The following day, when the shop was quiet with Harri put in charge, Jimmy told Mr Baxter about the man, relating what he'd said without mentioning how he'd been threatened with a knife, not wanting to scare him.

All the colour seemed to drain from Mr Baxter's face. His rheumy grey eyes appeared to be drooping more than usual this morning and he clung on to the arms of the chair as if his very life depended on it. He opened his mouth to speak but nothing came out and then he said, 'Arnold, that's who that must have been.'

'Arnold?' Jimmy raised his brows. 'So, you do know him then?'

'Oh yes. I met his mother before I met my wife. I was young and foolish, and I must admit...' His voice sounded shaky now. 'I was reckless too. I left that young woman in a right pickle and when I did decide to do the decent thing and marry her it was too late as she'd left my life. I remember him being a fine bonny boy, but I only got to know him for the first couple of years of his life. Then Olwen, his mother, disappeared. I don't know where they went to. I went to pay a visit one day and a neighbour said they'd left. She thought they couldn't afford the rent... I'm ashamed to say, I gave up on her after that and that's when I met my Lilian.'

'I expect maybe they ended up at the workhouse then,' said Jimmy in barely a whisper as he recalled his own experience there and how sad it had been.

'Aye, maybe,' said Mr Baxter, 'but I didn't care to find out. Back in those days, I was a selfish young man indeed!'

'You, selfish, Mr Baxter? I don't believe that for a moment. Look at the opportunity you've given me.'

He smiled. 'I've learned my lesson. That's why I've treated you like a son of late because I treated my own so badly.'

'Would you like to meet him now?' Jimmy asked tentatively.

'Aye, I would.' The old man nodded. 'Only thing is I don't wish to upset my wife.'

'That decision is yours. The bloke, I mean Arnold, said he'll call back to see if I've arranged a meeting in a couple of days.'

'Then do it, Jimmy, ruddy well do it. I'll just have to explain to Mrs Baxter what's gone on. I don't wish to lie to her.'

'I must warn you he got a bit threatening in the shop at first. He demanded money out of the till, and I thought he was a robber but, as we spoke, he calmed down. He said that money was owed to him.'

Mr Baxter nodded. 'I understand his feelings. If things had worked out differently, he would have been living a good life now. I do want to see my son, Jimmy. And thank you for telling me and calming down the situation. You're a good lad.'

8

It was a full week later before Arnold called to the shop again and he was shown into the back room to meet with his father. Jimmy insisted on being present to begin with as he feared for the old man's safety, but he needn't have worried as both men openly wept together and father apologised to son.

Arnold, who had taken the surname Evans, became a regular visitor to the shop after that and even began helping out. He seemed a natural at the trade like his father. Mr Baxter even passed a considerable sum of money over to him for his mother, so a doctor could be summoned and medication administered to bring the woman back to good health. Mrs Baxter didn't say too much about the subject, but from the flicker of pain in her eyes that Jimmy glimpsed from time to time whenever the man and his father were together, he could tell the woman was deeply hurt. Yet it was doing Josiah the world of good to have his son back in his life; Jimmy could see that.

The only troubling thing was, whereas Mr Baxter had paid Jimmy attention previously with the idea of him training to take over his place as his health declined, after some weeks it became clear he was mentoring Arnold now instead. Although Jimmy was pleased that father and son were reunited, he was beginning to feel like a spare part at the shop these days.

One afternoon, he was taken aback when Mr Baxter called him into the back room to tell him that he could no longer offer him the shop and premises after he passed away; they would go officially to Arnold. It was understandable, of course, but still painful to think that Arnold had walked into the shop out of the blue, and suddenly it would now belong to him. If Jimmy was being truthful he was jealous that Arnold had replaced him in the old man's affections. But the old saying proved true: 'Blood is thicker than water'. A true son was now expected to take over from his father. It felt like a death in a way, the way Arnold had taken his place.

'Try not to be bitter about it,' Mags advised when she noticed Jimmy looking particularly morose one day. 'It wasn't to be. You're a good cobbler and you might have your own place someday, lad.'

Jimmy nodded. 'Aye, maybe.'

'No maybes about it; if you want it enough, you'll find a way.'

'It's not just that though, Mags, it's the fact I feel I'm in the way at the shop now. I get along with Arnold well enough, but I think I need to leave and start a new round up, purchase my own utensils and establish new customers.'

'That's good thinking but where would you work from? You'd need some sort of pitch or shop.'

'I've been thinking about that. I'm not sure yet.' He paused for a moment. 'I wonder if Mrs O'Connell would have a word with the market inspector about me renting a stall like she does?'

'I'm sure she could, Jimmy. I'll have a word with her later.'

* * *

This was going to be the hardest thing Jimmy ever had to do: telling Mr Baxter he was leaving. The old man had been good to him and so had his wife. He really had no idea how the man would take it. Arnold and Harri had been working well together in the shop and now Jimmy felt like an outsider looking in. There wasn't enough room or work for both him and Arnold; Harri was still needed though to do the fetching and carrying.

Arnold now had enough money in his pocket to help his sick mother, so Jimmy guessed his intentions were good after all. And when the Baxters passed away, both cobbler shop and premises would belong to him. Jimmy was in no way bitter about it at all. He quite understood that family came first, and he was genuinely pleased for them. It was just that the vision he had for his future seemed to have gone up in a puff of smoke that drifted away into the ether.

Polly, too, had moved on from him. She was now courting a young fellow called Gethin Jenkins. Gethin lived in the Pontmorlais part of the town, and he worked in the tobacconist shop his parents owned. How she'd met the young man in the first place was a mystery to himself and Mags. She barely went anywhere and would most certainly have not stepped foot in a tobacconist shop. But she had mentioned to Mags he was a chapel goer, so she wondered if her parents had introduced her to the young man.

Wiping all thoughts of Polly from his mind, Jimmy entered Mr Baxter's shop where he was due to work for a few hours and then later make deliveries on the cart.

When he arrived, Harri was busy sweeping up the floor. Glancing up at him, he rubbed his brow.

'Good morning, Jimmy!' he said brightly.

'Er, good morning!' Jimmy forced a smile, feeling a little guilty now that he wouldn't be staying here for much longer. 'Where's Arnold?'

'I dunno.' Harri sniffed loudly. He was always doing that which was a habit that irritated Jimmy at times. Why didn't he just blow his nose properly?

'What do you mean you don't know? He's usually here before I arrive. Where the devil is he?'

This was all Jimmy needed. He wanted Arnold to be here to hear what he had to say to his father: that at the end of the day, when all the deliveries were completed, he could take over for good.

Harri shrugged and continued sweeping the floor.

Jimmy walked through the door behind the counter and made his way into the Baxters' living quarters. The first thing he heard was a loud sobbing, which sounded like Mrs Baxter. Oh no! Had Mr Baxter passed away? But then as he drew nearer to the living room door, which was ajar, he could hear her speaking to her husband.

'I can't believe someone has done that to us, Josiah!' There was more sobbing but no reply from Mr Baxter.

What on earth was going on? Tentatively, Jimmy rapped on the door with his knuckles, not wishing to just barge in on a sensitive moment, but something was going on here and he needed to find out what it was.

Mrs Baxter rushed to the door and drew it fully open. 'Oh, it's you, Jimmy,' she sniffed. 'Thank goodness you're here.'

Jimmy swallowed hard as he looked across at Mr Baxter, who was motionless, seated in his armchair staring into the flames of the fire crackling away in the hearth. Glancing up as Jimmy approached, he opened his mouth as if about to say something but then closed it again.

'Is everything all right?' Jimmy asked the pair.

'No, not really, Jimmy,' Mrs Baxter explained, shaking her head. 'We got up this morning to find the locked cupboard where we store the shop takings wide open, and all the money gone! There were a full month's takings in there. There's been so much going on lately that I didn't have time to bank it.'

Jimmy gasped. 'You mean someone's broken in here and robbed you? Has anything else been taken?'

'No,' sobbed Mrs Baxter. 'Whoever it was, was only after money. The back door was wide open when I got out of bed this morning. At first I thought I'd forgotten to lock it last night and it had blown open, but the thief must have entered that way.'

'Are you all right, Mr Baxter?' Jimmy asked, turning to him.

The man nodded with a sad expression in his eyes.

'This is bloody unbelievable!' Jimmy fumed. 'Where's Arnold this morning? Harri didn't seem to know where he is.'

'I've sent him to the police station to report it. He should be back soon,' said Mrs Baxter.

'That's good then.' Jimmy let out a little sigh. 'Let me make you both a cup of tea – you've had a nasty shock – and then we'll wait to see what the police have to say about this. Maybe Sergeant Cranbourne will send one of his officers here. How long ago did Arnold leave here?'

Mrs Baxter glanced at the mantel clock. 'I reckon it would have been about forty-five minutes ago. There or thereabouts.'

Jimmy frowned. The police station was only down the road. Surely Arnold should have returned by now. Deciding to keep his thoughts to himself, he forced a smile. All the while an uneasy feeling was forming in the pit of his stomach. 'Right, I'll make that tea then.'

By the time he'd brewed up and the tea was finished, and the dishes washed and put away, Arnold still hadn't returned.

'I'll tell you what,' said Jimmy, 'I'll pop to the police station myself to see what's keeping Arnold.'

Mrs Baxter nodded but said nothing.

'What's going on?' asked Harri as Jimmy brushed past him to leave.

'The takings were robbed from here last night. That's where Arnold is now, apparently speaking to the police, but he's been gone over an hour, so I'm going to check what's going on. You stay here and deal with any customers that arrive. Tell them I won't be long if they need to speak to me.'

Harri nodded open-mouthed, not the only one in shock that morning.

* * *

The Merthyr Central Police Station was a dark grey oppressive-looking building on Graham Street with a lamp above its entrance. Jimmy swallowed hard as he stepped over its threshold, making his way to the main long wooden desk where a constable stood behind it scribbling something into a large ledger.

He stopped writing and glanced up when he saw Jimmy. 'Can I help you?'

'I hope so. I've just come from Mr Baxter's cobbler shop; I work there, you see. He's been robbed of his takings and his son, Arnold, came here to report what's gone on.' Jimmy glanced at the large wall-mounted clock behind the main desk. 'That would have been a while ago but he hasn't returned. I'm wondering what's happening?'

The constable frowned. 'That's the first I've heard of this, but I've been on the desk most of the time except for a few minutes when someone else took over from me. I'll just check for you.' He left the desk and Jimmy watched him head off in the direction of a door down a short corridor. Rapping hard on it, the constable entered and closed the door behind himself. Then within moments he emerged with Sergeant Cranbourne in his wake. 'The sergeant will speak to you,' he said and then he retook his former position behind the desk.

'Hello, Jimmy.' Sergeant Cranbourne smiled warmly at him. 'You say Mr Baxter's son called here earlier to report a theft from the shop?'

'Yes, that's right.' Jimmy nodded.

The sergeant pursed his lips and then he sucked in a sharp breath through his teeth as he shook his head in a disapproving fashion. 'As far as I'm aware, Mr Baxter doesn't have a son and, in any case, no one has been here to report any sort of theft.'

A flicker of concern passed over Sergeant Cranbourne's face, so Jimmy explained the circumstances about Mr Baxter's son Arnold showing up at the shop and how both father and son had been reunited.

'I'm most concerned about this,' said the sergeant with a grave expression on his face. 'I think I'd better call to see the Baxters right away.'

* * *

It soon became evident after Sergeant Cranbourne had spoken with Mr Baxter that the old man had been the victim of someone who was out to dupe him. 'I think,' said the sergeant, 'this man was not your son at all, and it was he who took the money from that locked cupboard. He would have had the opportunity. Did he know where the key was kept?'

'Yes,' said Mrs Baxter, butting in. 'But we trusted him. He might have unlocked the back door before leaving through the main shop entrance last night, as he hung around until quite late here, while I prepared supper for us all.' She shook her head sadly. 'What I can't work out is how he knew my husband had fathered a child so many years ago?'

'That we don't yet know,' said the sergeant as he rubbed his whiskered chin. 'But I intend to do some digging to find out. What was the woman's name who gave birth to your child?'

Mr Baxter glanced dubiously at his wife.

'Go on, Josiah,' Mrs Baxter urged. 'It was a long time ago; you'll not hurt me now.'

Jimmy figured the woman had been hurt enough by the sudden intrusion of a 'stepson' along with mention of her husband's lover she'd known nothing about.

Mr Baxter nodded. 'It was Olwen Evans.'

'And where was she living when you knew her, when she gave birth to your son?'

'Pond Row in Abercanaid. She lived in one of the lower houses in the street that was below ground.'

'You mean it was a little like a cellar dwelling?'

'Well, sort of. Not the healthiest place to live either as it was damp and in recent years there was cholera in that area, with it being near the canal and all.'

Sergeant Cranbourne nodded. 'I'll go there myself and make some enquiries for you, see if any of the residents know what happened to her. Didn't you make any enquiries about Olwen and your son back then?' He narrowed his gaze.

'All I know is she couldn't pay the rent and moved somewhere but where I don't know. Might even have been the workhouse...' The old man shook his head sadly. 'I was just too selfish to go after her and my son to find out...'

Sergeant Cranbourne softened his stance. 'Please don't go chastising yourself, Mr Baxter. Discreet enquiries will be made to find out if this man is a son of yours or if he's some sort of scoundrel. Meanwhile...' the sergeant sucked in air through his front teeth in a reproving manner '... I'll check that all your door locks are secure. You'll need to find somewhere else to keep that money. I'd suggest depositing it in the bank more often than you've been doing and not leaving large sums around the place.'

'You're quite right, sergeant,' said Mrs Baxter with a look of concern on her face. 'I'm the one at fault here. When Josiah was taken ill my mind was all over the place and, I admit, I let things slip.' She turned towards Jimmy. 'If it wasn't for this young man here, I don't know what we'd do. He's stepped into my husband's shoes and really helped us out during a tough situation.'

Jimmy's cheeks blazed. He wasn't expecting such high praise.

The sergeant turned towards him and smiled, then he put a hand on his shoulder. 'You're an asset to Mr and Mrs Baxter, Jimmy. I've known you since you lost your mother and you've turned into a fine young man.' Then to Jimmy's surprise he stretched out his hand to shake his with a firm grip.

The sergeant turned towards the couple. 'I'll just check all your door locks before leaving and I'll make those enquiries I mentioned and report back to you. Meanwhile, do not, and I repeat this, do not allow Arnold Evans back on the property as, if my suspicion proves correct, he'll be after more than your shop takings.'

Mr Baxter nodded at the sergeant, but his wife put her hand to her mouth and all colour seemed to drain from her face.

How could Jimmy leave the pair of them now? He'd had permission to take over a market stall too; Mrs O'Connell had arranged it for him. Now he was just going to have to decline. After all, who else would look out for the couple? Harri was a great help, but he was far too young. No, he decided, it would have to be him. Thank goodness he hadn't got around to telling the pair he intended leaving after all. That in itself was a blessing in disguise.

'You've done the right thing, Jimmy,' Mags sympathised when he told her all about what had transpired earlier that day. 'The Baxters need you around. I don't like the sound of that Arnold Evans, if that's really his name, which I suppose it might not be now in light of what you've told me.'

Jimmy nodded. 'After supper I'm going back to the Baxter home and I'm going to stay there the night while that man is out there somewhere. There's something I didn't tell you about him...'

Mags lifted her eyebrows. 'Oh, aye? Go on then...'

'When I first encountered him at the shop a few weeks ago, he threatened me with a knife.'

'Oh, my giddy aunt! Have you told the sergeant?' she said, holding the palm of her hand to her chest as her mouth gaped open.

He shook his head. 'How could I? I didn't want to alarm Mr and Mrs Baxter. At the time, Arnold apologised for his behaviour, so I thought it was just the heat of the moment that had overtaken him. He went from a roaring beast to a gentle lamb and seemed quite vulnerable.'

'Vulnerable, my backside!' said Mags, her eyes glinting with anger. 'He might have harmed you and Mr and Mrs Baxter too. Jimmy, you should have told the old fella about the knife instead of persuading him to meet his so-called son instead.'

'Don't you think I realise that now? I've been very foolish, and my lack of action might have put Mr and Mrs Baxter in jeopardy.'

'The damage is done now but what you need to do is limit it. After your supper, before staying overnight at the shop, call to the police station and tell Sergeant Cranbourne exactly what you told me. Then you must tell the Baxters the same thing in case they are duped a second time if this "Arnold Evans" turns up with some sort of sob story.'

'I will.'

Mags nodded, then she smiled. 'By the way I have some interesting news for you...'

'Oh, what's that?' He quirked a curious brow.

'Polly and Gethin are getting wed!'

'It's a bit soon for all of that, isn't it?' Jimmy growled.

'Jimmy Corcoran, are you jealous or something?'

'It's not that. They've only known one another all of five bleedin' minutes and you know how naïve that girl is!'

'Aye, maybe. But she seems happy enough. It's none of our business either, and her parents have already given their blessing to the marriage taking place.'

Jimmy's eyes widened. 'You do surprise me!'

'It's because Polly's young man is a chapel goer as are all his family. He's respectable in the eyes of her parents.'

That doesn't prove anything about his character though, thought Jimmy.

* * *

If Sergeant Cranbourne was surprised that Arnold Evans had made threats with a knife, he wasn't showing it. He simply nodded at Jimmy when he dropped in to the police station later that evening. The place appeared strange and eerie, causing a shiver to skitter along his spine. It was the first time Jimmy had ever called in there at night-time. The wall-mounted gaslights cast a low glow over the place, giving it the effect of both light and flickering shadow, a bit like various criminals in the town, he supposed.

'I wasn't able to find out much,' explained Cranbourne as they stood near the main desk. 'It's correct though what Mr Baxter said about Olwen Evans moving away as she couldn't pay the rent. One neighbour thought she'd ended up at the workhouse like Mr Baxter guessed. So, that's my next port of call to check the records there.'

Jimmy nodded. Seemed sensible enough to him.

Cranbourne stared at him for a moment. 'Are you all right, Jimmy? You look a little disconcerted?' Jimmy had no idea what the term 'disconcerted' meant. Then as if the sergeant could read his mind, he said, 'I meant you look a little disturbed?'

Jimmy blew out a long breath. 'It's just that when that Arnold Evans came along, he was treated like a son, of course, and I felt like I was in the way. So, I decided I'd see if I could rent a market stall and work for myself. I was about to tell Mr Baxter when all that happened today. I'm glad I hadn't got a chance to mention anything now.'

Sergeant Cranbourne's features took on a grave expression. 'You're a good lad,' he said. 'Maybe it is best you stick around for a while; the old man's been good to you, training you up for a trade.'

'Yes, I realise that and I'm so grateful to him. I'm going to stop with the Baxters overnight in case that Arnold fella returns.'

'Very wise,' said the sergeant, nodding at him. 'I'll send a constable out on his patrol around the area tonight too, just in case. At least until the suspect is apprehended.'

Jimmy let out a sigh of relief. 'Thank you,' he said, now beginning to feel scared himself.

* * *

It was several days later before Sergeant Cranbourne turned up at the shop with the news that the old workhouse records indicated a woman called Olwen Evans, along with a young child, had been admitted there.

'But how do you know it's the right Olwen Evans, Sergeant Cranbourne?' Jimmy asked as Mr Baxter looked flummoxed in his armchair.

The sergeant smiled. 'The record showed her previous address as Pond Row, Abercanaid. But unfortunately...' He paused for a moment, which caused Jimmy and Mr Baxter to exchange anxious glances with one another. 'A different record showed that the child died a few months later. And, yes, he was a boy registered with the name Arnold Evans.'

'But what might have happened to cause his death?' Mr Baxter appeared agitated now, gripping on to the arms of his chair as though his very life depended on it.

'Well,' said the sergeant in a grave tone, 'there was an outbreak of some sort of illness that particular year and Master Aldridge, though not working there at the time, said that had probably caused the infant's death.'

Puzzled for a moment, Jimmy fought to think. He'd been told by Mags that the workhouse opened in 1853, so Mr Baxter couldn't have been all that young fathering a child even though he'd indicated he was. Maybe he wasn't telling the whole truth and he had been married at the time of his liaison with Olwen Evans. In any case, it was none of his darn business. It was a matter for Mr Baxter and his wife. But looking at the old fella now made Jimmy's heart go out to him. He must surely have regrets – if he'd taken care of Olwen and their baby maybe that child would still be alive now.

'But what I don't comprehend,' said Mrs Baxter, who'd remained unseen until now, stood near the door as she'd been minding the shop, 'is how whoever it was who posed as Arnold Evans knew all about my husband and the name of his child who died. It seems strange to me.'

All heads turned in the woman's direction.

'Not as odd as all of that after the information I've discovered. I returned to Pond Row as there was one resident there who wasn't around for questioning the first time. She told me she'd kept in touch with Olwen and that she later bore another son called Albert. I asked for a description of him, and the woman was able to provide one. It turns out that Albert Evans has had dealings with the police in the past, mainly for petty theft. Anyhow, we've got him in custody, and I'd like you, Jimmy, to come down to the police station with me and make an identification, if you will?'

'I can come,' said Mr Baxter, rising from his armchair.

'Maybe that's not the best idea,' said the sergeant, 'going by your current condition. Leave it to the lad for the time being.'

Mr Baxter nodded and then slumped back down in the armchair, looking defeated. He raised his brow. 'What about his mother? Is she still alive?'

Sergeant Cranbourne glanced at Mrs Baxter as though afraid of upsetting the woman. 'Yes, she is. She's living in Merthyr in the Morgantown area, and she's not sick either like he suggested to you when he said he needed money to help her – so that was a blatant lie and another theft from you by my reckoning! He fleeced you with that tale of woe, I'm sorry to say.'

For a moment, Jimmy noticed a flicker of pain and anguish in Mrs Baxter's eyes and then she forced a smile and said croakily, 'Well, it's good he's been caught anyhow, sergeant. Thank you.'

* * *

When Jimmy explained what had happened to Mags, the woman pursed her lips as, shaking her head, she blew out a surprised breath. 'You'd best hurry and get down the cop shop then,' she said.

'It's not like that, Mags,' he explained. 'I don't just go there where they show me a prisoner behind bars and I say, "That's him!" They're going to line up a group of men tomorrow afternoon and I have to see if I can pick him out.'

'Oh, I see,' said Mags. 'That shouldn't be too difficult, should it?'

'No, it shouldn't but I don't much fancy doing it, having to stare into his eyes again. That day he threatened me with a knife, he scared me so much.'

'You'll be all right with all those strapping policemen around. You'll not come to any harm, and it'll help him get put away.'

'Hopefully. He might even end up in Cardiff Gaol with Elgan!'

'Heaven forbid!' said Mags. 'I hadn't even considered that.'

As Jimmy sat eating his supper at the table, there was a knock on the door, which Mags went off to answer.

'Long time, no see!' he heard her saying in a bright tone of voice. Who on earth was that? 'Jimmy!' Mags called him. 'It's Betsan come to pay a visit!'

Jimmy pushed his soup bowl away from him and rose to see their unexpected visitor. Betsan looked so grown-up and smart these days. She wore a long violet dress with a matching cape edged with white fur, and a nicely trimmed bonnet with white gloves. Working at that Arden Brothers Factory had done a lot for her appearance. He guessed maybe she was allowed a discount from there on some of the goods as she helped to design them.

'And who is this young lady I see before me?' He chuckled.

'Oh, Jimmy, it's so good to see you both!' she said, her eyes shining with light and happiness.

'You'll stop for a cup of tea, of course?' Mags urged.

'Oh, yes please, Auntie!' Betsan nodded vigorously, and then Mags headed off for the scullery to brew up.

Jimmy watched as Betsan removed her bonnet and gloves and laid them on the table. She looked every inch a young lady these days.

Taking her by the arm, he led her over to the fireplace. 'Here, sit in Elgan's old armchair; it's the best seat in the house,' he said, and she did as told. He took the armchair opposite. 'So, what brings you here?'

'I wanted to tell you all about something I'm involved with,' she said excitedly. 'I've been asked to assist Francis Bradbury in a fashion show at the new Arden Brothers' store in Merthyr.'

'Oh, that's wonderful!' yelled Mags from the scullery.

'Thank you, Auntie!' Betsan shouted back, turning away for a moment.

Jimmy scowled. He couldn't bear that Bradbury bloke, but by the time Betsan had turned back to face him, he had pasted a smile on his face. 'That's good news indeed,' he said, rising from his chair and planting a kiss on her cheek. He watched in an amused fashion as she blushed profusely. Then he reseated himself. 'So, tell us all about it...'

It turned out that Betsan was allowed to invite some family members, and Mags and Jimmy were amongst those who would receive invitations. This didn't feel like something that would happen in Merthyr but in flippin' London or even Paris! But he was prepared to do anything to support the girl.

One person he knew who would have adored all of this was Enid. A pang of sadness washed over him as she came to mind but by the time Mags had brought a tray of tea to them and the three sat around the fireside chatting excitedly, there was no time to think of anything else except Betsan and her good fortune.

* * *

The men were lined up in the yard behind the police station. All were dressed in a similar fashion in flat caps, jackets and trousers and wearing mufflers around their necks. It seemed to Jimmy that they'd been told to dress in a manner of the description he'd given to the police.

From this distance, Jimmy could barely tell one man from another, so alike were they in appearance, and they were of similar height and stature too.

'Now I'm going to take you over there, Jimmy. I want you to take your time in looking at each one in turn,' Sergeant Cranbourne said. 'Don't feel intimidated by any of them as you're not in that position you were in where a knife might be used against you or anything like that.'

Jimmy trembled at the thought of it, and he wished Sergeant Cranbourne hadn't reminded him of the knife.

He nodded without saying anything, and then the sergeant led him over to the line. Each man held a small white board in front of him, which said number one, number two, and so on. As Jimmy peered closely at each man, all of whom stood there motionless with their hands gripping a board, staring vacantly at some point in the distance, he swallowed hard. Here, in amongst this line, would undoubtedly be the man who had threatened him and stolen from and duped Mr and Mrs Baxter. It was for them he was doing this, not for himself.

The first few men he shook his head at – most certainly none of them were him. Then when he came to man number six, he shuddered. It was Arnold all right, the man who had threatened him and stolen the shop takings from the Baxters. He noticed a nerve twitching at the man's jaw and then his eyes, instead of being fixed in the distance, now settled on Jimmy as he glared at him. It was such a look, both threatening and menacing that it sent a chill running down his spine, but Jimmy said nothing, and carried on inspecting the other men. At the end of it, and when they were far enough away from the line-up, he whispered to the sergeant.

'It's number six, Sergeant Cranbourne.'

'Are you quite sure, Jimmy?' he asked as he gazed intently at him.

'Yes, sir. It's definitely him. Also, he's the only man out of them all who looked into my eyes.'

The sergeant nodded and smiled, obviously pleased with how the line-up had turned out. 'Good lad, you've done well. I just want you to make a statement saying as such and about your dealings with Albert Evans, the man who called himself Arnold Evans, and then you're free to go.'

Jimmy breathed a sigh of relief. He just couldn't wait to get out of there. Before leaving, Sergeant Cranbourne said that the defendant would be up before the court first thing in the morning, and he and Mr and Mrs Baxter would be welcome to attend should Mr Baxter feel well enough.

'I don't think they'd attend,' said Jimmy. 'I might though, and I'll take Mags with me.'

'Good idea – she'll give you some moral support like you did with her when Elgan was in court.'

Fat lot of good that did her though, thought Jimmy. All that happened there was that Elgan got a sentence of one year in prison and he was still under lock and key.

* * *

The following morning as Jimmy and Mags sat in the courtroom, they discovered that Albert Evans was sentenced to one year in prison for the theft of the shop takings and conning the couple out of money supposedly for his mother's 'illness', one year for making threats with a knife, and another eighteen months for fraud by impersonating Mr Baxter's son. So, in all, a three-and-a-half-year sentence was imposed by the judge.

'But why would he do something like that?' Jimmy looked at Mags as they left the court.

'I don't know, Jimmy. People do odd things sometimes. It seems to me that he'd probably heard stories from his mother about how she'd given birth to a baby boy a couple of years before he was born, and who the father was. No doubt his mother had been bitter with her words. Maybe it was a way of paying back Josiah in some twisted way as well as trying to fleece the man.'

'Aye.' Jimmy nodded. 'If he'd kept his nose clean, he might have got away with that deception and inherited the business and premises. In a way, he scuppered himself!'

'True.' Mags smiled ruefully. 'I can't help feeling sorry for you, though, as Mr Baxter had promised everything to you before he came along.'

'I don't mind, Mags,' Jimmy said, forcing out the words because, truth be told, there was a little bit of hurt and anger inside him right now because that fraudulent fella had come along and changed everything. Still, he could return to the shop now and give the Baxters the news that Albert Evans was to be punished for his wrongdoing, but where did that leave Mr Baxter? Without a son and heir. It was in that moment, Jimmy realised, the hurt and anger he felt himself would be nothing compared to the betrayal the old man and his wife would be feeling right now.

10

It was just a couple of days later when Mags returned home with the news that Mrs O'Connell had offered them all the chance to move into the large house she owned.

Jimmy stood there open-mouthed for a moment as he digested the information.

'Yes,' enthused Mags, 'she's offered to rent us some rooms at the same price we're paying for this poky place. Just think, Jimmy, Mrs O'Connell's house has two large downstairs sitting rooms, four bedrooms, a nice-size kitchen and utility room and the privy is in the back garden!'

'Our very own privy!' gasped Jimmy. 'That would make a change from having to queue up for the few we have to share around here!' Then his face fell as something important came to mind. 'But what about Casper and Jasper? What will happen to them if we live with Mrs O'Connell?'

'That's the beauty of it. Bridget's neighbour owns a couple of horses, so she's going to ask him if we can pay him to stable both in his field. She's also suggested I run the sewing business from the house. Maybe Elgan can get involved in some way with deliveries on the horse and cart too when he comes out of prison.'

'That's great news!' enthused Jimmy. It was far better than he could possibly have hoped for.

Over the following few weeks, Jimmy was kept busy moving furniture and bits and pieces into Mrs O'Connell's home. Betsan had been offered a room there too while her father was still at the workhouse and had recently moved in with the woman. Being busy kept his mind off things. The Baxters had caused him great concern since all that business with Josiah's so-called son, but at least now the man would be safely under lock and key. Jimmy regretted ever persuading Mr Baxter to speak to the man in the first place, even though he'd assumed he was doing the right thing by arranging the meeting. What pain and trouble that had raked up for the Baxters. Now Josiah had said he would get the man's name removed from his will. It wouldn't have been legal in any case as he had been using a false name but whether a new will would be made making Jimmy sole beneficiary as before, he just didn't know.

* * *

The day of the move to Mrs O'Connell's house arrived and Jimmy, along with Harri, loaded up what little remaining possessions they had on the back of the cart, though three trips in all were necessary. Most of the furniture was owned by Richards the landlord, apart from Elgan's favourite armchair, a walnut wardrobe and a small stool that Elgan had picked up on his rounds in place of payment for his services. Mags ensured that her precious jug and bowl set he'd gifted her was safely on the back of the cart, well wrapped up with newspaper to cushion it – she wasn't taking any chances. Also on board were several colourful paintings of various Merthyr scenes along with pots, pans and crockery and clothing. The twins went on the final trip seated atop the cart with Jimmy, while Mags loaded up the donkey with some extra bags of clothing and other necessary items.

Mags made a final sweep around the house, to check if she'd left anything behind. Her memory drifted back to when she'd first moved in with Elgan after Thelma had passed away. There'd been no reason to hide their relationship after the woman's death. Jimmy, of course, had been familiar with the house long before Mags had taken Thelma's place in it. But to Mags, it was the home where she'd settled in well with Elgan, where she'd found the love of her life. And although it was difficult at first, as some of the neighbours gossiped about the pair living over the brush and shunned her in the street, eventually most came around. She and Elgan had married quietly not long afterwards.

Someone who had always supported her, even though she'd known Thelma, was Martha Hardcastle. She'd borne no ill will towards her, telling her she was good for him, and she could see the love they had for one another.

'Ah yes,' muttered Mags, as she turned the key in the lock for the final time. 'It's been a good home for us and those parish lads too.' She looked up at the sky. 'Now, Lord, I pray this house goes to someone who needs it, and that Mr Richards will give the new owners some grace if they have problems paying the rent on time...' Her thoughts were on the Hardcastle family as she glanced in the direction of their old home. There was a new family ensconced in their place now. She just hoped they wouldn't hit upon hard times like the Hardcastles had. But, still, the Hardcastles were doing so much better now. Martha and the kids had left the workhouse and gone to live with Enid at Beechwood House. And not so long afterwards, Arthur had joined them too, so the family were reunited. Maybe it was all meant to be.

Sighing, she gazed at the house one more time and headed off to the pub to return the key to Richards before walking Jasper, who was laden down with the rest of their belongings, over to Mrs O'Connell's house.

* * *

'To be sure it's good to see you all!' said Mrs O'Connell as she clasped her hands with happiness when Jimmy and the twins pulled up on the cart outside the house. She was stood behind her white picket fence with a lush green lawn bedded with colourful flowers behind her. This was the sort of home Jimmy and Mags had only had experience of in their dreams and now those dreams were about to become a reality. The woman had obviously been on standby awaiting their arrival, and now she was opening the gate to allow them access to her home. A new chapter in all their lives awaited.

Jimmy smiled and nodded and then he went to help Alys and Aled down from the cart.

'Come on, you pair!' He chuckled as he swung both, one at a time, onto the pavement. Then turning towards the woman, said, 'Thank you so much for taking us in like this, Mrs O'Connell.'

''Twill be you lot who'll be doing me a favour really. It will be lovely to have some company around the place again. I feel like I'm rattling around in this house.' She gestured to the tall building behind her, which was three storeys high, having a ground floor, top floor and attic.

Jimmy had to agree as it was huge in comparison with their little hovel in China, but to be fair to Mags, she'd made it a home with her warm persona and the way she'd tried to brighten it up. He could see why Mrs O'Connell wanted them all to move in with her though as she and Mags got on like a house on fire. It worked well too with Mags and Polly sewing and supplying garments for the woman's stall, so it all made sense.

Betsan had moved in a few days earlier, and even though he was looking forward to reuniting with the girl, he still felt a little betrayed that she hadn't informed him what was going on with regards to Enid. Even though Mags had insisted she knew very little, it explained a lot. All those awkward pauses whenever he asked about Enid. It was almost as though she'd been trying to shut him down, so he didn't ask any awkward questions. He appreciated that she was trying to keep Enid's confidence though.

He watched as Mrs O'Connell took both children by the hand, leading them up the garden path towards the house.

'Now I've baked some jam tarts especially for you both...' she was saying to them, 'and I've got a nice cold jug of buttermilk in the larder for you to drink.'

Aled and Alys knew her well enough by now to trust her, and in any case, Mags would be arriving soon. Jimmy wondered what Elgan would make of all this when he was released from prison and hoped he'd be able to settle down into his new home too.

* * *

Jimmy had already placed Elgan's armchair in a spot near the fireplace in one of the living rooms Mrs O'Connell had ascribed to them. She had a smaller one to herself. Mags felt it important the woman should be awarded some privacy in her own home.

Jimmy was in the middle of hanging some of Mags's paintings on the wall, using a hammer to bang in some nails to hang them, when she arrived with two bulging carpet bags in either hand, her face flushed, and her expression flustered.

'I'm not getting any younger!' she groaned as she placed the bags in the corner of the room. 'It wasn't all that easy leading Jasper here either. He didn't want to leave his stable, as stubborn as a mule that donkey was!' She chuckled. 'I hope he'll settle in at his new home.'

'Where is he now?' Jimmy furrowed a brow.

'I've tethered him to a post in the garden for the time being. Can you lead him up to the field later for me, Jimmy?'

'Yes, no problem. I have to take Casper there anyhow. I'll get them fed and stabled there for the night.'

'There's good you are to me. My feet are aching something chronic. This moving is hard work, and I've been on my feet at the market stall all day long as Bridget wanted to give this place a good bottoming before we all arrived.'

* * *

That evening, Betsan turned up at the house following her shift at the factory. She'd moved in there a few days ago, so was already settled in. It was so good to see her again as Jimmy had not seen much of her lately.

Betsan's eyes were shining brightly as she hugged him. 'It's wonderful to see you all!'

Jimmy took a step back to appraise her. 'You're looking so well these days.'

'Aye, my hair's grown back to its usual length now. It looked a right mess after they'd sheared it at the workhouse!'

'It's not just that though, you've grown so much lately. You're quite the young lady now!'

'Like you, I've had to grow up fast. I hear you've been working hard for Mr Baxter?'

He nodded. 'Yes. He's been training me up and he even took on board my idea of a delivery service to the big houses.'

'He must think a lot of you, Jimmy.'

Jimmy smiled. 'He does, I suppose. Not having any children themselves, the Baxters treat me like a son.'

'The son they never had!'

He was about to tell her all the trouble they'd had when Mr Baxter's bogus son had appeared on the scene but then they were interrupted by Mags calling him.

'I want you to pay Elgan a prison visit,' she said with a look of apprehension on her face, making him wonder if there was something wrong.

'Me?' Jimmy blinked profusely. In all the time Elgan had been inside there'd been no question of him visiting the man because the rail fare was too expensive. Mags, herself, had only been there twice. First when he was initially imprisoned and the second time more recently. So why would she want Jimmy to go there? It didn't make any sense whatsoever. He'd never been to Cardiff in his whole life. In his mind it seemed a million miles away. It was only twenty-five miles in distance though – so not that far in reality – yet as he pictured it in his mind, Mags might just as well be talking about London or Paris or Rome. It might as well have been the ruddy moon!

'Yes, Jimmy. You,' said Mags. 'The reason I want you to go there this week is that he's due to be released soon and I want him to have some tidy clothing to wear going out. Clothes maketh the man and all that. I want him to start as we mean to go on and from now on, he's not to be involved in any dodgy dealings! I'd go myself but I have quite a big order to complete at the moment and going to Cardiff would take the best part of a day for me. A day of work I can't afford to lose out on!'

Jimmy frowned. 'But why would he need new clothes? He was wearing a perfectly decent suit when he was arrested.'

Mags nodded. 'That may be so, but his clothing got a bit roughed up at the police station...'

She'd never imparted that information before. 'You mean he was beaten up in the police cell?'

'No, nothing like that!' She shook her head as though disgusted he'd even consider the constabulary would treat Elgan like that. Then she let out a little sigh. 'He'd been drinking is what it was, we both had, and he fell a couple of times and vomited. It's not just that though, that suit will no longer fit him anyhow. He'll look like a clown wearing it these days, he's lost so much weight.'

'Oh, I see,' said Jimmy, understanding now. 'Yes, of course I'll take some new clothing to him. How can you afford it though?'

'I didn't need to buy him anything new. Mrs O'Connell's husband, Shamus, was thinner than Elgan was before he went to prison, so she gave me a bundle of his clothing that should fit him; they're in good condition too. After all, where Shamus has gone...' she glanced heavenward for a moment '...he's not likely to need them, is he? May his soul rest in peace.'

Jimmy supposed not. 'Mags,' he said, his forehead creasing into a frown, 'you'll have to run me through all the train stuff though. I've never been on one in my life nor been to Cardiff neither.'

Mags blew out a breath. 'No, I know you haven't had much opportunity to go farther afield than Merthyr, lad. Don't worry, I'll run you through the drill and tell you which station to get off at and how to get to the gaol.'

He nodded, grateful for any advice she could give him. Elgan and Mags had been so good to him, so he didn't mind doing this little favour for them at all. 'I'll have to ask Mr Baxter for permission to take the day off though. I expect Harri can fill in for me for a few hours.'

'Thank you, lad.' Mags smiled and lightly touched his shoulder. 'How would I ever manage without you?'

* * *

Jimmy was on his way to Cardiff with a bundle of clothing for Elgan beneath his arm. The package was well wrapped in brown paper and secured with string, Mags insisting on giving everything a quick press with the iron before neatly wrapping it all up.

As he stood on the station platform, he glanced down the valley and at the surrounding majestic hills. Imagine, most of this area had once been mainly farmland but now the population had grown thanks to the influx from the ironworks. The steam train was already on the platform with its engine running. Jimmy could hear the hiss of it and climbed on board, securing himself a seat near the window. As it was his first trip on a train, he didn't want to miss a thing. He glanced around at his fellow passengers. Some looked like businessmen wearing smart jackets or coats with astrakhan collars; others appeared to be well-to-do ladies wearing fancy bonnets. All these people and all with a destination to go to!

After a few minutes of people scrambling to get on board and a mad dash to get themselves seated before departure, there was a rhythmic chugging sound as the engine's pistons fired, propelling the train wheels forward. Then a release of steam through the train's whistle, creating a loud shrill sound that was ever so exciting. The train was off, all the way to Cardiff.

* * *

The man before him seemed a shadow of his former self. They were in a room where prisoners were sitting at tables with visitors seated opposite them. The room was large, and people's voices seemed to echo off the walls.

'Thank you for coming to see me,' said Elgan, glancing up with tears in his eyes. 'My, how you've grown. You look like a man now, no longer a lad...'

Jimmy chuckled. 'You'd better tell that to Mags when you get out of here then, as she still insists on calling me "lad".'

Elgan smiled. 'Mind you, you've always been like a son to us, Jimmy. You know that, don't you?'

Jimmy felt his heart surge. 'And you've been like a father to me ever since I lost my own.'

Elgan nodded with understanding. 'How are the twins doing?'

'Aw, they're great they are,' said Jimmy enthusiastically. 'Right little rays of sunshine. We've all moved into Mrs O'Connell's place now.'

'Aye, Mags did write to tell me. Just as well, as I'd have left here and gone back to China otherwise, wondering where you'd all disappeared to!'

There was no disputing it, Elgan looked like he'd aged ten years since being in prison. There were rings beneath his sad-looking eyes, his hair had greyed at the temples and his cheeks appeared hollow.

'I've brought a package of clothing for you when you leave here next week,' said Jimmy brightly in an effort to cheer him up.

'Mags bundled some of my old stuff up, has she?' said Elgan, glancing at where Jimmy had left the package on the table.

'Oh no, this is new, well, almost. Mrs O'Connell gave all these to her, and Mags has pressed them for you.'

Quite suddenly, Elgan grabbed Jimmy's forearm with some urgency. 'Tell me how she's doing, Jimmy? Is Mags missing me?'

Startled, Jimmy drew a breath before releasing it. What a strange question to ask. 'Yes, of course she is – it goes without saying.'

Elgan loosened his grip and removed his hand from Jimmy's arm. 'It's just Mags is a good-looking woman who could have her pick of men. I feared...' He glanced down at the table and shook his head.

'You feared you might lose her to someone else while you've been inside?' Jimmy couldn't believe what he was hearing. There was no one more devoted to Elgan than Mags was.

Elgan looked up and made eye contact with Jimmy. 'Yes, I did. I do.'

'Now, let me tell you, you have no fear on that score. All Mags has done since you've been in here is work her ruddy guts out with that sewing business of hers and take care of the twins, and me too. She has no eyes for any other man but you; talks about you all the time she does.'

Elgan let out a loud groan. 'Oh, Jimmy, I'm so sorry for even asking you. It's just this place does things to a man's mind. There's too much time to think in here and reflect on things. The days aren't so bad, as there's some sort of routine going on, even though the tasks are mindless and monotonous like turning the crank or walking on the treadmill wheel. Most of the prisoners think they're punishments to crush our spirits so we don't reoffend, but I welcome those bloody tasks, Jimmy. I really do as they provide me with a routine. It's the nights that are the longest for me, and it's then I awake with all sorts running through my mind. There's a man banged up here called Tommy Morris. He hadn't been inside two minutes when his young wife was off with another man. Now he finds out she's pregnant with the other man's child and he has no home or wife to return to!'

'That's terrible!' said Jimmy. 'But you have no fears on that score, let me tell you!'

Elgan, looking relieved, suddenly appeared much younger, his skin seeming to smooth out. 'Thank you for that, Jimmy,' he said, letting out a little breath of relief. 'Please don't tell Mags I ever doubted her, will you?'

Jimmy shook his head. 'Of course I won't. Look, before you know it, you'll be back home with us and reunited with your twins.'

'I'm really looking forward to that, son.' He wiped away a tear with the back of his hand.

What on earth had being incarcerated in this place done to Elgan?

* * *

Jimmy stayed for a good hour but after that he noticed visitors begin to drift away, and one guard kept glancing at his pocket watch, so he guessed that was his cue to leave.

'You're sure now you'll be able to get back home safely on your release from this place?' asked Jimmy as he rose from the table.

Elgan nodded. 'Aye, yes. The governor told me my train fare back to Merthyr would be taken care of and a guard will accompany me to the station.' Then seeing the look on Jimmy's face, he chuckled. 'Have no fear, the guard won't be coming all the way back to Merthyr with me, mind!'

'Phew! That's a relief at least!' Jimmy smiled. He felt like rushing over to him and hugging him tightly like he did when he was a little boy, but realising that wouldn't be allowed, he extended his hand across the table and shook hands instead. 'Don't worry, you'll be back with us soon!' he said cheerfully. 'And I, for one, can't wait for that day to arrive.'

Elgan gripped his hand as though his life depended on it. It was then Jimmy noticed that Elgan's eyes were brimming with tears, so he turned and walked towards the door without a backward glance, realising that if he turned back towards the man, he'd start crying himself.

* * *

When Jimmy arrived home, he related how the visit had gone to Mags as they both sat in front of the fireplace in the living room.

'Elgan's in good spirits there but, as you feared, he's lost a lot of weight. So, it's just as well you got those new clothes for him. He's very grateful an' all. The only thing that concerned me...' He watched as she chewed on her lower lip.

'Is what?' She was sitting forward in her armchair, leaning in to hear what he had to divulge.

The crackling of the flames from the hearth seemed to increase the tension between them.

Swallowing, he continued, 'Elgan's not the same man any more. He's a broken man, Mags.'

Mags frowned. 'You can't expect him to be the same, Jimmy. I noticed that the last time I visited him.'

'It's more than that though; he was crying to me today an' all.'

'He's always been an emotional so-and-so, but he didn't cry at my last visit a few weeks ago, only the first one of all and that was to be expected. So, what are you really saying?'

'What I'm really saying is this... when he returns home soon, it's going to take time for him to adjust to being around folk and that sort of thing as well as living in a new house.'

Mags nodded her agreement. 'So, it's best he doesn't start his round up again right away?'

'No, I don't think it would be a good idea, particularly as I can't help him right now either as I'm working long hours for Mr Baxter. I think he just needs a few weeks to find his feet again.'

'Jimmy!' said Mags with some surprise. 'When did you turn into a young man?'

'Funny you should say that, but Elgan said something similar.'

It was strange to think how people were no longer viewing him as a boy, even if Mags continued to call him lad. Was it just because his voice had deepened of late or because of the way he conducted himself, he wondered. Whichever it was, it cheered him to know that both his mentors now viewed him as a fine young fellow, making him immensely proud of the way he'd turned out.

11

It was a few weeks later after Elgan had been released from prison that Jimmy was sent on another errand to Cardiff, this time by Mr Baxter himself who had run out of his supply of shoe leather. His supplier in Cardiff hadn't answered any correspondence, so Jimmy had taken it upon himself to visit the premises, feeling confident now that he could find his way, having recently visited Elgan in prison.

After locating the dark grey building, which was just off St Mary's Street, he managed to speak to a foreman there, who explained that the person dealing with the correspondence had been ill lately, so he took the details of what was needed from Jimmy with a promise that the leather would be delivered to the Merthyr shop by the end of the week. Meanwhile, he scribbled down the name of another person in the company they could write to instead who was now dealing with all correspondence – 'in an efficient manner' the man had said – which made Jimmy wonder if the previous person was really ill or had been sacked for incompetence. Still, none of that mattered now. What did matter was that the supply of leather would be delivered to them soon and Mr Baxter would be pleased with that. His employer took pride in his work and always ordered good quality supplies. There was no scrimping or cutting corners in his shop.

Job done, happily, Jimmy headed for home, but there was a delay as he waited for the Merthyr train. When he enquired at the ticket office, he was informed it was something to do with some goods train that needed to travel through on the same track, so people were moaning and grumbling loudly. As a result of a long wait though, more people crowded onto the platform and Jimmy was standing cheek by jowl with folk, realising this train back home would be packed to the rafters with passengers.

Finally, he heard a familiar chugging sound and could see puffs of steam arising in the distance. The train was about to pull into the station. Everyone surged forward on the platform to secure a seat, but Jimmy let them all carry on with it as he figured he might be better off standing anyhow as he didn't want to feel hemmed in as people hovered and jostled around.

The train had gone past a couple of stations, and on the third stop, Jimmy absently gazed out of the window as passengers alighted. There weren't so many leaving this time and he noticed now there were a couple of spare seats available, so he was about to make his way over to one, when he glanced again out of the window. A young woman marching briskly across the platform caught his attention as she held her head erect and had a familiar-looking stride. She'd evidently just alighted from the train. No, it couldn't be, could it? That was Enid!

This time he was convinced it was her – the long red hair bouncing on her shoulders as she walked off with extreme purpose – his heart began to pound and his breath hitched in his throat. He knew in that moment he had to get off the train and follow her. But in his haste, other passengers had now embarked and were headed towards him, forcing him to jostle past them as he elbowed them out of the way, which caused comments about how rude he was.

Rude he was not though. It was an eagerness in not ever losing sight of Enid ever again. He didn't even know what time the next train was, but he was prepared to take a chance and if there was no other train, then he'd walk all the way back home to Merthyr if necessary. Heck, he'd spend the night on the platform if he had to and set off for home the following morning.

The platform was milling with passengers and, to his dismay, he could no longer see Enid. But the crowd was all headed in the same general direction of the exit, so that's where he went too, walking as fast as he could. There was no way he could even run after her as there were just too many people in his way. Eventually, as the throng arrived at the platform's exit, through a brown and white gate as people made off in all sorts of directions, he spotted her, glimpsing her blue jacket in the distance.

He carried on trailing a few yards behind. What would he say, though, when he caught up? The couple walking behind her turned off to head down another road, but Enid appeared to be walking towards a wooded area along a small path. Deciding not to shout after her, he slowly decreased the distance between them and noticed as he did so that she began to walk faster with her head down. When they were young, he had a habit of putting his hands over her eyes to surprise her, so walking as fast as he could, he did just that and he felt her tremble. And then to his horror, she screamed loudly. It was a guttural-sounding scream, one he'd never heard before, almost animalistic, and then he felt awful.

'I'm so sorry for scaring you. Enid, it's me, Jimmy,' he said softly when she'd finished screaming and she turned towards him with tears in her eyes. Recognition dawned and then she fainted in his arms.

'Come along, let's sit you down here,' he said, lightly tapping her face to rouse her.

Her eyelids flicked open. 'Jimmy? Is it really you?' she whispered.

'Yes, it's me. Come on,' he said, steadying her as he led her over to an old, felled tree trunk.

She slumped down on it and put her head in her hands and wept. Jimmy had never seen anyone cry so hard before, except for maybe his mother when she was told of his father's death. He sat beside her and gently rubbed her back. Then reaching into the top pocket of his jacket, he handed her a clean cotton handkerchief that Mags had only given him that morning.

'Here, wipe your eyes with that,' he whispered.

She did as told and then, sniffing, said, 'I'm so sorry for being like this, Jimmy. It's just I wasn't expecting to see you of all people. I feared I was being followed and that I'd be attacked.'

'It's me who should be sorry. I should have thought better of it, creeping up on you like that without a word of warning. It's just that it used to be my way to surprise you – to put my hands over your eyes – so I thought you'd have guessed it was me.'

'No. You were the last person I'd have expected it to be.'

She shook her head as tears spilled down her cheeks, then he took the handkerchief from her hand and dabbed gently at them. 'I'm sorry, but I'm so glad I found you again, Enid. I've tried to find you for so long. You never replied to my letters and the next thing I knew you'd been sent to Cardiff. I even called in to see Cook at Hillside House about you.'

'You did?' She quirked her brow. 'You did that for me?'

'Of course, I did. I loved you then and I still love you now.'

She began to sob again so he put his arm around her shoulders, pulling her close to him and then he lifted her chin with his thumb and forefinger to plant a kiss on her lips but she pulled away.

'No!' she said firmly. 'I can't do this!'

'Why ever not? Didn't you miss me in all that time we've been apart? I missed you so much I thought my heart would split in two at times,' he said, frowning now. This was making no sense at all, unless... 'Is there someone else?' he asked, narrowing his gaze.

She vehemently shook her head. 'No, there's no one else but there is *something else*, something that when I tell you, you'll not want me again, ever.'

'Please let me be the judge of that,' he said as he caressed her face.

She nodded at him. 'Not here,' she said. 'There's a small coffee shop across the way. Let's go there.'

'Yes, of course.' He took her hand and helped her on to her feet, all the while thinking what on earth could be so bad that he'd never want her again? He couldn't imagine anything that might cause him to want to keep away from her, ever.

* * *

When they were seated in the coffee shop and waiting for their order of a pot of coffee to arrive, Jimmy reached out, taking Enid's hand across the table. She looked so upset to him, still. Her eyes looked huge and watery, but it wasn't just that; there was a sadness in them that he'd not seen before.

'What happened, Enid? Something's obviously occurred since we last met, something I'm not aware of. Has someone hurt you?'

She nodded. 'Y... yes.' She bit her lower lip so hard that it appeared almost white until she released it and the colour returned.

Jimmy sensed this was difficult for her, so he vowed to go slowly, allowing her to tell him at her own pace. 'Go on...'

She was clasping and unclasping her hands now as if not knowing quite what to do with them. 'It's the reason I was dismissed from Hillside House, yet it was me who was the injured party not the master's son...'

Jimmy frowned, perplexed. This was making no sense whatsoever. 'Just tell me what happened in your own time,' he said, glancing up apprehensively as the waitress arrived with their order. She set the pot of coffee down on the table with the cups. 'Thank you, miss,' Jimmy said, turning his attention away from Enid for a moment.

'Shall I pour for you, sir?' she asked, looking at him as she quirked her brow.

Jimmy flicked a hand of dismissal. All he wanted was for her to leave them alone. 'It's all right, I'll sort it. Thank you,' he said curtly, not wanting her to fuss over the table.

The waitress nodded and left them to return to the counter where no doubt another order waited for her to attend to.

'Here,' said Jimmy. 'I'll pour our coffees and you just take your time.'

Enid nodded and when the coffee had been poured, she took a sip as if to steady her nerves and then, after setting her cup down, her hand flew to her mouth as though horrified.

'The coffee's bitter?' Jimmy wanted to know.

'Oh, it's not that. For a moment there, it reminded me of when I took coffee that time with Mr and Mrs Clarkson. It was after I'd been summoned into the drawing room to see them. It was that awful incident involving their son.'

Jimmy tilted his head to one side, puzzled. 'What happened?'

'I didn't want to tell you this, Jimmy. That's why I stopped all contact with you. After being sent to the Cardiff workhouse for a spell, I'm now working as a maid at another house and I'm happy there as I don't have any sort of threat hanging over my head. I'm no longer living in fear. You see, when I arrived at Hillside House, I was so looking forward to it. Master and Matron Aldridge from the workhouse had chosen me out of all of the other girls especially to work there. You remember me going there, don't you?'

'Yes, I do, Enid. You even visited me one Sunday on your afternoon off...'

'I know, but I didn't tell you what had been going on there at the time. You see, as soon as I arrived, I was warned by one of the footmen to take care around the master's son, Anthony.'

'In what sort of way?' He narrowed his gaze.

'It was implied that he had wandering hands, that sort of thing, and to be wary of being left alone in a room with him. Late one night, before I was setting off for bed, he returned from a business trip, and it was obvious he'd been drinking alcohol as he accosted me in the drawing room.' She swallowed hard.

'What did he do to you?' Jimmy could feel his hackles rising. The man was obviously some sort of chancer.

'It wasn't that night he did anything other than to threaten me with robbing me of my virginity!'

'The bastard!' said Jimmy, then he banged his fist on the table. Realising he'd raised his voice, he glanced around the coffee shop, but no one appeared to have noticed. 'I'm sorry, I shouldn't have used that word, but I feel so angry on your behalf!'

'If that's all it had been, I'd have coped, I think. Even though the threat of it made me fearful, at least I was on my guard around him. But what I wasn't prepared for, was one evening, I was out taking some air in the grounds around the house, and it was getting dark, so I took a shortcut back to the house through a wooded area...'

Enid placed a clenched fist to her mouth and tightly shut her eyes as though it was all too painful for her.

'I'm guessing he followed you?' Jimmy said as he lowered his voice.

It was a moment or two before her eyes flicked open and she made eye contact with him and nodded. 'And then he carried out his threat...'

'Oh no!' said Jimmy, now realising what had occurred. 'You mean he raped you, Enid?' he whispered so as not to be overheard and draw any unwelcome attention to them for her sake.

Slowly, she nodded, and in that moment, he longed to take her in his arms, telling her everything would be all right from now on. To think of his beautiful sweetheart violated in such a horrific manner was beyond comprehension.

'It was dreadful,' said Enid. 'He took me by force. I couldn't seem to fight him off, Jimmy. It was as if my emotions were bottled up inside me. Why didn't I shout for help? Why couldn't I fight him off? I blame myself sometimes...'

'Oh, please don't say that, Enid.' He reached out and took her hand across the table, giving it a reassuring squeeze. 'You were petrified. Who wouldn't be? You were probably shocked inside and somehow trying to get out of there alive as no doubt he could have killed you. Most probably your survival instincts kicked in. How awful for you, and I wasn't even able to protect you, my love.' He tilted his head to one side in a gesture of sympathy.

She nodded. 'So, do you see why you wouldn't want me now? I'm no longer your pure little sweetheart.'

'Please, Enid, don't talk so daft. I've loved you since we were children and I've wanted you for ever such a long time. This makes no difference to me. I feel both sad and angry for what happened to you, but I still want us to be together someday. There is no other girl for me – only you.'

'Oh, Jimmy!' she cried, but now she had a smile on her face as he recognised those were tears of joy to hear him say such a thing.

* * *

After leaving the shop hand in hand, Jimmy walked Enid to her final destination. She told him she was going to visit her friend, Annie, whom she'd met in the Cardiff workhouse. The girl had recently settled down and married someone, who apparently had been a regular customer at the tea room where she worked. As they walked along, Enid filled Jimmy in on all the details of how both girls had tried to help another workhouse inmate called Connie, who had got herself in a load of bother at Tiger Bay.

Jimmy couldn't believe his ears about what Enid had relayed to him. 'I wish I could have helped you with all of that,' he sympathised. 'But one thing I'd love to do is punch that Anthony Clarkson fellow squarely on the jaw!' he said, gritting his teeth. 'After what he did to you and to Connie too, he deserves a right thrashing!'

'Oh, believe me, he got his comeuppance in the end,' said Enid as she clung on to Jimmy's arm as they walked along. 'Not only did my new master, Mr Darling, give him a severe horsewhipping in front of folk, but he later died the day before the court case where all those girls gave evidence about him and that Mr Sharpe.'

'He died?' asked Jimmy, stopping mid-step. 'But how?'

'He followed me one day as I was crossing the road to visit the pharmacy shop. I think he was lying in wait for me. He'd just made threats, grabbing hold of me and striking me hard across the face, but I managed to get away and ran across the road to the shop. I had to weave in and out of the traffic and almost got run over, but when I got to the safety of the shop, I turned, after hearing a woman's scream. I was afraid to look but when I did so, I saw his lifeless body lying on the ground and a horse reared up on its hind legs, trampling him to death. He didn't stand a chance...' She shook her head.

'Oh, my dear, Enid,' he said, taking her into his arms now, 'life has been so very tough for you of late, but that man deserves no sympathy. And everything that happened to you was most definitely not your fault.'

She gazed at him through eyes brimming with tears. 'I'm so grateful you've found me, Jimmy,' she said, looking up at him. He lowered his head to plant a kiss on her lips. This time there was no resistance as she responded. Enid finally drew away and then pointed across the road. 'That's Annie's house,' she said. 'She's expecting me.'

'Well, you can tell her it's my fault you're a little late.'

She smiled at him. 'She's half expecting me not to arrive on time anyhow, the way the trains are running of late. That goods train was a right nuisance earlier, but that sort of thing happens now and then.'

'Wasn't it just.' He nodded his agreement. 'But if that hadn't happened, making my train late, I might never have met you again, so thank you, goods train!' he yelled, lifting the flat cap off his head in acknowledgement.

'Jimmy,' Enid said with a note of urgency to her voice, her eyes wide now. 'I just remembered, you'll need to rush to catch the next train up to Merthyr as there's not another for three hours after that!'

'Oh!' he said. That had taken the wind out of his sails. 'But how will we keep in touch now we've found each other again?'

'That will no longer be a problem. I promise I will write to you this time and I'll send you the address where I work as upper housemaid. I'm sure we can manage to meet up now and then. Or perhaps we can meet halfway in Pontypridd or something.'

He smiled at her. He told her his new address and she made a mental note of it.

'I'll write that down as soon as I go inside,' she said. 'Annie must have a scrap of paper and a pencil somewhere.'

He nodded at her. 'Be sure you do. I don't want to risk losing you again.'

'Go now, quickly!' she yelled. Then she blew him a kiss and he returned it.

'So long for now, my love!' he said, then he turned his back and ran as fast as he could towards the station. Somehow, he floated on air all the way back. Just knowing that Enid still cared for him was enough to keep his hopes up.

12

Mags was waiting for Jimmy with her hands on her hips when he arrived home.

'Just where have you been, lad? I was about to send a search party out for you!' she quipped, but by the twinkle in her eyes he could tell she was just having him on.

'You will not believe what I am about to tell you, Mags,' he enthused as he removed his jacket and cap and hung them on the back of the door, then he turned around to face her.

'Well go on, then...' she said eagerly, sitting down in the armchair.

There was a long pause before he blurted out, 'I've found Enid, Mags! I couldn't believe my luck.'

Jimmy watched as the colour appeared to drain from Mags's face. What was going on here? Wasn't she pleased for him?

'B... but how did you manage that?' She swallowed hard.

'The Merthyr train was late, something to do with the line being needed for the goods train. More and more people flooded on to the train and when it pulled into one station, I was standing and looking out through the window and then I caught sight of her walking along the platform...'

Mags's features appeared to smooth out and she let out a little sigh.

'Oh, that's what it was like the last time, Jimmy, when you thought you saw Enid in Merthyr. You saw someone who resembled her.'

'No! No!' he yelled. 'It really was her this time. I got off the train and followed her – that's why I'm so late getting home. You're not going to believe this, but we ended up talking and I took her to a coffee shop where she told me why she'd left Merthyr in the first place...'

What was happening here? Mags was now dabbing at her forehead with a handkerchief and her jaw had slackened somewhat, but he carried on relating the tale to her anyhow.

'It's not a happy story either,' he explained, 'but I finally found out the reason why she was banished from the Clarkson House. It's so awful, Mags, bleedin' awful.' He was prepared to steel himself now to inform Mags what had occurred.

'I know, lad,' she said with a great deal of sympathy in her eyes. Then, pulling herself out of the armchair, she wrapped her arms around him. 'I wanted to tell you myself for such a long time.'

Suddenly, he withdrew himself from her embrace. 'You mean you knew all this time?' She nodded. 'And you didn't think to tell me? To at least put me out of my misery?'

'I'm so sorry...' She was shaking her head now. 'I wanted to tell you, really I did, but I was sworn to secrecy by Betsan and Mrs Hardcastle.'

'Mrs Hardcastle keeping it a secret I can understand, but you and Betsan? Why did you both lie to me?'

'We didn't lie to you, Jimmy. It was made clear to the both of us that Enid didn't want you to ever find out, as she thought you'd reject her, I suppose. She even met up with Betsan recently for coffee in Merthyr and she told her the full story then. Believe me, Betsan didn't know the entire truth before that – only I did. All she knew was that Enid had been sent away due to something to do with the master's son.'

'How on earth did you know then?' The emotion inside him made his voice sound croaky. He glared at her.

'Mrs Hardcastle told me herself. I asked to see her at the workhouse as I thought I might find out where she was because you were so upset. The problem was Martha swore me to secrecy and I couldn't break that promise.'

Jimmy nodded, his earlier pent-up emotions now drifting away as he realised what an awful predicament Mags had found herself in. No doubt the woman had been conflicted by omitting to tell the truth and holding a dreadful secret at bay.

'The main thing is you've found one another now though, Jimmy. There'll be no more secrets between any of us. And you still feel the same way about her?'

'Of course, I do, Mags,' said Jimmy with tears in his eyes. 'I love her; she's the only one for me...'

* * *

True to her word, Enid wrote to Jimmy. The tone of her letter was warm and grateful to him for finding her. It was obvious that she'd never stopped loving him, despite all that had happened to her since leaving Merthyr.

He wrote back to her, taking her up on the idea to meet in Pontypridd one day as it was halfway between Merthyr and Cardiff. The town had swollen in population as several collieries, mills and breweries had sprung up there in recent years. It was described as a 'rising town' and Jimmy guessed maybe it was the knock-on effect of being in close proximity to Merthyr where travel was easy with the canal, railway and roads running all the way from his home town to Cardiff docks.

'I'm meeting Enid this Saturday,' he told Mags.

'Oh, that'll be nice. Do you have enough money for the train fare though?'

'Yes. It won't cost as much as to Cardiff as we're meeting halfway in Pontypridd.'

'That's a good idea,' she said, nodding her approval. 'You'll be able to visit the marketplace too if you go on Saturday.' He'd heard all about that large outdoor market that brought people from neighbouring towns and valleys to it.

'I was thinking of buying Enid a little present,' he said, 'maybe I'll get her to choose something for herself at the market. Is there a little jewellery stall there?'

'A jewellery stall? Good grief, lad! You'll be telling me you want to buy her a wedding ring next!'

A soppy smirk plastered itself on Jimmy's face. 'Would that be such a bad idea? I'm seventeen years old next month and both you and Elgan have said I've matured into a man.'

'Of course you have, but you don't need to rush into marriage yet. Get a bit of money behind you first. It's only in recent years you've gone into long trousers!'

Jimmy nodded. 'All would have been well if that bogus son of Mr Baxter's hadn't shown up. Before that he'd made his will out to me should anything happen to him.'

'I know,' said Mags, grimacing. 'That was most unfair. I don't suppose the old fella is in the mood to sort out a new one?'

'He hasn't mentioned it, no.' He shook his head.

'And, of course, you wouldn't like to approach him about it either?'

'Absolutely not. I'm not helping the Baxters for what I can get out of them. It was just for a time, I felt I wouldn't have to worry about my future if I owned that shop. Then when the golden child arrived, I thought I'd set up my own cobbler stall on the market and work hard to achieve it and possibly rent my own shop someday instead, but I can't abandon Mr and Mrs Baxter and do that right now, can I?'

'No, you can't, and I wouldn't want you to either, Jimmy. You've been a good support to me and Elgan over the years. It's what we both love about you. You are so kind and thoughtful towards folk, and you will make a good husband to Enid someday, but please, wait a while longer, won't you?'

He nodded, knowing she was speaking sense.

* * *

Jimmy stood on Pontypridd platform waiting for Enid's train to pull in. It was already five minutes late and he wondered if that darn goods train was causing problems yet again. But within moments, he heard the familiar chugging sound as puffs of steam emerged from the approaching train as passengers got ready to alight and those on the platform surged forward, preparing themselves to get on.

As the carriages drew up, he scanned them to see if he could catch a glimpse of Enid. It was hard for him to tell if she was on it or not as the carriages were quite full. So he stepped back and decided to wait for her to get off. But there was no sign of her. Didn't she realise this was her stop? As the last passenger boarded, he began to panic, running up and down the platform peering inside the train as he called out her name. But still, no one else disembarked. Instead, a middle-aged lady wearing a large hat that shaded part of her face scowled at him through the carriage window as though he were a madman on the loose. Then there was a hissing sound, then chug, chug and the shrill sound of the train's steam whistle and it began to pull out of the station in the direction of Merthyr.

A sharp pang of disappointment hit him in the gut in that moment. A feeling so empty and desolate that it brought tears to his eyes. Had he lost Enid yet again? He could wait for the next train. Yes, that's what he'd do in case she'd missed this one. But what if she wasn't on that one either?

His sense of despondency was so strong he just didn't know what to do with himself. A voice within told him to buck up and find somewhere to have a cup of tea while he waited. He was just about to head towards the town when he saw someone walking towards him, waving. No, it couldn't be. Enid?

Yes, it was her, with a big smile on her face.

Relief flooded through him.

'Oh, Jimmy, I'm so pleased you hadn't left the platform!' she said.

Then he ran towards her, arms outstretched, and they hugged. 'What happened? Why weren't you on that train?' he said, holding her at arm's length as he searched her eyes.

She smiled. 'Mr Darling has some business in Ponty to attend to today, so he told me to save my train fare and he'd take me in his coach instead. I should have been here much earlier but there was a problem with one of the horse's hooves. It's all sorted now but we were held up a good ten minutes. No one realised – that's why the horse appeared lame at first until Mr Darling inspected his hooves and found a small stone lodged in one of them. He managed to dislodge it with a pocketknife, fortunately.'

'Thank goodness you got here, but I would have waited until the next train anyhow,' he said, taking her by the arm and escorting her from the platform and in the direction of the town.

Enid beamed. 'I've got a good few hours here though as I told Mr Darling I'll catch the train back home as he's going on to Merthyr later.'

Jimmy quirked a brow. 'Merthyr? How come?'

'He's going to visit Mr Clarkson senior.'

Jimmy froze suddenly. 'I don't understand why he'd bother with the family of the man who violated you, Enid. And not only that but you seem all right with it.'

'Believe me, I am. Donald Clarkson and Mr Darling have been friends for a long time. He was disgusted with how his son treated me when he discovered the truth and he tried to make amends to me. In fact, it was he who secured employment for me at Beechwood House. He also helped me get away after that big trial in Cardiff when a few men, including Cornelius Sharpe, were up in court. He realised what an ordeal that must have been.'

'Oh, he sounds a good sort then,' said Jimmy thoughtfully. 'Where did you go to, Enid?'

'To a place near the sea in West Wales,' she said, 'to stay with his sister as he thought it would do me good.'

'And did it?'

'Oh, yes. I was able to have lots of peace, fresh air and walks by the sea. And the best part was that before I'd left, I was concerned about Connie – the Irish girl I told you about – she'd gone missing after the trial; anyhow she was located, and Mr Clarkson sent her as a surprise to stay with me at the cottage. It was so kind of him.'

'He sounds a very caring person. What about his wife though? She wasn't so nice to you, was she?'

Enid shook her head. 'No, she wasn't. If Anthony had said black was white, she'd have believed him. But I bear her no ill will as, after all, she's lost a son who was very dear to her.'

'But so has he – Mr Clarkson, I mean.'

'That's true but I think he recognised the darkness in his own son's soul whereas his wife did not.'

Not wanting Enid to dwell too long on painful memories, Jimmy changed the subject. 'I thought we could have a stroll around the shops and visit the marketplace, too. If that's all right with you?'

'That sounds lovely.'

Taking her by the arm once again, Jimmy led her towards the main high street.

Excitedly, the pair glanced in shop windows hither and thither. There was a gentlemen's outfitter with smart-looking shirts and long woollen coats for toffs in its window and a lady's department store with the most fabulous gowns.

'Hey, look at this store,' Enid said as she dragged Jimmy by the arm over to a display window, which showed off a lilac taffeta gown with a nipped-in waist and low neckline with matching beading along the short puffed sleeves and flounced body. 'No surprises for who influenced this gown!' she said as she tapped the side of her nose.

'Eh?' Jimmy frowned.

'You clot, Jimmy!' Enid laughed. 'What does that sign say above this shop?'

Jimmy looked up and squinted to see that it read in fancy lettering: *Arden Brothers Fashions.*

'Oh, I see,' he said, smiling now. 'The Arden Brothers must have opened another store after the Merthyr one. So, you reckon Betsan had something to do with that design?'

'You can count on it! By my understanding, Betsan has a lot of sway there and makes suggestions to James Bradbury.'

Jimmy nodded. 'She's come a long way. It's just a pity she doesn't get more credit for her work.'

'How'd you mean?' Enid wrinkled her nose.

'From what Mags told me, sewn into each piece of work is a label marked as "Bradbury Designs" – no mention of Betsan's name whatsoever!'

'I see what you mean, but I suppose although she has some fantastic ideas as she watched her mother at the sewing machine as a young girl, she's not a qualified designer like he is. She told me he trained at the House of Worth in Paris for some time.'

'Mags told me that. But I don't know, what if the guy is ripping her off?'

Enid shook her head. 'I don't think so. Betsan's done very well, and she speaks highly of him in her letters. She even told me he's thinking of taking her to Paris to meet the man himself.'

'Charles Worth?'

'Yes. Now if he was ripping her off, wouldn't he want to keep her away from someone like that?'

'I suppose so. I have to say I'm very protective of Betsan due to the family connection between her and Mags. She's like a sister to me.'

'Yes, I realise that. But you have no need to fear, Jimmy. Betsan is a big girl now and for someone of her age she's done very well for herself as a supervisor at the clothing factory. She's got plenty of mettle as they say!'

Nodding, they both continued on their way until they reached the outdoor market.

'Mags wasn't kidding when she said this place is bustling on market day!' quipped Jimmy as he surveyed the various stalls set out with all manner of goods and the potential customers vying to get at them. Spotting a small jewellery store sandwiched between the stall selling faggots and peas and the other selling Welsh flannel goods, Jimmy took her hand. 'Come with me,' he said as he led her through the throng.

Wide-eyed, she followed him to a stall that displayed all sorts of costume jewellery. None of it was precious metal or fancy jewels from what Jimmy could see, which was just as well as he couldn't afford that sort of stuff. These were just cheap trinkets made from glass and paste to imitate the real thing.

Finding a little tray of silver-coloured rings with varying-coloured stones, he looked at her and asked, 'Would you like me to buy you one of these, Enid?'

A small smile crept over her lips. 'Why, Jimmy, that's so kind of you but I wouldn't expect you to spend your hard-earned money on me; they're sixpence each!'

He jangled some coins in his trouser pocket. 'I want you to have one.

Pick the prettiest for me, please! It will make me so happy if you accept one.'

Spotting a potential sale, the female stallholder addressed them both. 'They're such pretty rings, aren't they, miss? I only got those in just the other day. But I suspect they'll all be sold by the end of the week, and I don't know if I can get any more.'

That was enough to tempt Enid, so she nodded eagerly at Jimmy.

'Would you like to try a few on to see if any of them fit you?'

'Oh, yes please!' Enid's eyes scanned the tray. 'I like that turquoise one there,' she said, pointing to it.

The stallholder smiled as she handed it to her.

'Here, allow me,' said Jimmy, taking the ring from Enid's outstretched palm. He slipped it over the fourth finger of her left hand.

'Oh, Jimmy!' she enthused. 'It fits perfectly.' She held her hand up and waved it back and forth as she admired the ring.

'Then I shall buy it for you, my sweet!'

He exchanged a few words with the stallholder and slipped a silver sixpence into her outstretched palm. Then he led Enid towards a small shop that had scrumptious-looking cakes in the window – iced buns, cream horns, scones and chocolate eclairs.

'Let's take tea in here,' he said. Once they were seated at the table, he gazed lovingly at her. 'I bought you that ring and slipped it on your ring finger as I want it to be a promise ring.'

'A promise ring?' Enid's eyes widened.

'Yes. I can't afford to buy you an engagement or wedding ring as yet and maybe we shouldn't rush right into marriage anyhow, as we are still young, but it's my promise to someday make you my wife!'

'Oh, Jimmy, I never thought I'd hear you say that, particularly after...'

'Ssh, my love,' he said, placing his index finger to his lips. 'To me you'll always be my sweetheart, my wonderful Enid, whatever happens to you.'

She nodded, tears in her eyes, as she studied the pretty ring on her finger.

It was a while before the emotion of the moment calmed for them both. But finally, as they were ravenous, Jimmy ordered a pot of tea and some cheese and cucumber sandwiches along with some fancy assorted cakes.

'This is truly the best day of my life,' said Enid as she gazed at him adoringly.

'Mine too,' added Jimmy.

For the rest of the afternoon, it felt to Jimmy as though he was walking on air as they strolled around the town, and they managed to sit near the riverbank to watch the water flowing fast towards Cardiff. They smiled as they watched a kingfisher dipping its beak in the water. It was only twelve miles from Merthyr but that afternoon it felt a world away. He remembered the times he'd sat at the same river with Enid but on a different bank in Merthyr. All of that seemed so long ago, yet it wasn't that long really – less than two years. It felt like a different world for them both back then, a world where nothing bad would have ever come between them. But darkness had ensued and out of that darkness emerged a world that, although not feeling quite as safe as previously, now felt full of hope for the future.

13

When Jimmy returned home after having seen Enid safely on to the train bound for Cardiff, he was in for a shock. Elgan was seated in the armchair in the living room with Mags fussing over him.

'B... but I thought you weren't due out for a few days yet?' Jimmy blinked. 'I was going to take the horse and cart then, to collect you from the railway station.'

Mags quickly ushered Jimmy to one side out to the hallway and, with a concerned look on her face, whispered, 'It's Elgan's condition, see; that's why they sent him home early.'

'I don't get it?' Jimmy furrowed his brow. He'd been bursting to tell someone all about his meeting with Enid and now he was being prevented from doing so.

'He's a bit morose, 'tis all,' said Mrs O'Connell as she passed the pair on the way to her living room, a folded newspaper beneath her arm. The woman liked to pick up a newspaper after her long day at the market-place. Mags always reckoned the woman was reading old news by purchasing one so late in the day. But Bridget O'Connell said it was the best part of the day, reading the newspaper at home, feet up with a cuppa without the incessant chat from customers and other stallholders – it was her way to unwind from the day's stresses by blocking out all the noise.

'Elgan hasn't snapped out of it since your last visit, Jimmy,' warned Mags. 'He turned up here and got emotional as soon as he saw me. I haven't even taken his own kids to meet with him yet in case he upsets them, so they're in Mrs O'Connell's living room at the moment. I'd been looking forward to introducing them to each other an' all.'

'Never you mind,' said Jimmy. 'Look, you go and have a break. I'll speak to Elgan to find out what's going on with him.'

'Would you, Jimmy?' Tears were brimming from her eyes. 'He's barely spoken a word to me since he got home.'

But it's hardly his home, is it? Jimmy thought to himself, but decided it was better not to say aloud.

'Thank you.' Mags shot him a tentative smile.

'Yes, go and have a cuppa with Mrs O'Connell and I'll see what he says to me,' Jimmy reassured as he patted her shoulder.

Mags nodded her thanks and then headed for the kitchen.

'Elgan, what's the matter?' he asked as he approached him. Then he took a seat in the armchair opposite. He could tell the man was dispirited and defeated by his demeanour.

Elgan, who had his head lowered, raised it so their eyes met. 'I just feel so inadequate.' He paused for a moment.

'Inadequate? In what sort of way?'

'In that I should have been providing for you all, not leaving you to it while I went to prison...' He took a painful breath. 'And the twins...'

'But you knew about them when Mags got pregnant?'

'I did, yes, Jimmy, but because Gwennie and David had taken them on and as Mags was in no fit state to, I sort of put them out of my mind. I was just thankful they were being loved and cared for... but...'

'But what?'

He shook his head. 'I don't even know where to begin to be a father to those little mites.'

'Oh, Elgan, of course you do. You were like a father to me when my own died and I was young back then. I couldn't have wished for better. You just need time to adjust to all the changes that have come into your life, that's all.'

'Do you think so?'

Jimmy huffed out a laboured breath. 'All right, it will take time for you to get to know one another, and this house...' his eyes scanned the room '...is new to us all but it's much better than our poky place back in China. And as for your work on the horse and cart, you can still do that eventually. Jasper and Casper are being stabled in a neighbour's field close by. I've kept the cart in working order for you. Well, I've had to really as I set up a collection and delivery service for Mr Baxter at some of the big houses in the area...'

Elgan's eyes widened with surprise. 'I'm so proud of you, Jimmy.'

He nodded. 'So, you see, we're all starting anew here. Later, Mags will fetch the twins. They're in Mrs O'Connell's living room right now. They'll take your mind off things for sure.'

Elgan smiled but the smile didn't quite reach his eyes.

* * *

Later that evening, Jimmy watched as Elgan met Alys and Aled, his own offspring. At first both children were wary of him but, eventually, they approached him, and Jimmy noticed how a light seemed to flick on in the man's eyes. It was at that point that he realised, although it would take time for Elgan to adjust after spending a year in prison, there was hope there for him in the form of his own offspring.

14

Elgan had been home for about a fortnight when Jimmy decided it was time he got back to his round.

'Don't you think you're rushing him a bit?' asked Mags as she watched Jimmy attach Casper to the cart. He began to load up bits and pieces belonging to Elgan, which had been stored in Mrs O'Connell's garden shed. Today he was loading up an old trestle table, four matching chairs and some old ornaments.

'No, there's no time like the present! Mr Baxter has allowed me the morning off so I can help set Elgan back up on his round. He's lost a lot of his confidence since being in prison. If I go out on the round with him, even just now and again until I'm sure he can do it alone, it should be a big help.'

'I hope so,' said Mags with a worried frown on her face. 'He was starting to settle in living here. He loves tending to Mrs O'Connell's vegetable patch and taking care of her flower beds too.'

'That's all fine and dandy,' said Jimmy as he loaded the final box of ornaments to the cart, 'but it's not healthy for him to be at home all day long. A man needs to earn a living. In any case, he can still tend to the garden too.'

'I suppose you're right, lad.'

'Besides,' said Jimmy brightly, 'if he gets into any trouble, I'm with him. It's a good way for me to keep an eye and assess just what he's capable of now. Will you fetch him for me? He does know he's going.'

'Of course,' said Mags as she wiped away a tear. 'It's just it's been so long since he last did anything like this.'

'I know,' said Jimmy as he laid a hand of reassurance on her shoulder. Then he watched as she entered the house to summon Elgan.

Within a minute or two Elgan was stood outside gazing at the horse and cart almost in disbelief as though he thought he'd never see either again. Jimmy feared the man would change his mind about embarking on his old round, but instead he nodded at Jimmy. Then he patted the horse's soft muzzle, and with watering eyes, laid his head against the horse's head, whispering to him, 'I've missed you, old boy!'

Drawing away, and facing one another, Casper looked at his master and Jimmy could have sworn the horse had tears in his eyes too, but then Jimmy blinked and, turning back towards the scene before him, thought he must be imagining things.

He watched Elgan climb aboard the cart and then Jimmy did the same, taking up the reins.

Mags handed Elgan a muslin-wrapped package. 'These are bread and cheese sandwiches for your lunch, both,' she said.

Elgan smiled lovingly at her. 'As thoughtful as ever, my sweet.'

Then they were off. Jimmy steered the horse in the direction of Plymouth Street. He'd done his homework and had been told that a Mrs Wilson was interested in a second-hand table and chairs. Betsan had told him about that as the woman was one of her old neighbours.

Elgan, who was sitting quietly throughout the journey, shivered, and Jimmy wondered whether it because there was a nip in the air or because he was nervous. The truth was he didn't quite know how to handle things for their first trip out, as he was used to Elgan being the one in charge, but now with his shoe repair deliveries he was used to being his own boss.

But he needn't have worried as Mrs Wilson was very pleased with the table and chairs and, before he knew it, Jimmy noticed Elgan having a little bit of banter with the woman, as he did with customers in the old days. A little joke here and there and a quip about the weather, making the woman chuckle. The light was slowly returning to his eyes, and he seemed to be enjoying himself. Yes, Jimmy's instincts were right all along; this was the right thing to do, to throw the man in the deep end.

Mags was waiting for them both when they returned later that afternoon.

'Well, how did it go then?' she asked as soon as they emerged through the front door.

'*Da iawn! Chwarae teg!*' Elgan, forgetting himself, expounded in the Welsh language, then remembering that Jimmy spoke mainly English as did a lot of younger people in the town, said, 'Very good, fair play, Mags. I managed to convince our first customer of the day to purchase that old table and chairs, then she said one of her neighbours might be interested in some of the ornaments, then Jimmy sold that old stool and some cushions and then...'

'Slow down!' Mags laughed. 'I can't keep up with you.'

She had a twinkle in her eyes, and Jimmy could see how relieved she was to see all was well and that some of the old Elgan had returned.

'I've made some stew and dumplings for your tea,' said Mags. 'You need a bit of feeding up, Elgan. You need plenty of flesh on those bones!'

He nodded at her. 'Being out on that cart in the fresh air has really given me an appetite.' Patting his stomach, he asked, 'Now where are my Aled and Alys?'

'In the living room. Go and get changed out of your work clothes and wash and brush up, then you can go and read them a story.'

He smiled and Jimmy could tell he couldn't wait to see them. They were both giving him a new lease of life. Elgan even seemed younger these past couple of weeks, but Jimmy did wonder if he'd ever go back to his old ways of associating with criminals. He sure hoped not.

* * *

The days settled into a pattern of Jimmy helping on the cart for a couple of mornings a week and then, one day, he just left Elgan to his own devices, which seemed to work out well. The man even acquired a few new customers. Of course, the cart was still needed for footwear deliveries, so Jimmy came to an arrangement with Elgan of the best time to borrow the cart, which was usually around four o'clock in the afternoon as Elgan tended to stop work around that time of day. Yes, life was sweet indeed.

But it was while Jimmy was resting on his laurels that fate took a dramatic turn. Polly, who had since married Gethin a couple of weeks previously, turned up at the house one day with her head lowered and in a distressed state.

'Oh, my goodness!' said Mags as she let the girl in through the front door. 'What on earth has happened to you?'

Polly lifted her head to display a swollen and cut lip, which quivered as she stood there trembling, unable to utter a single word.

'What's gone on, *cariad*?'

Tears welled in Polly's eyes, and she swallowed hard. 'Oh, Mrs Hughes. I didn't know marriage was going to be like this. My parents think the world of Gethin so I can't tell them what he's done to me. He's a chapel-going man they approve of and soon he's to be appointed as one of the chapel deacons.'

'There, there,' said Mags as she took the girl into her arms and soothed her gently as if she were comforting Aled or Alys. 'Chapel-going or not, no man has a right to lay a finger on you.' She held her at arm's length for a moment and, as she did so, she noticed some bruising on Polly's wrists. The girl winced as though Mags's touch had caused her some discomfort. Mags narrowed her gaze. 'Are there any more bruises on you beside your wrists?'

Polly nodded. 'They're hidden under my dress but they're on my back too.'

'Here, come with me into the kitchen where I can get a good look at them. You're all right – there's no one home right now and the twins are at school.'

Polly followed Mags into the kitchen where she removed her dress for her to carefully inspect the bruising.

'I've got some tincture in the cupboard I can apply to those,' she said.

'I'll go and get it and then I'll make you some chamomile tea for your nerves. It'll help calm you down.'

Polly smiled gratefully. 'Thank you. I didn't know what to do as I can hardly go and see my parents. They think the sun shines out of my husband. To them he can do no wrong and it was my own father who suggested Gethin become a deacon at the chapel.'

Mags shook her head, tutted and then muttered under her breath, 'Oh dear, what are we going to do?'

Polly winced as Mags applied the tincture to her bruises. Then she slipped her dress back on and sat at the kitchen table while Mags brewed up. Mags placed a cup of the tea on the table for her and she sat opposite the girl.

'Polly, you must promise me something.' Mags sighed. 'You're not to go back to your husband if he's going to treat you like this. It's just not safe. How did it come about anyhow?'

Polly grimaced. 'He was good to me before we wed but after our wedding night, he began to snap at me over little things. Nothing is ever good enough. I can't cook like his mother does; he reckons I'm sloppy around the house, too. It's really affecting my confidence...' She began to weep.

'I'm not surprised,' said Mags. 'You've no need to go back there though. You can stay here for a spell until you get your head together. I'm sure Mrs O'Connell won't mind.'

'I should have married someone like your Jimmy,' she said, smiling through her tears. 'He'd have treated me well.'

'Maybe you should have at that,' sympathised Mags, 'but Jimmy's reunited with his old flame, Enid, now, love.'

Polly nodded and swallowed hard. 'The good ones always get away. I regret now that I didn't see what was in front of me. I might have been Jimmy's girl once upon a time. My head was turned though when I was introduced to Gethin. I put pleasing my parents over pleasing myself, and he had such good prospects as he'll one day inherit the family business. What a fool I've been.'

Mags sincerely doubted Polly would have been Jimmy's girl as from what she'd been able to tell, although he was very fond of her, after getting to know her, he'd had reservations, realising she was very naïve and would never match up to Enid in his eyes. She'd never dream of telling Polly that though. She didn't want to hurt her; she was hurting enough as it was.

* * *

Jimmy was surprised to see Polly at the house when he returned from work and even more so to see the state of her swollen lip. When Mags filled him in on what had gone on, he was furious, wanting to head over to Polly's house to confront her husband. Polly was a lovely young lady who had never hurt anyone; she didn't deserve this.

'Now, settle down, Jimmy. You can't go rushing over there like a bull at a gate,' advised Mags, closing the living room door so Polly wouldn't over-hear them. 'That sort of thing won't do any good and you might come off worse. I thought something was up. Their marriage seemed to be conducted in secrecy. There were no real wedding guests. I thought I'd at least be invited but I wasn't. The only people who attended were both sets of parents and the bride and groom themselves. I got a bit suspicious when Polly told me, not long afterwards, that her new husband was trying to get her to give up working for me. The girl loves her job; it gives her a real sense of purpose. That husband of hers is trying to separate her from all her friends, Jimmy, and that's not good. So, I've told her she's to stay here as long as she likes, though she'll have to make a bed up on the living room couch every night.'

Jimmy shook his head. 'No, Polly can have my bed if she wants it. I'll take the couch.'

Mags smiled and, lightly touching his arm, said, 'Enid is lucky you found her again, Jimmy. You'll make her a fine husband someday.'

He returned the smile and blushed. 'I hope so,' he said, staring through the window, far away in his thoughts about the young woman he loved.

* * *

Jimmy spent a restless night tossing and turning on the living room couch while Polly slept in his bedroom. He didn't think he'd miss his bed so much but he'd slept on far worse. The beds at the workhouse had been narrow and hard, so even the couch was a luxury compared to those coffin-like structures. It wasn't so much the lack of comfort that was keeping him awake, as no matter which way he turned, his neck felt stiff and his limbs numb at times; it was because he was concerned for Polly. Society dictated that a wife did her husband's bidding and, as the girl had explained to him, her parents would be likely to take his side as they saw him as being a godly man. Well, in Jimmy's book, striking a woman – or come to that a man or child – was most ungodly. If the man could do something so dreadful at the beginning of the marriage when all in the garden should have been rosy, goodness knew what he'd end up doing next.

He managed to drift off to sleep for an hour or two when he was awoken by a clatter outside the window. Wondering if it was a cat prowling outside, he went to look and, when he opened the front door, became alarmed to see a dark shadow. For a moment he feared it was Mr Baxter's son out to cause bother for him, but then he remembered the man was safely under lock and key and in any case wouldn't know he'd moved in with Mrs O'Connell.

'Who's there?' he asked, finding his courage at last.

'It's me, Gethin Jenkins, Polly's husband.'

'I know who you are!' yelled Jimmy, annoyed to have been woken out of his sleep by the man who had thumped his wife. 'But what are you doing here and at this hour too?'

'I've come to take my wife back home with me!' he said as though Polly were a piece of his own personal property. 'Is she here?'

Jimmy swallowed. Was he to tell the truth or not? He decided to lie as it might give Polly more time to get away to some other place of safety. 'Your wife is not here. Go home and go back to bed.'

'She must be here. I've looked everywhere for her. She hasn't gone home to her parents, and she's got no friends to speak of.'

Aye, you've put paid to that, thought Jimmy. As far as he was concerned this relationship with Polly and Gethin had happened all too quickly; it had been a whirlwind romance. Neither he nor Mags had even been introduced to the man.

'Are you sure she's not here?' growled Gethin.

'Perfectly sure, now go on home and look for her in daylight in the morning,' commanded Jimmy.

To his surprise, Gethin nodded and left without another word. It was then Jimmy wondered if the man had been drinking alcohol to call at the house at this hour of the morning. Had his alcohol consumption been anything to do with the bruises on Polly?

Breathing out a long, hard breath, Jimmy returned inside the house and, as well as locking the front door, he bolted it too.

* * *

The following morning Jimmy related his surprise encounter to Mags, who frowned.

'Oh dear, I don't think Polly is safe here now, Jimmy. We're going to have to find somewhere else for her to go for the time being.'

'I know, Mags. I was thinking the very same thing myself. But where?'

'I'll have a word with Elgan. He used to collect money for landlords sometimes; he might know of a property she can rent.'

'That's a good idea.' Jimmy nodded. 'She won't be safe here now he's got an inkling where she is.'

Elgan though couldn't come up with somewhere for the girl to stay. He'd lost a lot of his contacts since being in prison and preferred to keep away from many of them lest he slip back into his old ways.

'I suppose Polly will have to remain where she is for now,' Mags advised. 'At least she's safer here than going back to that beast.'

Jimmy had to agree with that. 'We'll just have to ensure she's not left on her own. Elgan and I are out most of the day; at least you can keep an eye on her, Mags, when you work.'

'Yes, now the sewing machine has been moved from Betsan's house to here, I'm able to conduct all business from this premises. Unfortunately...'

'What?' He blinked.

'What about when I'm at the market stall covering for Bridget?'

'You'll just have to take Polly with you, I suppose.'

It wasn't going to be easy. Jimmy would have preferred them not all to be concerned in Polly's affairs but, on the other hand, he couldn't watch her return home either. There seemed little choice in the matter for now.

* * *

Polly had settled well into living at the house and there seemed strangely no more contact from Gethin, which made Jimmy feel suspicious, until one afternoon, while he was at work, he saw a familiar-looking man pass the shop window accompanied by a young blonde woman. No wonder Gethin wasn't going to search for Polly any longer – he now had someone else! Finding it hard to concentrate on his work, he asked Harri to mind the shop for a moment while he went in search of Polly at Mrs O'Connell's clothing stall in the market. Polly seemed in her element, as he watched her exchange a few words with a customer she'd just sold something to. A feeling of unease overtook Jimmy as he realised he was about to shatter her world further, particularly as the girl had recovered of late. All the bruising and her swollen lip had now disappeared.

'Hello, Jimmy!' she said brightly as he approached. 'Come to check on me, have you?' She chuckled.

Oh dear, this was going to be harder than he'd imagined.

'Er, sort of,' he said, exchanging concerned glances with Mags. 'I need to speak to you about something.'

'Yes, what is it?' She blinked.

'It's your husband.'

'You haven't had another encounter with him, have you?' She looked concerned now, her soft features hardening with fear.

'No, not at all!' He waved a hand. 'I just saw him passing the shop when I was at work, but he wasn't alone, he was accompanied by a pretty young blonde woman.'

'Oh, that sounds like Millicent Roberts from chapel,' she said. 'She's a regular chapel goer.'

'Well, she didn't look much of a chapel goer to me, associating with a married man!' said Jimmy, tersely.

'How'd you mean?' Polly bit her lip.

Jimmy hesitated before replying, realising how much this would hurt the young woman. 'He had his arm around her waist. It's my thought that's why you haven't seen him of late, as he has someone else.'

A strangulated sound emerged from Polly's throat and then she swallowed hard. 'No, no!' She shook her head as her eyes enlarged with horror. 'You must be mistaken!'

'I'm sorry, I'm not. They looked most intimate with one another. What would your parents make of him now? Did they provide you with some sort of dowry when you married the man?'

Polly nodded slowly as she replied in a croaky tone of voice. 'Yes. My father gave us some of his life savings to set us up.'

'Then you have got to tell your parents, Polly. This isn't right at all. Not only has the man physically abused you but now he has your money to spend on other women. All the while, acting like an upright member of society!'

Jimmy thought he'd cause Polly to cry, but instead she held her chin erect. 'You're quite right. Gethin is making a fool out of me, and this can't continue. I shall leave here right now.' She looked towards Mags. 'I'll call to see my parents and tell them what's gone on. Would you come with me, Jimmy?'

Jimmy gulped. This wasn't what he intended at all but now Polly seemed to view him as some kind of white knight. He didn't like being put in that position because the only person he ought to be one of those to was Enid. Reluctantly, he found himself nodding. 'I can't be too long, mind you, as I've left young Harri in charge of the shop. He's a good lad but there are some things he's not trained to do.'

'We won't be too long, Jimmy,' said Polly, taking him by the arm. 'It's just a short walk over to Georgetown.' Jimmy knew full well how far away the place was, and he had very bad memories of it after being boarded out to that cruel grocer some years back, but he said nothing of it.

Feeling helpless for once, he made eye contact with Mags, who shrugged her shoulders. She, too, must now feel all this Polly business was getting terribly out of hand.

15

'*Dewch i mewn, cariad,*' Mrs Samuel was saying as she held the front door open for the pair to enter. Polly glanced nervously at Jimmy but at least the girl's mother wasn't being hostile towards her. Considering Polly hadn't seen her parents in weeks, Jimmy wondered why the woman wasn't more pleased to see her daughter.

Mrs Samuel led them down a dark passageway and into the living room where there was a small fire kindling in the grate. On the walls were various emblems of their faith. One was a painting of a chapel with the words 'Honour thy Father and thy Mother' and another read 'The Wages of Sin is Death'. Jimmy swallowed. He got the impression from things Polly had told him that this was a strict, authoritarian household.

'Won't you both have a cup of tea?' the woman offered, her grey eyes large and unblinking.

'No, thank you. We can't stop for long as Jimmy has to return to the cobbler shop where he works. There's something I need to discuss with you both. Where is my father?'

'He's just out in the backyard, chopping some sticks for firewood. I'll go and fetch him,' said Mrs Samuel, looking alarmed by the urgency of her daughter's request.

It was not a couple of minutes before the woman returned with her husband by her side. The man was shorter than his wife, which Jimmy wasn't expecting. He didn't know why but he'd anticipated a much taller man. His hair was neatly combed back and kept in place with what looked like pomade. Even though he'd been cutting wood in the yard, he wore a pristine white shirt, grey waistcoat and a tie. If he donned a jacket and a hat, he wouldn't have looked out of place stepping into a chapel. Indeed, Jimmy didn't know anyone who dressed like that around the home; Elgan sure didn't.

'Hello,' Mr Samuel said stiffly. 'Why do we have the pleasure of your company this afternoon, Polly, when we haven't seen you for weeks?'

Polly swallowed hard. 'I haven't been living at home with Gethin, Father. I left and I'm now living at Mrs O'Connell's house.'

'Pardon?' said Mr Samuel, his face flushing bright red. 'And why have you left your husband's side?'

'B... because he hurt me, Father. He beat me. I went to stay with Mrs Hughes, who I work for, at Mrs O'Connell's house. And now, since I've left him, Gethin has been spotted with another woman walking up the high street – someone from chapel, actually... Millicent Roberts!'

Mr Samuel sucked in a sharp breath through his front teeth and shook his head. '*Duw duw.* I don't know what this world is coming to...'

Jimmy thought for a moment the man was going to say something harsh about his son-in-law's behaviour but instead he turned towards his daughter and, wagging a finger, began to chastise her.

'You march in here like a frivolous hussy in the company of another young man who is not your husband! Who is he anyhow?' Mr Samuel narrowed his eyes.

Jimmy cleared his throat to speak up for them both as he fixed his gaze on Mr Samuel. The man was talking about him as if he wasn't in the same room, which he found rude and distasteful – no wonder Polly had married at such an early opportunity if these were the sort of parents she was coming home to. She'd jumped out of the frying pan into the fire.

'It's all true what your daughter is telling you, Mr Samuel. I saw the bruising on her and her swollen lip too, and I was the person who saw your son-in-law, not an hour since, in the company of another young woman about the town.'

'Well, is it all that surprising?' yelled Mr Samuel with a gleam in his eyes. 'When his own wife has abandoned him? The good book says that a wife is to yield to her husband. And who are you anyway, young man?' He glared in Jimmy's direction.

Jimmy lifted his chin and, staring the man in the face, said, 'I'm Jimmy Corcoran, the person who helped your daughter get a job sewing with my auntie.'

'So, don't tell me, you also live under that Mrs O'Connell's roof?'

'Yes, sir.' Jimmy nodded, all the while wondering why the man should question this.

'A hotbed of sin, by the sound of it...' he said in a low growl, causing Jimmy to grit his teeth.

Jimmy didn't wish to lose his temper, not here, not right now, but the man was provoking him into it. 'Look here, Mr Samuel, Polly could do without this nonsense. I saw her the day it all happened and let me tell you, she was badly beaten up by her husband. It seems to me you are only thinking of yourself and how society might view your daughter for leaving him.'

Polly, who had now taken herself off to a corner of the room, began to sob uncontrollably as she brought her hands to her eyes, her body convulsing from the upset of her father's cruel words. Her mother appeared distressed at not knowing what to do, not wanting to incur her husband's wrath even further, but in Jimmy's view, any mother worth her salt would comfort her daughter, not take her husband's side.

'Get out of my house and don't darken this door ever again!' yelled Mr Samuel as he pointed his finger at Polly. 'You're not fit to be called a daughter of mine!'

'Come along, Polly,' said Jimmy gently as tears rolled down her cheeks. 'It's evident your father can't bear to hear the real version of events and will take the side of a wife beater over his own daughter.' Looking the man in the eye he carried on, 'I pity you, sir. I really do. But I believe your daughter is better off living with us than either an uncaring father or a violent husband. Good day to you!'

Without waiting for a reply, he quickly ushered Polly out of the door, where outside in the street, she collapsed into his arms at the upset of it all.

* * *

Polly said little on the short walk back to the marketplace. When they returned, Mags didn't even need to ask how it all went; she could see by the state of Polly how upset she was – by her red-rimmed and swollen eyes.

'Take her home, Jimmy,' she instructed. 'Make her a hot drink and put her to bed, please. I'll only be here another hour or so. Then you can return to work. I don't want you getting into any trouble with the Baxters over this.'

Jimmy nodded, then something occurred to him. 'But that will mean she'll be alone in the house. Elgan won't be home from his round yet. Isn't it important she's not left alone?'

Mags shrugged. 'Nothing we can do about that, but it's unlikely her husband will seek her out this afternoon, not if he's with another woman,' she added as a whisper. 'Maybe that's the reason he never returned to look for her in any case.'

'It seems that way,' said Jimmy, fixing his gaze on Polly, who was now leaning on the wooden stall for support. What a contrast. An hour ago, she'd been full of joy, thoroughly enjoying herself as she made sales with customers, and now she was a crumpled mess. He led the young woman away in the direction of the house, supporting her beneath her arm. Some men in society had a lot to answer for, one of them being Polly's father and the other her husband.

* * *

Jimmy had written to Enid to invite her to Sunday dinner. He hadn't seen her since their visit to Pontypridd and he felt it was time for them to meet again. He even offered to recompense her for her train fare, but she replied saying she was able to afford it. He realised if they wanted to see more of one another then maybe one of them needed to move a little nearer to the other. But now that seemed impossible as Enid was doing so well at Beechwood House. Her letter told him that Mrs Sowerberry, the housekeeper, would be retiring soon and the woman had recommended she take over as housekeeper instead, which along with more responsibility would mean more pay for her. Also, it seemed nigh on impossible that Jimmy could desert the Baxters right now, even if he wanted to, unless a suitable replacement was found. Harri was too young and inexperienced but in a couple of years the lad might well fit the bill.

Sunday afternoon soon arrived, and Enid stepped off the train, looking even more beautiful than he last remembered. The sun was high in the sky and seemed to illuminate her Titian-coloured hair, which made her appear almost angelic. His angel. Taking her by the hand, he pecked a quick kiss on her cheek. He'd loved to have taken her in his arms there and then and kiss her properly, but that just wouldn't do as there were too many people milling around them. Some people used the train on a Sunday to attend church and chapel services in various parts of the valley, so to get caught locked in a passionate embrace particularly on the Lord's Day would be seen as sinful. How he wished they were already married and living in their own home.

'Mags and Mrs O'Connell are making a lovely dinner for us!' he enthused. 'Mags has roasted a leg of lamb and prepared all the veg and Mrs O'Connell has baked an apple pie for afters,' he said, rubbing his stomach in anticipation of the veritable feast that lay ahead.

'How is Polly?' asked Enid. Jimmy had kept her informed of the girl's predicament in his correspondence.

'She's improving day by day but I'm sorry to say this, she relies on me far too much. Since that incident where I sent her husband packing and spoke up to her father, she's got it into her head that I'm her knight in shining armour!'

'Oh,' said Enid, appearing taken aback. 'That doesn't sound good, does it?'

It was then he decided he'd best come clean and tell her all about his previous relationship with the girl.

'...so, what started out as a possible relationship, didn't really happen at all,' he concluded. 'We were more like brother and sister in my mind. And of course, I never really got over losing you.' He squeezed her hand in reassurance.

'The trouble is,' said Enid, 'what's going on in Polly's mind? It seems to me that maybe she has designs on you, Jimmy. She knows what it's like to be treated badly by someone of the opposite sex and now, she's obviously placed you on a pedestal.'

Jimmy gulped. 'Do you really think so?'

Enid nodded. Then pasted a smile on her lips. 'Come on,' she said, 'one thing we mustn't ever do is allow someone to come between us.'

He nodded in agreement and then, taking her by the arm, walked her to his home.

* * *

Aled and Alys ran out to greet Jimmy and Enid when they arrived at the house.

'Hello, you two,' said Jimmy as he stooped to give them a big hug. Then pulling himself up to full height, he turned and gestured towards Enid. 'I've brought someone to meet you. This here is Miss Enid Hardcastle.'

Alys put her head down shyly, resting her chin on her chest, while Aled beamed at Enid.

'Hello, you two,' said Enid, smiling at the pair. 'I've heard a lot about you both.'

'What have you heard?' Aled wanted to know.

'Jimmy told me you're both twins and that you now go to school?'

'Yes, that's right,' replied Aled. 'I'm a big boy now, the biggest in my class!'

Alys looked up. 'Did Jimmy tell you about my rag doll, Joanna?'

'No,' said Enid. 'But when I was your age, I had a rag doll too.'

'Did you, Miss Enid?' Alys smiled at her. 'What was her name?'

'Molly Mae.'

Alys's eyes were huge and shiny now. 'I'll show you mine if you like.'

Enid nodded and smiled as Alys stretched out her little hand for her to take.

'Go inside with her,' whispered Jimmy. 'She wants to take you to their bedroom to show you. She doesn't often take to people right away, but it appears she likes you.'

Enid did as told and Aled, not wishing to be left out, followed the pair inside.

Jimmy set off towards the kitchen to see if Mags or Mrs O'Connell needed any help, but when he got there, he found it was Polly who was keeping an eye on things.

'Where are Mags and Mrs O'Connell?' He fixed his gaze on her.

She beamed when she saw it was him standing there, her large dark eyes glistening. 'Mrs O'Connell is having a spell on the bed, as she put it, and Mags has gone on the cart with Elgan to see if she can pick up some fresh mint. She forgot all about that to go with the lamb. They should be back soon.'

Polly began to close the space between them, which made Jimmy feel a little awkward. Then, looking up at him, she placed a hand on his shoulder.

'Would you like a cup of tea while you wait, Jimmy?'

'Er, not for me, thanks. I'm just going to see what Enid and the twins are up to...'

'Oh?' Polly took a step back. It was almost as though she'd forgotten he'd invited his girlfriend to Sunday dinner. Seeming deflated now, she turned her back on him and began to stir something in a bubbling saucepan on top of the stove.

Jimmy hoped Mags and Elgan would hurry home.

When he got to the top of the stairs, he noticed the twins' bedroom door was ajar, and Enid, who had removed her jacket, was seated on the floor between them both, reading them something out of one of their picture books. He realised the reason she was so good with children was probably because she had younger siblings. He stood silent for a while unobserved, marvelling at what a great mother she'd make someday, and, in that moment, he saw a vision of her cradling their own children. His heart swelled with love and pride for her. Then there was the sound of the front door opening and closing and voices down below, making his daydream disappear.

Mags and Elgan were home and wasn't he glad of that!

* * *

When all of them were finally seated around the large table in Mrs O'Connell's dining room, Jimmy continued to feel uncomfortable as he noticed the strange looks Polly was giving Enid. If looks could kill, poor Enid would be dead in the water. He'd never really seen this side of the girl before, but then again, maybe she'd never had reason to feel jealous previous to this.

Everyone around the table seemed oblivious to what was going on except for himself and Polly. Enid happily chatted to Mags who was seated beside her while Elgan and Mrs O'Connell were discussing the marketplace. Bridget was explaining how there was a new market inspector who didn't stand for any nonsense. The twins, who were seated at the end of the table beside one another, seemed happy enough, quiet for once as they shovelled large forkfuls of the delicious roast lamb meal into their mouths.

This was a rare treat indeed as usually they made do with a small chicken most Sundays. Yet Jimmy couldn't really taste his food properly as he was far too concerned what Polly might do or say. She hadn't seemed herself of late since leaving her husband. Mags didn't appear to notice it much, but he had. Those nights when Polly had risen several times from his bed, where she'd been sleeping while he still made do with kipping on the living room couch. He had no idea what she was doing at night but, whatever it was, she was disturbing his sleep as he'd hear her opening and closing the kitchen door or her footsteps on the stairs. Once or twice, she'd even opened the door as though she were watching him sleeping, then closed it again. It was as if she was wide awake at night and listless by day. Once he'd even caught her asleep, slumped over the sewing machine one morning, and had to rouse her with a cup of coffee to ensure she stayed awake to complete her work – Mags would have been furious if she'd known that.

Why couldn't people see what he saw? Mags made no reference to the girl's work so he assumed she must be putting the hours in and turning out garments of a reasonable quality. Betsan hadn't joined them for dinner today as she'd gone somewhere with that Bradbury bloke. If she'd been here, he knew she'd have noticed something. She was very observant about that sort of thing, and he didn't want to worry Enid too much. He just wanted her to enjoy herself; she worked so hard throughout the week.

As he glanced down at her hand, his heart swelled with pride that she still wore the ring he'd bought for her. In fact, he just thought to mention it, so Polly realised how serious he was about Enid.

'Mags,' Jimmy said, laying down his knife and fork on his half-finished meal. 'Do you like the ring I bought for Enid?'

Everyone stopped in their tracks as attention was drawn towards Enid. There was the clinking of cutlery as some paused to lay down their utensils and Jimmy watched as the young woman's face suffused with heat. He hadn't wanted to embarrass her for all the world, but he wanted to make a point.

'Here, let me see, *cariad*,' said Mags, smiling as she took Enid's hand. 'My, that ring is ever so pretty, isn't it?'

Enid nodded.

'It's a promise ring,' said Jimmy.

Polly glared at him. 'What's a promise ring? Never heard of one of those before!'

'It's a ring to make a promise that someday I'll marry Enid.'

Jimmy watched as Polly's mouth gaped open and snapped shut again. 'But that's what an engagement ring is for, Jimmy. It will take you ages to save up for one of those.'

'Yes, it will take some time. But it will happen. I'm putting away a little money from my wages every week to save for our wedding,' he said as he took Enid's hand and they both made eye contact with one another and smiled. 'In fact, if I had my way, there'd be no engagement as we'd marry immediately!'

'Well, I think it's marvellous!' said Elgan as he raised his glass of blackcurrant cordial. 'You can't beat the love of a good woman! And I'm so glad I found mine!' He winked in Mags's direction and now it was her turn to blush.

'I'll just clear the table for the pudding,' said Polly in a clipped tone of voice.

Jimmy realised she now felt uncomfortable and was using it as an excuse to dismiss herself from them all.

'I'll help you,' offered Enid, but Polly dismissed her with the wave of her hand.

'I can manage. I'm not a cripple, you know!' she snapped, leaving Enid's bottom lip trembling.

Jimmy squeezed her hand in reassurance. Polly was behaving badly, and it didn't sit right with him. He knew she wouldn't have responded like that if Mags or Mrs O'Connell had offered help. Her hurtful remark left an uneasy silence at the table while the girl began to scrape and stack the dishes. When she'd left the room to head for the kitchen, Jimmy let out a long breath.

'Sorry, folks, I don't know if I can put up with this much longer.'

'What do you mean?' asked Mags, her eyes full of concern.

'Polly's really latched on to me lately and it's now obvious she's full of spite towards Enid.'

'Don't you think you might be imagining things?' asked Mrs O'Connell. 'She seems all right to me.'

Jimmy stood and closed the door so Polly couldn't overhear. 'No, she's not right at all. She's up at all times of the night wandering around the house. Maybe I'm the only one who is disturbed by this as I'm sleeping downstairs.'

'All right, Jimmy,' said Mags as she cast her eyes on the door for fear Polly might emerge through it at any moment. 'Maybe this isn't the best place to discuss this. We'll chat later in case she overhears.'

He nodded. 'Thank you. I just wish her parents had taken her back in as I'm doubled up on that old couch at night.' He glanced at Mrs O'Connell. 'Sorry, but it's fine for sitting in, not sleeping in.'

'I hear you, Jimmy,' said the woman. 'Maybe we can get you a second-hand bed from somewhere?'

Jimmy shook his head. 'With all respect, Mrs O'Connell, that's not the point.'

The elderly woman furrowed her brow. 'Then tell me what the point is?'

He huffed out a breath as everyone except for the twins watched him. 'The point is she shouldn't still be here.'

16

Everyone glanced at one another, not knowing how to respond. Enid seemed to squirm around in her seat while Elgan glanced at the ceiling as if somehow the answer to the problem lay there. It was only Mags and Mrs O'Connell who kept their eyes on Jimmy.

Finally, after an awkward pause, Mags said, 'I think you're right, Jimmy. Although the girl is a great help to our business...' she glanced at Bridget, who nodded '...if she is going to start to cause trouble because she has a liking for you, then it needs to get sorted. Agreed, Bridget?'

Mrs O'Connell nodded. 'Aye, I like young Polly well enough, but I think maybe she now needs to get out from under this roof. We're already full to bursting.'

'Oh, I'm sorry, Bridget.' Mags looked at the woman. 'Have we over-stayed our welcome here?'

'No, not at all. 'Tis not any of you lot I'm referring to, as you're all like family to me. It feels like Betsan and Jimmy are my own children and the twins my grandchildren. And you and Elgan, well, you're like a sister to me, Mags. And Elgan my brother-in-law. But, when I think of Polly, she doesn't really belong here. And if she can't return to either her husband or her family home, then we'll have to come up with a solution. I won't have her kicked out on to the street.'

Everyone murmured in agreement though Jimmy now felt like a bit of a heel for raising the topic in the first place.

'I've got an idea,' said Enid and all heads turned towards her.

'Yes, go on,' urged Mags, as she rested her chin on her closed fist.

'What if I ask Mr Darling if he'd take her on at Beechwood House? There's a scullery maid leaving soon as she's getting wed. It's a live-in position. It would give her more to think about than Jimmy, not that he's not worth thinking of, mind you,' she said, playfully digging him in the arm. He blushed. 'That way she'll be far enough from that hateful husband of hers and her parents who have such disregard for her welfare.'

'That sounds a really good idea, Enid. We'd better run it past the girl first though. Put it to her in such a way that it's for her own good and not Jimmy's, if you get my drift.' Mags blew out a breath, looking positively relieved.

Jimmy thought the others probably got her drift very well. It seemed a good idea, but he couldn't help worrying in case Polly turned a bit nasty towards Enid if she were to be secured a position at the big house, as they'd both be working together there and he wouldn't be around to keep an eye on events.

* * *

Polly jumped at the idea, which surprised Jimmy as she'd had so much trouble at the last place she worked. By solving one problem though, another was created as Mags would now have to look for a new sewing assistant.

It was while Jimmy was working at the shop, hammering some tacks into the sole of a boot, that he heard a heavy thud upstairs. Knowing that Mrs Baxter was out shopping, and it couldn't be her, he exchanged concerned glances with Harri.

'Mind the shop for me,' he said, to which the lad nodded, and then he burst through the door leading into the Baxters' living quarters and hurried up the stairs. Hearing a groan, he rushed up to the landing and noticed Mr Baxter lying prone with his one arm outstretched. The man barely walked anywhere these days. Usually, it was with the assistance of his wife. Jimmy was quite sure the woman would have seen to her husband's needs before leaving the house, so why was he out of bed?

'Mr Baxter, are you all right?'

The man groaned again.

Jimmy went back to the top of the stairs and shouted down, 'Harri, come quickly! You're needed here; there's been an accident!'

It wasn't long before the lad was by his side and they somehow managed to roll Mr Baxter onto his back and carry him into the bedroom, Jimmy lifting beneath his armpits and Harri taking the man's legs. After a little huffing and puffing, both managed to steer him towards the bed, where they gently laid him down. Mr Baxter was breathing heavily as Jimmy propped up his pillows for him and covered him with blankets.

'But what happened, Mr Baxter?' asked Jimmy, sitting on the bed as he looked at Josiah's face. His skin looked pale and crepe-like and his eyes sunken into their sockets.

'I... was just coming down to help you in the shop...' gasped the man.

Jimmy frowned. 'But you haven't been working in the shop for months now. Don't you remember? That's why me and Harri are working there to help you.'

Mr Baxter put his bony hand to his temple and began to weep.

Jimmy had never seen the man cry before, and he wasn't sure what to do. Realising it must feel a little uncomfortable for Harri too, he looked at the lad and said, 'Go and fetch Mr Baxter a clean glass from the kitchen and fill a jug with water. He looks a bit poorly to me.'

Harri nodded and then made his way out of the room.

'Do you know what day it is?' Jimmy asked.

Mr Baxter shook his head. 'Is it my birthday then?'

'No, today is Wednesday.'

Feeling concerned that the man didn't seem to be aware of what day of the week it was, whether it was his birthday or not, and had forgotten he no longer worked at the shop, Jimmy decided he'd better have a word with his wife on her return. He fumbled in his pocket to locate the clean handkerchief that Mags had given him only that morning.

'Here, dry your eyes with this.'

Mr Baxter, accepting the handkerchief, sniffed loudly. 'I don't know what's happening to me, son.'

When Mrs Baxter returned home, Jimmy explained what had happened, while Harri sat in the bedroom to keep an eye on Mr Baxter.

Initially, she avoided eye contact with Jimmy but then said, 'I'm sorry. I should have told you this some time ago, but Josiah seems to be getting forgetful lately. I didn't want to worry you; that's why I never mentioned it. I thought maybe it would pass as he's been unwell of late, but it hasn't.'

Jimmy nodded with understanding. 'I don't know what to say...' For once he was unable to think clearly about the situation.

'Please will you carry on with what you're doing, running the shop for us?'

'Yes, of course I will. But he must have had a heck of a fall. I heard that loud thump all the way from the workshop.'

Mrs Baxter's face clouded over with concern. 'I'll go up and see how he is.'

Jimmy lightly touched the woman's hand and spoke softly towards her. 'He seems all right. We put him back to bed and I've told Harri to sit with him for a while. You put your shopping away and have a cup of tea. You need to think clearly what to do about the situation. Maybe getting some help for him might be a good idea. You know, someone who can keep an eye on him when you're not around?'

Mrs Baxter bit her bottom lip and tears formed in her eyes. 'I don't know what I'd do if anything ever happened to him. We've been together for ever such a long time and Josiah's been a good husband to me.'

Jimmy nodded. He'd been a witness to the high regard the couple had for one another. While he could soften the blow of her husband's deteriorating health by being supportive and helping to run the man's business, what he couldn't do was to bring him back to good health and be the man he once was.

* * *

Help came from the last person Jimmy imagined – Polly! While she was waiting to be taken on at Beechwood House, as the maid who was leaving worked out her notice, she offered to sit with Mr Baxter and help in general at the house. At first, Jimmy wondered if she was doing it out of the goodness of her heart, even though she was being paid a nominal sum for her services, but quite soon he was to realise that she had another motive and that was himself. By working for the Baxters, she was now in close proximity to him, even though her work was conducted either upstairs caring for Mr Baxter, or in the living quarters cleaning and tidying. If Polly was downstairs, she never missed an opportunity to pop her head around the door and offer Jimmy a cup of tea. Initially, he was pleased to have a mid-morning or afternoon brew, but it became a constant interruption, so much so that it affected his work and he found himself snapping at the young woman. At one point he even wished she'd go back to her husband but then felt bad for thinking that way.

Polly's behaviour was beginning to grate. It was one thing tolerating the young woman at Mrs O'Connell's house and putting himself out sleeping on that uncomfortable couch, but quite another having her around him at his workplace too!

'I don't know if I can cope with this for much longer,' he moaned to Mags when he arrived home that evening.

Mags laid a sympathetic hand on his forearm. 'It won't be for much longer, lad. She'll be off to Cardiff soon.'

Jimmy rolled his eyes. 'Then poor Enid will have to put up with her!'

Mags shrugged. 'What can you do though? It's either put up short term or risk her going back to either a violent husband or an uncaring father? It won't be for much longer and she's doing the Baxters a big favour!'

He had to admit that Mags was right. Mrs Baxter told him she found Polly a godsend as now she could go out shopping or pop to the bank without having to worry about Josiah. And to be fair, Polly appeared to be taking good care of him too. He seemed to like her. If it wasn't that it involved his workplace then Jimmy would have suggested that Polly forget all about going to Cardiff and move in with the Baxters instead. He found himself fretting enormously about the situation and would wake up at all hours mulling over Mr Baxter's deterioration and Polly's persistence in hanging around the shop floor.

This time it wasn't the discomfort of the couch that awakened him but the thoughts flooding through his brain.

'I don't know what to do though, Mags. Polly is being a right pest when I'm trying to do my work. She even interrupted me when I was in the middle of seeing to a customer the other day.'

'How'd you mean?' Mags frowned.

'The man is a good customer of Mr Baxter's, has been for years. She insisted on brewing up and giving both me and him a cup of tea and kept nattering away about all sorts of nonsense...'

'That might be a good idea of Polly's, though, offering good customers a nice cuppa?'

'No, it bleedin' wasn't!' yelled Jimmy. 'The man didn't even want one! He drank it in the end out of sheer embarrassment, I think. It's a cobbler's not a blinkin' tea shop!'

'Oh, I see.' Mags nodded. 'Either someone needs to have a quiet word with her or maybe you need to explain what's happening to Mrs Baxter herself.'

He nodded. 'I'll do it first thing in the morning.'

A strong sensation of being 'disconcerted' – as Sergeant Cranbourne had once put it to him – was working its way at his gut and gnawing at his sense of peace. Jimmy didn't know quite what was going on, but it was an uneasy suspicion that something bad was about to happen.

17

While Polly was out of earshot tending to Mr Baxter upstairs, Mrs Baxter listened with interest as Jimmy explained the situation. The woman was quite understanding and said she'd have a quiet word with the girl about not disturbing him at work or any customers come to that.

So, for the following few days, things were relatively peaceful for Jimmy at the shop as he barely got to see Polly at all. But unfortunately, a few days later he received a letter from Enid informing him that the job she'd lined up for Polly had fallen through as the young woman who was leaving was heartbroken as her fiancé had suddenly called off the wedding without warning. There was no explanation given and Jimmy wondered to himself if the young fellow in question had found someone else. Life could be so cruel at times. He imagined how the poor young woman, who had the hope of a future cruelly snatched away from her, must be feeling right now. Although he'd been looking forward to Polly leaving and being far enough away from him in Cardiff, his sympathies lay with the poor girl who must be bereft. Work would be her salvation to keep herself active.

But what now? He was going to have to break it to Polly that there was no longer a position available to her. How would she take it? But he needn't have worried about confronting her as Mags offered to do so and, afterwards, she claimed Polly took it very well. Mrs Baxter had offered her a permanent position and made it a live-in one too.

At this, Jimmy breathed a sigh of relief. At least he could get his bed back now. Maybe things would work out for the best after all. Polly no longer bothered him at work now that she'd been reprimanded by Mrs Baxter.

Inroads too had been made between Polly and her parents. She'd called around to the house one Sunday afternoon and was surprised her father was no longer hostile towards her. Then she discovered that he'd heard the gossip for himself – about his son-in-law and his new young 'female friend' – which was enough to change his mind about the entire situation. Though why the man couldn't have taken Polly's word for it, Jimmy just didn't understand.

So now things were beginning to settle down once again.

* * *

'Just the young man I want to see,' said Mrs Baxter, smiling as she entered the shop.

'Oh yes!' chuckled Jimmy as he glanced up from the boot he was repairing. 'There's not many who would want to see me!'

'Go on with you. You know how many young women give you a second glance when they call into this shop. You're a very handsome young man.'

Jimmy felt himself blushing down to his boots. He was aware of it, of course. At least none of those young women were as forward as Polly had been.

'What can I do for you, Mrs Baxter?'

'I'm going to visit my sister-in-law in Aberdare tomorrow as I need to have a word with her about something. There's a wagon going over there first thing in the morning, and I should be back by teatime. I was just wondering...' She hesitated for a moment.

'You were just wondering if I might keep an eye on things as Polly will be left all day with Mr Baxter?'

The woman nodded slowly. 'That's about the crux of it, yes.'

'Of course, I'll keep an eye out when I'm not working. Or would you rather I shut the shop and give him all my attention, instead?'

'There'll be no need for that; it's just that sometimes, as good as young Polly is, she doesn't quite have enough common sense, if you know what I mean?'

He did know very well what the woman meant. 'You'd just feel reassured if I pop in the back or upstairs from time to time to check how she's getting on with things?'

The woman let out a little breath of relief. 'Something like that, yes. All feels fine when I'm on the premises, but I wouldn't want to leave her to her own devices for too long. But of course, that will involve you having dealings with her that day. Can you cope with that?'

'If it's just the one day then I'm sure I will!' he said brightly.

'Good lad.' She nodded approvingly and then turned her back to return to her living quarters.

When Mrs Baxter had departed, the doorbell tinkled as Harri came rushing in in a highly excitable state, florid and slightly breathless.

'What's up with you?' asked Jimmy, feeling amused. 'You managed to get that dye for me, didn't you?'

'Oh yes!' said Harri, smiling as he placed the pot of dye down on the counter.

Jimmy narrowed his gaze. The way the lad was grinning it felt almost as though he were about to burst out with laughter, as though he had some sort of secret he was dying to spill.

'Well, go on,' urged Jimmy. 'What's happened?'

'When I was out, I just paid a quick visit to my mam,' said Harri. 'I know I'm not supposed to go back home when I'm at work, but I got the dye quick; there was no queueing up like the last time...' he said, huffing out the words.

'You know that's fine for you to call to see your mother, Harri. I know she hasn't been well of late, and I did tell you if she needs you, to pop back home.' Harri resided in the China area, so it wasn't far from the shop.

He nodded. 'Anyhow,' he sniffed loudly, 'when I got to my house there was quite a commotion going on. People were outside their doors as a fancy carriage was rumbling across the cobbles.'

Jimmy tilted his head in a puzzled fashion. 'Huh?'

'At first I thought maybe it was royalty come to Merthyr!' He chuckled. 'But then someone said it was a lady and gentleman from one of those posh houses. People what are well off.'

'Yes, go on. What were they doing?'

'The gentleman and his wife were visiting the wash house of all places!'

'But what on earth were they going there for?' It was the last place that Jimmy would expect anyone of their ilk to visit. The place was full of women who were down on their luck as his mother had been. He couldn't imagine what they'd find of interest there.

'Dunno to be honest!' Harri shrugged his shoulders. 'When I let myself inside my house and saw my mam, she said she didn't know what they could be doing there either as the place is full of fallen women!'

It was a mystery indeed.

'How is your mother feeling now?' asked Jimmy.

'She's a lot better,' Harri enthused. 'The medicine Dad got for her from Doctor Llewellyn seems to be working. Her cough has almost gone now.'

That was a relief. Jimmy didn't want young Harri to lose his mother as young as he had lost his.

* * *

The following morning Mrs Baxter was to catch the early wagon to Aberdare at seven o'clock, so Jimmy decided to come in to work a little sooner than was normal for him. He was relieved when he did as Polly was up and dressed and boiling a couple of eggs for Mr Baxter.

'Good morning, Jimmy,' she said brightly. 'What brings you here so early this morning?'

'Oh, I've got a lot of work on for a couple of the big houses in the area, so I want to make an early start,' he fibbed. He could hardly tell her the purpose of him coming in early was to keep an eye on her.

'I've just brewed up for Mr Baxter. You should be able to squeeze one out of the pot,' she said as she spooned the eggs into the waiting cups, then lifted the tray with the man's breakfast on it ready to leave the room. 'I should be some time as I need to supervise him eating his breakfast.'

Jimmy nodded. So far so good; Polly appeared to be on the ball. He poured himself a cup of tea and took a seat at the table. In the distance he could hear her speaking to Mr Baxter and then there was silence for a spell; he figured the old man was eating his breakfast.

Jimmy drained his teacup and then took it to the sink. Before getting on with his work though, he loitered at the foot of the stairs, listening in as Polly spoke softly to the man, telling him that after breakfast she was going to get him washed and dressed.

Smiling to himself, he turned away and pushed open the door that led to the shop. The aroma of leather was so comfortable and familiar to him, and he wondered why Mrs Baxter had decided to spend the day with her sister-in-law in Aberdare.

* * *

By the time Harri arrived, the shop was beginning to bustle as people came in either to drop off repairs or to collect them. It was mid-morning when he had the time to go and check on what Polly was up to. But he needn't have concerned himself as the girl's arms were submerged in washing suds in the old stone bosh.

'I'm just swilling a few things out for Mr Baxter,' she explained, smiling at him. He returned the smile. 'He's just dropped off to sleep. I thought maybe it would be a good idea when he wakes up to put him out in the yard outside, on a chair, warmly dressed up of course, as it's such a nice day. Would you help me with him later?'

'Sure,' said Jimmy, nodding, pleased he could help in some sort of way. 'You tell me when you're ready and, providing there are no customers, I'll move his favourite armchair outside in the yard and Harri and I will help him down the stairs.' He pondered for a moment. 'On second thoughts, as he's not so steady on his pins, I'll do it all. I'll carry him down if he'll allow me. That might be safer. You just make sure all the doors are open and there's nothing obstructing my path.'

Polly nodded eagerly. 'Yes, I'll give you a shout later then, Jimmy,' she said, nodding as she wrung out Mr Baxter's shirt, squeezing out as much excess water as possible before hanging the garment out on the line in the backyard.

Funny, thought Jimmy as he returned to his work, *Polly seems more normal these days, less obsessive towards me. Maybe things will turn out all right after all.*

It was about half an hour later when Jimmy was explaining to Harri how he was going to move the armchair outside to the yard that he became aware of something going on in the back room. Fearing Mr Baxter might have taken it upon himself to get out of bed again, alarmed, he rushed through the door to hear Polly's cries of protest.

'No, you're not coming in here; I shall get the police!' she was shouting as frantic hammering was coming from the back door. Biting her lip, her face deathly pale, she turned to Jimmy. 'It's Gethin. He's trying to get in here!' she said, panic-stricken, the whites of her eyes now on show.

'Oh, is he now?' Jimmy said as he gently moved her to one side. 'Go away!' he yelled through the closed door, but the banging continued and then he heard a shout.

'I want my bloody wife!'

By the slurred sounds, Jimmy guessed he'd been drinking alcohol.

He unbolted the door to confront him. 'Go home and sleep it off!' he shouted at him. 'There's a very sick, elderly man living here.'

'But I only want my wife,' said Gethin, who was weeping now. 'I made a big mistake. I love you, Polly. I want you to come home to me!' he shouted over Jimmy's shoulder.

Polly folded her arms. 'I'm not coming! You've got a new woman, that Millicent Roberts now.'

'Oh, her!' Gethin waved an arm of dismissal as though he were waving away a pesky fly, then he hiccupped loudly. 'That was just a little dalliance while you were gone. I didn't think you were ever coming back to me. It's all over now. I won't ever hurt you again, I promise.'

With mounting fear, Jimmy studied the expression on Polly's face and, to his horror, she was blushing and smiling.

'Don't go with that swine!' Jimmy hissed. But it was too late. She removed her pinafore and flung it on the counter.

'I have to go with my husband,' she said, looking at Jimmy. 'He still loves me; that's all I need to know. Can you take care of Mr Baxter for me and thank Mrs Baxter for putting me up?'

Jimmy nodded. 'I suppose I'll have to, won't I? But I'm warning you you're making a big mistake, Polly.'

Polly shook her head. 'I'm not, Jimmy. I've never felt more certain in all my life.' She turned her back on him and followed her husband through the open door. Jimmy closed the door behind the pair, firmly bolting it, feeling in some ways he was closing a door on a chapter in the young woman's life.

How foolish of Polly to return to the man who had hurt her so badly. Now he was going to have to either shut the shop while he took care of Mr Baxter or maybe send Harri to look after him, while he worked alone. Neither sat right with him. Polly had been employed to take care of Mr Baxter and if she felt so strongly about going back home to Gethin she could at least have waited until his wife returned.

Another feeling of foreboding filled Jimmy's veins.

* * *

When Mrs Baxter returned from Aberdare, she was most alarmed to hear that Polly had gone back home to her husband and shocked she'd walked out on the task allotted to her that day. 'What on earth possessed her?' The woman sighed as she placed her basket, which was full to the brim with shopping, down on the kitchen table. 'I picked up some provisions in Aberdare market and my sister-in-law, Cissie, baked a lemon sponge cake, so she wrapped it up for me to take home. We can have a slice later. How's Josiah been, anyhow?'

'He's been fine today and, despite Polly abandoning him, before that she was caring very well for him. She'd made him breakfast, fed and washed him and even rinsed through some of his clothes, which she hung out on the line. I'm as shocked as you are about her going off like that though. She had asked if I might help her to get him to sit outside as the weather has been quite nice today.'

Mrs Baxter pursed her lips. 'Easy come, easy go, I suppose. One thing's for sure, she won't get another chance with me now after this. I've lost all trust in her. We gave her a roof over her head and fed her too. I know she worked for her keep but she won't step another foot in this place if I've got anything to do with it. I shall pack up all her belongings so they're ready to go if she comes knocking for them.' The woman sounded angry now and, Jimmy had to admit, he couldn't blame her. Due to Polly's neglectful and cavalier responsibility towards Josiah, he hadn't got the chance to sit outside after all.

* * *

Later that evening, when Jimmy told Mags what had occurred, she shook her head in despair. 'What a foolish girl! After everyone trying to help her an' all. And you, Jimmy, you even gave up your bed for her. Suffering sleeping on that old couch for weeks on end, so you'd wake up with a stiff neck and aching back in the mornings!'

Jimmy remembered it well. It was so nice to be back in his old comfy bed that he appreciated it more than ever.

'It's not that so much though, Mags. I fear for her safety now; I really do. As much as Polly was a bit of a pest towards me at times and I wished she'd leave me alone, I didn't want her to return to her husband.'

Mags laid a sympathetic hand on Jimmy's shoulder. 'We must all forget about the girl now. We did our best for her; I even gave her a job. I'm going to have to get someone in to help me though, as I'm finding it hard to keep up with what I do. I'll say one thing for Polly, she was a good worker on that machine.' She glanced at her sister's sewing machine in the corner of the room. 'Betsan has told me I can use it for as long as I like if she can make use of it too. Oh, I know it really belongs to her. She says she has access to other machines at work, but it's special. Maybe in some way it belongs to us both as it keeps us linked with her mother.'

Jimmy glanced at the sewing machine. 'If a sewing machine could talk, eh? I bet that could tell a tale or two.'

'Oh yes. It could probably tell a few secrets an' all!' Mags laughed as she tapped the side of her nose with her index finger.

'So, what are you going to do about getting a new assistant?'

'I might advertise in the newspaper. Though those ads cost money. Could you put the word out for me, Jimmy?'

Jimmy raised his eyebrows and grimaced. 'Me? How?'

'You get plenty of customers calling into the shop. A quiet word wouldn't go amiss, and I can ask customers at the market stall if they know someone who'd like a sewing job.'

When he was busy dealing with customers in the shop, Jimmy didn't think about things like that; his mind was focused and he'd fear being too intrusive, so instead, he said, 'How about I write out an advert for you and place it in the shop window? I'll have to clear it with Mrs Baxter first though.'

Mags nodded eagerly. 'That's a great idea, lad.'

'Thinking about it, Mrs Baxter could do with someone too to replace what Polly was doing for Mr Baxter. So, I could do that same thing for her by placing another ad in the shop window at the same time.'

'Now that is enterprising.' Mags smiled. 'You really have some good ideas, don't you?'

Jimmy blushed. 'Oh, I don't know about that.'

'You do, like that time you thought about setting up a delivery business. You don't just wait for things to happen; you get out and do them!'

Jimmy supposed Mags had a point; he'd pursued Enid, after all. Initially, he'd tried to find her himself and when that hadn't worked and he'd spotted her that day on the platform, he hadn't just stayed on the train and missed his opportunity. He'd got off it and followed her and won her heart all over again. He wondered what Enid would make of all of this 'Polly business'.

He was soon to find out as he was meeting her on Sunday. This time he was travelling on the train to see her in Cardiff. He'd been saving up for the fare, not wasting his money on trivialities like he sometimes did. He'd foregone his usual pokes of peppermints from the sweet shop and held off buying himself a new jacket until next month. Borrowing Elgan's jacket again would have to suffice for now.

* * *

Enid and Jimmy were strolling arm in arm around the grounds of Cardiff Castle. 'I couldn't imagine what it would have been like to live in this place!' Jimmy enthused. 'It has so much history.'

'Apparently, according to Mr Darling, it's a medieval castle but its history goes back even further than that as it was built on the site of a Roman fort.'

Jimmy nodded, impressed by Enid's knowledge. 'That's interesting but I need to change the subject for now. I've something to tell you about Polly...' He related what had happened to the girl.

'That's dreadful, Jimmy. It's a shame that job at the big house here fell through. It might have been the making of her.'

'Possibly. But I suppose we must keep out of it now. We all tried to help her in some respect, and it's as though everything we did was thrown back in our faces.'

'Aw, don't look at things like that,' said Enid, frowning. 'You all helped her through a difficult time and if she's made the decision to return to her husband there's nothing that can be done about it. She's a grown woman after all.'

He nodded, supposing Enid was right. Who knew what Polly's parents would make of it though as she'd recently made things up with them and they were finally on her side about her leaving Gethin.

'At least there's one good thing to come out of this...' said Enid.

'Oh, yes?'

'You're sleeping in your own bed again!' She smiled.

'Aye, there is that, I suppose.' He gave a wry chuckle.

They continued to walk arm in arm around the grounds, passing other couples who were out for an afternoon stroll, until they came across a pride of peacocks.

'Just look at those birds!' exclaimed Enid, pointing, totally in awe. 'Aren't their feathers such beautiful colours?'

Jimmy had to agree. 'Particularly that one over there spreading hers out to show off!' Jimmy laughed. 'Typical woman!'

'Actually, I think that's a male not a female.' Enid shook her head.

'How'd you know that?'

'Mr Darling explained to me about the peacocks when I told him we were coming here this afternoon.'

Jimmy tilted his head to one side and stroked his chin. 'This Mr Darling of yours seems to impress you such a lot, Enid. Are you sure he doesn't have designs on you?'

'Oh, don't you start!' She playfully punched him in the forearm, realising he was only teasing her. 'To be fair, he's been so good to me. I feel I might have to let him down though after all he's done to help me.'

'How so?'

'I'm thinking of turning down the housekeeper's position I was offered after all.'

'But why on earth would you do so?' Jimmy stopped in his tracks and turned to face her. 'You love working at the house!'

She nodded and then chewed her lower lip. 'I did, I do. It's just I've been thinking about things. You mentioned that Mrs Baxter is looking for someone to help take care of her husband?'

'Aye, she is. But what would that have to do with you not accepting that housekeeper position? I don't understand.' He stared at her blankly for a moment and then his gaze averted to a peacock, strutting around on the well-manicured lawn, being followed by another larger bird. Maybe it was mating season.

'I've been thinking...' She huffed out a breath. 'Connie, my Irish friend I told you about, she'd be capable of taking over the position at the house. I'd be doing her a favour if I didn't take it. Also, if I asked Mrs Baxter if I could work for her instead then I could live in at her place and we'd get to see more of one another.'

Jimmy could hardly believe what Enid was saying. 'That's a marvellous idea, Enid. Though you wouldn't get much pay and you wouldn't need to work full-time helping with Mr Baxter. It would be seeing to his needs, so you'd get some time off. But I'd feel awful taking you away from a job where you have worked so hard and have such good prospects.'

She shook her head. 'Have you forgotten your promise to me then, Jimmy? When you gave me that ring? That you want me to be your wife someday?'

'No, of course I haven't. I still want that with all my heart.'

'The way I look at it is this. If we both save to one day marry and set up home together then our money will soon fritter away as we have to keep spending it on train fare. If, though, I move back to Merthyr and have a little job, then we can both prepare for our future.'

'Oh, I do love you, Miss Enid Hardcastle!' Jimmy's lips curved into a smile as he swept her up into his arms, not caring a fig who saw them.

'Jimmy... that's the first time you've ever told me you love me,' Enid said breathlessly.

'But I do. I always have ever since I saw that little girl sitting on the doorstep outside her house back in China. She was always too shy to speak to me though!'

Enid blushed now. 'I suppose I was back then, but you soon won me over when Thelma brought you around to our house to meet me.'

'Come on, let's celebrate. I'll buy you an ice cream from that cart over there!' He pointed to a wooden cart with the name 'Bellini's Ices' painted on the side of it.

Enid appeared to freeze in her tracks, her eyes widening. 'Oh!' she gasped.

'What's the matter? Don't you want an ice cream?'

'It's not that. Seeing that Bellini's Ices cart just reminded me of a bad time in my life.'

He frowned. 'Why? What happened?'

She explained to him the memory: how in the run-up to the trial where she and Connie were to give evidence of the goings-on in Tiger Bay, she'd been on an afternoon out with Sam, the footman, when she thought she'd spied Anthony Clarkson on the other side of the lake.

'Sam had gone to buy some ices from a cart like this one and when he saw me drop my parasol with fear and how distressed I appeared, he left the queue to come bounding over to my side.'

'And was it him? Clarkson, I mean?'

'No, but it shook me up as bad as if it had been.'

'You poor darling,' he said, now hugging her to his chest. 'You've never mentioned this Sam to me before. Who was he to you?'

She sighed. 'He works at Beechwood House. We got very close to one another but then he started to push things.'

'How'd you mean?'

'Well, I was going through so much following the rape and about to go through a court trial that I found it suffocating as he was rushing things and he even asked me to marry him.'

'Really?'

'Does that surprise you that someone who knew all about the fact I'd been raped still wanted to marry me? Some girls would have taken him up on that, but not me. It was all too much too soon.'

'Maybe he just wanted to protect you,' said Jimmy softly.

'Maybe. But I feel like I let you down, Jimmy.'

'But why?' He furrowed his brow.

'Because I should have waited for you and known you'd find me again someday.'

He took her hand and planted a kiss on the back of it. 'How were you to know? In any case, don't feel too bad; I was involved with Polly for a short time, wasn't I? I thought at first she was a potential girlfriend for me after you'd left, but then I realised she could never compare to you, Enid.'

He looked at her with such longing and as she gazed up at him his heart swelled with love for her.

'Look, we'll leave those ice creams if they bring back bad memories for you.'

'No,' she said firmly. 'I never got to have one that afternoon as I was so fearful. Afterwards Sam took me to a tea room to calm me down and it was there he proposed. Let's have those ice creams so I can create a new memory.'

'That's a good idea,' he said, taking her by the arm and escorting her over to the cart.

* * *

A fortnight later, Enid began working for Mr and Mrs Baxter, and she was a great help to the pair of them. Although Polly had done the work to the best of her ability and had made a decent enough job of things, Enid was more thoughtful as she'd sit with Josiah, patiently listening to his tales of what Merthyr was like in the old days. It was a bonus too as Josiah remembered her and her family as they'd lived close by and were visitors to his shop. There was a bond of trust there that the elderly couple would not have with strangers.

Jimmy, of course, was in his element to have Enid near at hand. They often spent the odd ten minutes, if the shop was quiet, having a little chat with one another, and he trusted her if he had to leave the shop floor as she was good with customers and able to take payment from folk. He left Harri from time to time, but the lad got a bit flustered when there were a lot of customers in the shop vying for attention. Besides, Harri loved Enid and she'd taken to him too. So for once it felt as though things were going well for everyone concerned.

But this was not to last. Just a few weeks later, Jimmy had started work for the day when he became aware of Enid standing behind him. He pivoted on his stool to face her. There was something about her demeanour that told him something was up, the way she stood with her head lowered and then, as she raised her eyes to meet with his, he could see tears in them.

'What's the matter, Enid?'

'I... It's Mr Baxter,' she said quietly.

'Has something happened to him?' Jimmy stood, fearing the old man had fallen yet again.

'I w... went to w... wake him, and he wouldn't wake up,' she stammered. 'Mrs Baxter is with him right now. His hand was so cold when I touched it, Jimmy. He might have been dead for hours.'

'Someone needs to fetch the doctor,' said Jimmy gravely. 'Even if he appears dead to the both of you, he needs to be declared deceased by a doctor.'

He felt like running upstairs and crying and throwing himself on the bed. Josiah Baxter was one of the kindest men he knew. But he couldn't make a show of himself in front of Enid like that. He could see she needed some support right now as she'd had a nasty shock.

Enid nodded wordlessly.

Taking her in his embrace, he softly said, 'Now, you go and make a cup of tea for yourself and Mrs Baxter as there's nothing else either of you can do. Meanwhile, I'll put up the closed sign in the shop window. Harri won't be in for a bit yet. There's no need for him to come in today at all. I can call to his house to tell him later.'

Enid nodded. 'Yes, I'll boil the kettle.'

'Good,' said Jimmy. She was obviously knocked off balance so boiling the kettle to brew up would give her something to focus her attention on. 'I'll just pop upstairs to tell Mrs Baxter I'm going for the doctor, then.'

He watched Enid leave the shop floor, heading off for the kitchen. He just couldn't take it in. Mr Baxter had passed away. It felt like the end of an era.

18

Josiah Daniel Baxter was pronounced dead by Doctor Llewellyn at precisely fifteen minutes past nine o'clock that morning. Jimmy could hardly believe it as he stood in the doorway of the couple's bedroom staring at Mr Baxter's lifeless form on the bed as the doctor removed his stethoscope from around his neck and packed it away in his leather bag. Then he raised the bed sheet over the man's head, so that it covered his whole body, causing Jimmy to swallow hard.

Ushering both Jimmy and Mrs Baxter outside the door, the doctor spoke in a quiet tone of voice, almost as though he disliked being over-heard by the deceased, but then Jimmy guessed maybe he was doing it out of respect for the old man as many folk in Merthyr had great admiration for Josiah.

'It's his heart I suspect,' said the doctor gravely. 'It gave up in the end. Also going by the blue pallor on his skin...' he paused for a moment for Jimmy and Mrs Baxter to digest what he was saying '...we in the profession refer to it as "cyanosis", I would suspect he had respiratory issues too, which often go hand in hand with a weakened heart. He reached a good age, mind you.'

Jimmy glanced at Mrs Baxter who was standing with the heel of her hand to her chest, almost as though she might be suffering a heart condition too, and in a way, maybe she was. The pair had been married for more than fifty years, and although the woman hadn't known anything about her husband having fathered a child by someone else until recently, she had been the love of his life. That much was evident.

Enid was downstairs in the shop as a precaution because in Jimmy's experience even though there was a large notice with bold black letters on the door that declared the shop was closed, it didn't stop people hammering on it from time to time with the expectation that someone might emerge from the living quarters to answer a query. Usually it was 'When will you be open again?' or 'I need to pick up my shoes urgently. Can't you just get them for me?' He sighed inwardly. Whichever it was, if it happened this morning then it would disturb the peace and Jimmy didn't want that. So Enid had promised she'd keep an eye out and tidy up the shop as there were sure to be visitors calling to see Mrs Baxter when they found out her husband had passed away. The shop door was the main entrance to her home.

The doctor replaced his bowler hat on his head. 'Give her a strong cup of sugared tea for the time being,' he said to Jimmy, as though Mrs Baxter was deaf. 'But if she needs anything for her nerves, let me know. It's usual for people not to be able to sleep properly for a while, so I shouldn't worry too much about it.'

Jimmy nodded and he followed the doctor down the stairs to the front door of the shop. He recalled how he'd supported Mags and Elgan's application to take him on as a parish orphan. He was a good sort was Doctor Llewellyn.

The doctor paused thoughtfully for a moment at the shop door as Jimmy opened it for him. 'I wonder what'll happen to this place now?'

Jimmy wondered that himself, of course, but he was prepared to keep the shop going for Mrs Baxter's sake as it provided an income for her. 'I'll help out as much as I can until Mrs Baxter makes a decision what to do,' he said.

'Good, good,' said Doctor Llewellyn, smiling now. 'She'll need all the support she can get at this terrible time. Does she have any relatives that you know of?'

Jimmy shrugged. 'Not really, apart from a sister-in-law, that is, who lives in Aberdare.'

'That's something at least. Miss Hardcastle,' said the doctor as he nodded his head in Enid's direction. 'Jimmy, I'll bid you both good day!'

As Jimmy closed the shop door behind the man, ensuring it was locked, he thought how odd it was that the doctor said that – it was anything but a good day, especially for Mrs Baxter. But then again, it was only a turn of phrase, a throwaway remark people often said without even thinking about it.

Enid caught Jimmy's eye as she rested her forearms on the broom she'd been using to sweep the floor. 'What did the doctor say?'

'Mr Baxter's heart just gave out and he probably had some sort of respiratory condition too.'

She nodded at him. 'Maybe it's a blessing in a way for him to have passed in his sleep like that...'

Jimmy smiled ruefully. He didn't like to see anyone suffer. When he was a little boy, after his father had passed away, Thelma – Elgan's first wife – had often taken care of him while his mother worked at the wash house. He'd noticed how Thelma often got out of puff; she'd had a dodgy ticker too. 'Oh, the doctor said we should make a nice strong brew for Mrs Baxter with plenty of sugar. So, I'll go and make one now. Would you like another one?'

'Yes, please,' said Enid. 'It's been a dreadful start to the day. I'll go up and check on Mrs Baxter while you attend to it.'

'Thanks, Enid,' he said as he reached out and touched her hand. She had such a caring, thoughtful nature and had been that way ever since he'd first encountered her when she was seven years old. It was Enid he'd been able to speak to about his father's death, not the other lads he used to knock around with. She never judged him either or called him a 'cissy' when he burst into tears. Those lads had taunted him mercilessly but, then again, none of them had lost a parent so they didn't understand what it was like. Enid had been the one who patiently listened to how he felt and never, ever judged him. That's what he liked most about her.

* * *

The day of Mr Baxter's funeral had a gloomy start. Dark, dismal-looking clouds had gathered overhead as though a storm might be approaching. Mrs Baxter said she didn't think their living quarters were suitable to hold some kind of reception before and after the service, so instead people were asked to go directly to the chapel where the minister would conduct a service and then, after the men had visited the graveside, there would be a bit of a do at a local hotel. Jimmy understood the Baxters had enough money to host such an occasion, and it was expected to be a good turnout as Josiah was well thought of by the town's folk.

The shop was shut for a few days and the blinds closed out of respect, and Mrs Baxter had worn a black dress ever since her husband's death. Enid too had worn a long dark but serviceable dress while Jimmy had opted to wear dark attire and a black armband over his white shirtsleeve. Even young Harri would be expected to wear some sort of dark clothing for a time when the shop reopened. So far, Mrs Baxter hadn't said anything about how she wished to proceed, nor did Jimmy expect her to. She seemed to be in a world of her own, and as much as he liked the woman, he felt that Enid was the best person to deal with her. And so Enid was the one who took endless cups of tea with Mrs Baxter, listening to her concerns. She was the one who answered the door to callers who wished to show their respects, showing them inside the property, and she was the one who helped the woman make funeral plans. Although having no experience herself, she'd contacted the undertaker, booked the time and date of the funeral, spoken with the minister at the chapel and booked the hotel room for the afternoon. If Mrs Baxter had a daughter, she couldn't have done any better than Enid had and Jimmy was so proud of her.

Maybe it was a blessing in disguise that Polly had left shortly before the man's death as she'd have been useless in this sort of scenario. She might have given the woman added grief, especially if that husband of hers had come knocking too.

Cecilia Baxter, otherwise known as 'Cissie' from Aberdare, Mrs Baxter's sister-in-law who had never married, came to stay at the property. Enid had gleaned from Mrs Baxter that her sister-in-law had been proposed to twice as a young woman and had both times turned each suitor down though no one seemed to know why. The last suitor she'd even become engaged to and then she'd called the wedding off just the week before. No doubt the woman had her reasons. Marriage wasn't for everyone, though if Jimmy had the chance to marry Enid, he'd do so in a heartbeat. There was no opportunity for that at present. Although he knew Mrs O'Connell would take the couple in to start their married life at her home if they asked, he realised it would be most unfair as the house was crowded enough as it was. Besides, he didn't earn enough to support a wife yet; he realised that.

Jimmy was astonished how many well-meaning women had presented Mrs Baxter with various home-baked cakes that week. There were succulent slabs of *Teisen Lap* and *Bara brith*, Welsh cakes and even mouth-watering apple and custard tarts. And if they'd all had the appetite for them, they'd have polished off the lot, but none of them had much of a yearning to stuff their faces right now. The suddenness of Josiah Baxter's death had floored the lot of them.

A crack of thunder brought Jimmy back to reality. It was going to bucket down soon and on the day of the funeral too. Could anything be more miserable than walking to the chapel with rain running down everyone's necks? Or standing at the graveside being deluged in a veil of tears from up on high?

Thankfully, Enid had the presence of mind to book a funeral coach for Mrs Baxter, the woman's sister-in-law and herself to get to the chapel. Afterwards they'd go directly to the hotel as women in the Welsh valleys did not attend the graveside funeral; it just wasn't the done thing. The same coach, though, would be used to transport himself, Elgan and Harri to the cemetery. Jimmy guessed some of the masters from the big houses would probably be attending too, using their own coaches. Those masters would be men who had taken up the delivery repair service that Jimmy had started. He wondered if Donald Clarkson would make an appearance. It seemed like the whole of Merthyr would be attending Mr Baxter's funeral, though of course that was simply not the case. Glancing around the congregation, he saw no sign of Polly in attendance, and for that, he was grateful.

Someone Jimmy had forgotten when he'd mentally run through the list of possible attendees was Sergeant Cranbourne, but when they arrived at the chapel, the man was at the entrance dressed in full uniform with two constables flanking him either side, almost like a guard of honour.

Josiah's coffin was removed from the horse-drawn glass funeral carriage and transported on the shoulders of four men into the chapel. A large wreath of white lilies lay on top of the coffin and all the mourners' heads bowed as it passed them by, as men rushed to remove their hats as a sign of respect and the women lowered their heads.

'It's a sad day for Merthyr Tydfil,' he heard one old man say.

'Aye,' said another, 'we'll not see the likes of Josiah Baxter as a cobbler in the town again. That man went above and beyond to help people.'

Jimmy had to agree with that. He had ever such a lot to thank the man for – providing him with a trade, for one thing.

While it gladdened Jimmy's heart to hear people speak that way about his former employer, it also created a huge lump in his throat.

* * *

On entering the chapel, where the outside of each pew was adorned with white roses and strands of ivy, Jimmy noticed all the bobbing heads turn in their direction as he took Mrs Baxter by the arm. He hoped the woman wouldn't faint. She'd been particularly quiet all morning. Enid and Cissie were just behind them and Harri behind those. Mrs Baxter, whose face was barely visible beneath her black veil, trembled as they headed towards the front pew that was reserved for the chief mourners. This was an unwritten rule that everyone knew about. No one would have dared to have seated themselves there.

At the front of the chapel, set on a trestle before the pulpit, was Mr Baxter's gleaming oak-wood coffin with the large spray of white lilies and trailing green ivy on top of it. The organist was playing a piece of music Jimmy thought he recognised, something by Mendelssohn. Strange, he thought as he realised he was correct, it was the same composer who'd written 'The Wedding March' and now he remembered this piece of music was called 'The Funeral March'. Both were striking pieces of work, yet this piece had an ingrained sadness about it. He knew the couple had married at this chapel and now one of them was having their funeral service here. Life went by in a flash. He'd realised that a long time ago by losing both parents at such a tender age.

When everyone was seated, the minister began his address. 'Dearly beloved, we are gathered here today to mark the life of Josiah Daniel Baxter...'

Jimmy hardly heard what was being said next though, as his eyes filled with tears. He hadn't wanted to cry but somehow this was reminding him of his father's funeral. Elgan had taken him along to that, much against Thelma's protests that he was too young to attend, but Elgan had been right, he'd needed to go. Although quite young at the time he remembered the man being by his side, a fatherly presence when he'd needed it. The memory of it all suddenly resurfaced and played through his mind like he was watching a magic lantern show but with sound.

Elgan had explained to him there'd be no further pain for his father in heaven and what a beautiful place it really was, somewhere where the sun always shone from blue skies, not like grey old Merthyr. His father would be looking after him and his mother from heaven.

But sadly, as it turned out, his father hadn't looked after his ma for long from heaven because she'd ended up working at that wash house in China and got hooked on the bottle, which in its turn led to her mixing with some bad sorts until she was doing a bad thing herself...

He glanced at Mrs Baxter beside him. The woman was staring towards the pulpit as though she was wearing blinkers, her focus fixed ahead, almost unaware of what was going on around her. Maybe it was the shock of it all, as that's how he'd felt when he'd lost his father. He remembered it like it was only yesterday. It had been different when his mother had passed though, as there'd never been any closure for him about that. Sergeant Cranbourne had told him at the time that she'd slipped and hit her head on a rock while she'd been in the River Taff. But what on earth would his mother have been doing there? He'd known she was petrified of water, especially the fast-flowing kind like the Taff. She'd warned him often enough to keep away from it.

In later years, he'd heard the rumour that his mother was murdered by one of the China bullies, probably double-crossed one of them it was thought. Maybe she'd not coughed up enough of her earnings, or not had permission to go it alone and work for herself. He'd remembered a time when his mother had left the wash house and seemed to be doing well for herself. There'd been more food on the table, new clothing for them both and there'd been a male visitor at night to the house. But there were also times when Jimmy had been left alone overnight. It all pointed to prostitution. He often shuddered at the thought of it and would have to push it as far from his mind as possible.

The congregation were now singing 'Abide with Me'. Shaking himself out of his reverie, he tried to concentrate on the words of the hymn.

> Swift to its close ebbs out life's little day
> Earth's joys grow dim, its glories pass away
> Change and decay in all around I see—
> O Thou who changest not, abide with me

Then the minister spoke about dying as though it were passing through a doorway into another life. Jimmy liked the sound of that as this life could be truly terrible at times. What sort of lives did either his mother or father have – being cut cruelly short like that?

* * *

A couple of days after the funeral, Mrs Baxter went to stay with her sister-in-law in Aberdare, and so Jimmy was left to his own devices at the shop, which he didn't mind too much though it seemed odd not to think of Mr and Mrs Baxter in their living quarters. Harri proved to be a real asset to him, and he began to teach the boy simple tasks like how to hammer a few tacks into a leather sole and how to properly polish repaired foot-work afterwards. The thought being that if he became overly busy then Harri would be able to help out. Maybe next year he'd allow the lad to take the horse and cart out to collect and deliver footwear.

Enid remained on at the shop and she now tended to deal with customers, which left Jimmy free to work at all the repairs that needed doing. She also kept Mrs Baxter's living quarters spick and span for the woman's imminent return. Though when that might be, no one had a clue.

Meanwhile, Mags had taken on a new sewing assistant to replace Polly. A lovely young lady called Netty Burns from Lower High Street who proved to be an asset. No more had been heard of Polly since the time she abandoned her duties at the shop to return home to her husband. Days turned to weeks and weeks to months, and it was sometime after Christmas, when Elgan had been on his round collecting some furniture from the lower end of town, that he'd sworn he'd seen Polly being thrown out of the Star Inn. Mags related the tale to Jimmy, shaking her head and pursing her lips in disapproval.

'A right state she was in an' all according to Elgan.'

'What did he say to her?' Jimmy furrowed his brow. No matter what Polly had done, he somehow didn't see her as the inebriated sort. It seemed most out of character.

'Hang on,' said Mags. 'I'll call him in now; he's just tending to the garden.'

'Aw, don't disturb him,' said Jimmy. 'I know how much he loves tending to it.'

'Go outside and have a word with him then,' said Mags.

Jimmy nodded, realising that Elgan viewed looking after Mrs O'Connell's garden as some sort of solution for his recent troubles. He found him at the bottom of the garden, near the stone-built wall, with his shirtsleeves rolled up to his elbows, shovelling up tumps of earth.

'What do you plan on doing there then?' Jimmy asked, tilting his head to one side in puzzlement.

'I thought I'd plant some turnips, here,' Elgan said decisively as he paused to take a break.

'Oh, that's a good idea. You're turning this into a real market garden what with the potatoes and carrots you've grown of late.'

'Aye, I enjoy it an' all,' said Elgan as he rested one arm on the handle of his shovel.

'I hear from Mags you came across Polly being thrown out of the Star

Inn,' said Jimmy. 'Are you sure it was her though?' He remembered that time the master of the big house she'd worked at had tried to ply her with drink and Polly had seemed disgusted by that.

Elgan's weather-beaten face creased into a frown. 'Yes. It was around lunchtime today. I was in the area, had to go to Gillar Street to collect some items when I noticed a woman being tossed out from the pub. I didn't recognise her at first though. She looked a right bag of old rags, she did. Dishevelled-looking clothing and, worst of all, she was wearing that rouge and lipstick. The type of stuff nice girls in this area wouldn't be seen dead in!' He sucked in a breath between his teeth as he shook his head in a disapproving manner.

'What did you make from that?'

'That maybe she's importuning for men. I don't like to make that suggestion, Jimmy. But it appeared that way to me as then I noticed the landlord throw a man out after her. I'd have gone over to check on her, but she brushed her clothing down and then walked off with the man in question.'

'Maybe it was her husband,' said Jimmy thoughtfully as he stroked his chin.

'I don't think so. This man looked twice her age. I think I recognised him an' all. Sups ale in the Vulcan Inn and has a yearning for young women from China, if you get my drift.' He tapped the side of his nose.

'Poor Polly,' said Jimmy.

Elgan continued. 'It looks as if things fell through with that husband of hers and she's ended up as a nymph of the pave. Mags suggested we ask Sergeant Cranbourne if he knows what's gone on with her, as he knows everything. You know what Mags is like with waifs and strays; she wouldn't want to see anything happen to the girl.'

Jimmy nodded, feeling so sad to hear of what had happened. 'If only she hadn't left with her husband when he came hammering on Mr Baxter's back door that time. She had a decent job and was good at it.'

'Speaking of jobs,' said Elgan. 'What about Enid now the old fella has passed? What will happen to her?'

'I received a letter from Mrs Baxter just the other day and she says it's fine for Enid to stay on and help out in the shop for the time being.'

'Must be a worrying time for you though, Jimmy. You can't be assured of a future in that shop now in case the woman wishes to sell up.'

The truth was he had considered that. He could well be left without a job and Enid could end up out on her ear too. 'I have thought about things,' said Jimmy. 'At least I have a trade behind me and if it turns out I must leave the shop, then I'll go back to my idea of renting out a market stall to work from. Enid, though, I don't know about as she'd be left without a job, though she's a clever and adaptable sort so I'm sure she'd find employment somewhere.'

'Aye, she would an' all,' said Elgan, smiling. 'And Mags and Mrs O'Connell wouldn't see her out on the streets either. They'd give her a roof here if she must move out from living above the shop.'

Jimmy thought about the kindness both women had shown him. It was a pity that Polly hadn't repaid their kindness by sorting out her life and getting away from that horrible husband of hers.

He watched Elgan return to the task in hand, realising the amount of progress the man had made since leaving prison. He had fretted about him for a time and so had Mags. He'd seemed a shadow of his former self when he'd first returned to Merthyr. Persuading Elgan to get back out on the horse and cart and returning to work was the best thing he'd ever done.

19

The following week, Mrs Baxter returned home from Aberdare to tell Jimmy she had some news for him. She wanted him to carry on running the shop for the foreseeable future, but she wasn't too happy about Enid sleeping on the premises on her own, especially after what had happened not that long ago when her husband's 'so-called son' had robbed the place. That incident had made the pair more nervous.

'Well, that's no problem,' said Jimmy. 'I can stay overnight too to keep Enid company.'

'Oh no!' Mrs Baxter shook her head. 'That wouldn't be seemly, Jimmy. Enid has her reputation to think of.'

He honestly hadn't considered that as he'd been thinking of Enid's safety and not seen it as a chance to be alone with her. 'But I wouldn't have done anything improper towards her,' he explained.

'Nevertheless, even if you were entirely virtuous, it's what folk might think – that you are living over the brush together and taking a married man's privileges.'

'But what if I married Enid, Mrs Baxter? It would be all right then, wouldn't it?' The words were out of his mouth before he'd even thought of them.

He noticed the gleam in the woman's eyes.

'Yes, yes! That would be most acceptable,' she said, nodding approvingly. 'If you were husband and wife, you could both live on the premises and you'd be managing the shop for me at the same time.'

Jimmy's head was spinning as it seemed the ideal solution. Would Enid even want to marry him right now anyhow? It was a lot to ask of her as he'd always given her the impression it would be a couple more years yet before they married. He wouldn't have the money for them to have a nice wedding anyhow. It would have to be done on the cheap.

As if reading his mind, Mrs Baxter said, 'You've been very good to us both – myself and Mr Baxter – so if you do decide to marry, I'd like to give you a little gift of some money to spend on your wedding. Just think, Jimmy, you could have a spring wedding!' Mrs Baxter clasped her hands together with delight.

Although Jimmy was still young, he did know of another lad who had wed at his age; it wasn't unknown, but in that case the young fella was pushed into it as he'd got his girlfriend pregnant.

What would Mags and Elgan think? And more importantly, would Enid even accept his sudden proposal?

As he walked back home to the house that night he mulled it all over in his mind. He didn't have the horse and cart as Elgan had needed it to help with a house move.

When he returned to the house, Mags was at the kitchen table watching Aled and Alys eat the bowls of stew she'd just dished up. If she didn't watch them, she could never be certain if one of them had allowed the other to eat theirs as they were prone to little tricks like that if they weren't in the mood to eat.

She looked up as he entered the kitchen. 'Had a good day, Jimmy?'

'Not so bad,' he said, grinning as he ruffled the twins' hair before sitting down at the table himself and removing his cap.

"Ere, what's up with you? You've got a grin like a Cheshire cat on your face!' Mags laughed.

Jimmy's face suffused with heat. He wasn't quite sure how to tell Mags, so he hesitated for a moment.

'Go on, lad. Spit it out!' she urged.

'I... I think I might be getting married!' There, he'd said it now, come hell or high water. The statement was out of his mouth and left hanging in the air like the aroma of something that couldn't quite be detected. The sort of aroma where folk might ask when a cake was in the oven: 'Is that cinnamon or nutmeg I can smell?' But when the answer came, it was neither, totally different to what the person who asked the question expected to hear.

'Married?' said Mags, holding the palm of her hand to her chest as though wounded in some way. 'But I thought we'd already discussed this, Jimmy. You're too young to get married right now. You were going to wait a couple of years to save up enough money to set you both up.' She narrowed her eyes for a moment. 'Hey, you've not got Enid pregnant, have you?'

Alys looked at her mother with wide eyes and then asked, 'What's pregnant mean?'

'Never you mind. I'll tell you when you're twenty-one!' quipped Mags.

Jimmy shook his head. 'No, there's nothing like that going on. It's just that Mrs Baxter doesn't like the idea of Enid sleeping alone at the shop, particularly after what happened with that man pretending to be Mr Baxter's son worming his way in and stealing money from them. It's made her consider the shop's security. I offered to live in with Enid, but Mrs Baxter won't hear of such a thing. She said folk will talk.'

Mags nodded. 'Well, she's right there. When me and Elgan were living over the brush for a time, some folk at China took against me and refused to even look my way for a long while. Once we were wed it was a different matter though; they accepted me then. But seriously, Jimmy, are you doing the right thing in getting wed? Enid could always move in here with us if you don't mind kipping on the old couch again.'

Jimmy shook his head. 'I would do that if it made things easier, but Mrs Baxter doesn't want the shop left unoccupied overnight.'

'If she doesn't want that to happen, then maybe she ought to move back home!' said Mags as her chin jutted out in defiance. She was obviously miffed that the woman should suggest marriage as a prospect to Jimmy just to sort out someone staying at the shop.

'To be honest, I think she likes living with her sister-in-law; they're company for one another, and besides the change of scenery seems to be doing her some good.'

'I'll not deny that,' said Mags. 'But to ask you to marry Enid just to keep the girl company is preposterous!'

Jimmy inclined his head and then he looked up to face Mags. 'Er, she didn't suggest it; I did and then she got all excited about it. The words were out of my mouth before I'd properly thought it through. In any case, I haven't even spoken to Enid about this yet.'

'I've got an idea,' Mags said, smiling. 'How about you kip over the shop and Enid live here? That would solve everything and that way you won't have to rush into marriage. You can take your time.'

Jimmy forced a smile. Mags was right of course, but part of him had wanted to wed right away. There were times lately when he was in Enid's presence alone that he felt that strong yearning to know her body and soul, to be as one with her. He excused himself and left the kitchen feeling thoroughly deflated, so desiring that 'married man's privilege' that people spoke of.

* * *

Mags was standing on the market stall feeling ravenous. She'd had little to eat that morning and now that customers were finally ebbing away, she guessed it might be the best time to pop over the road to a little shop that sold warm pies and hot drinks. She had just served her final customer of the morning and was about to go, leaving another stallholder to mind hers, when she was approached by a smartly dressed man wearing a long coat and a bowler hat.

'Mrs Hughes?' the man enquired, tipping his hat towards her and then replacing it on his head.

Mags narrowed her gaze as she dropped a few coins into the small leather purse on a string around her neck. Safely tucking it out of sight beneath her blouse, she paused for a moment, deciding that the man looked decent enough before replying to him. 'Yes, that's me. Who wants to know?'

'I'm Mr Samuel, Polly's father...'

'Oh, I see,' said Mags, stiffening up, wondering what on earth the girl's father would want to see her for. 'But how can I help you? I haven't seen Polly in a long while. I tried my best to help your daughter by giving her a job and taking her in, we all did – Mrs O'Connell who ran this stall too – but she threw everything back in our faces by going back to that good-for-nothing husband of hers.'

Mr Samuel's face reddened. 'I know,' he said softly. 'A lot of it is my fault as I took her husband's side when she came to visit me with your Jimmy. But I did learn my lesson and I was in touch with her after that. I've been a silly old fool.' He shook his head and Mags could see a sadness behind the man's eyes.

Giving him the benefit of the doubt, she asked, 'So, are you still in touch with Polly?'

'No. I was hoping you might be and that you might know where she is?'

'I'm sorry I don't, Mr Samuel.' She bit her bottom lip, deliberating on whether she ought to tell him what Elgan had said recently, what he'd seen. But then again that might hurt the man. Honesty was supposedly the best policy, so she threw caution to the wind. 'Actually, my husband saw Polly just last week.'

'Oh yes?' said the man, brightening.

Mags sighed. 'But when he saw her, she was being thrown out of a pub at the lower end of the high street, the Star Inn.'

'I know of it. But what on earth was she doing in a place like that?'

'I've no idea but as Elgan put it, she appeared like a bag of rags, dishevelled and she was in the company of a much older gent.'

'Oh?' Mr Samuel's forehead furrowed into a frown. 'That doesn't sound like anyone I'd know. All the men at the chapel abstain from alcohol apart from the odd glass in moderation. I wonder what she was up to.'

'No idea,' said Mags, huffing out a breath. She didn't want to be the one to tell him his daughter might be involved in prostitution; he could discover that for himself if he began a little detective work. Thinking of which, if she mentioned Sergeant Cranbourne then the man might have a word with him. 'You could try calling to the police station, Mr Samuel. See if the sergeant knows anything about her whereabouts.'

Mr Samuel nodded. 'That's a good idea. Thank you for your help, Mrs Hughes. If you hear of anything, will you please let me know?'

'Of course.' She handed him a notepad she used to calculate customers' bills along with a pencil. 'Write your address down in my book and I'll let you know if she turns up.'

Hopefully, there'd be no need for any of that as Sergeant Cranbourne would fill the fellow in on any necessary details, but she felt she had to show willing.

When the man had departed, heading off in the direction of the police station in Graham Street, Mags realised that she no longer had an appetite to eat anything. Polly was such a concern to everyone. No matter how let down Mags felt by the young woman, she could never turn her away. It was a shame it was Elgan who had seen her being booted out of that pub and not herself, as she'd have taken the time to talk to her. To get her to tell her what she was doing and where she was residing right now. But she couldn't blame Elgan; he hardly knew Polly even though they'd been under the same roof for a few weeks.

* * *

Before Mrs Baxter left to stay with her sister-in-law in Aberdare again, Jimmy reassured the woman that while he'd be moving in above the shop, Enid would not; she'd be taking his bed at Mrs O'Connell's house instead. The woman seemed happy enough with that arrangement and if she was disappointed that Jimmy had put off his plans to marry Enid, she wasn't saying so. Enid, of course, knew nothing about any of this as Jimmy hadn't got around to speaking to her.

Still, Jimmy realised he'd need to avoid being left alone somewhere like this with Enid to keep his desires at bay until they wed. So it was quite out of the blue when he had locked up the cobbler shop for the night and was about to bolt the back door to retire for bed when there was a persistent hammering on it. Startled, wondering if Polly's husband was there, he cried out, 'Who is it?'

'It's me, Polly!' called the voice on the other side of the door. 'I've come to pick up the things I left behind, my clothing and such.'

Relief flooded through him as he unlocked it to see her standing there. There was no sign of her looking like 'a bag of rags' as Elgan had described. She looked quite clean, presentable and attractive. He inhaled as she brushed past him and stepped inside the premises. He wondered if she'd been drinking alcohol but all he sniffed was the pleasant aroma of perfume. Polly's appearance was different to how he remembered – her dark hair was nicely coiffed into a neat chignon on top of her head instead of being loose on her shoulders, making her appear stylish and somewhat sophisticated for her age. Her clothing appeared well cut and he wondered if her matching dress and jacket were purchased from the Arden Brothers' Fashion store, probably designed by that Bradbury bloke with Betsan's assistance.

'Hello, Polly,' he said, genuinely pleased to see her though baffled why she was calling at this late hour. 'You're looking good. Fallen on your feet, have you?'

'In a manner of speaking, yes.' She smiled. It was then he noticed she was wearing some kind of lipstick though it was not the garish kind that Elgan had described. Had he made a mistake, and it was only someone who looked like Polly he'd seen being thrown out of the pub?

Jimmy drew in a breath and let it out again. 'So, tell me then, where have you been this past couple of months? We've all been very concerned about you.'

'Do you have something to drink? I'm parched,' she said as she placed the palm of her hand on her throat, obviously not in any rush to tell him where she'd been and why she'd chosen now of all times to call to the shop. How did she know he'd be here alone?

'Yes. I can make you a cup of tea or coffee. I was just on my way to bed, mind you, but I can spare a half hour or so.'

'Oh, Jimmy, I hope you can spare me more than that,' she said, fluttering her eyelashes at him. 'And by drink, I meant something a little more adult.'

'Oh, I see,' he said. 'There were a couple of bottles left over after Mr Baxter's funeral as Mrs Baxter asked me to get some in for any callers to the house...' He turned to face her. 'You did hear he had passed away?'

'Yes, so sad.' She nodded. 'That's how I knew you'd be here alone. A customer who calls to the shop told me she'd popped in here one day to see Mrs Baxter and Harri explained she'd gone to Aberdare to stay for a while. I noticed the light on at this hour as I passed by so guessed if the woman was away, it must be you.' She followed him into the living room where he found a bottle of brandy on top of the sideboard and poured her a generous amount into a glass tumbler and then handed it to her. 'Aren't you going to join me?' She pouted.

'I don't usually drink alcohol,' he said, but looking at the disappointment on her face, he wondered what would be the harm in joining her, so he poured a small amount for himself and then they sat opposite one another at the hearth.

In the fireplace there were now just glowing embers of the roaring fire that had been going all day. Jimmy would stoke it up again early in the morning and add some lumps of coal to it to keep it going throughout the day. He had extra responsibilities here that he didn't have at Mrs O'Connell's house as the womenfolk there attended to the fire, feeding it all day long.

'So, what happened to you when you left here with your husband that day?'

'All went well for a while,' she said, sighing, 'but Gethin started up again, belting me.'

'But why didn't you come back to Mrs O'Connell's?' Jimmy asked with some alarm, raising his brow and shaking his head. To think of all Polly had been through with that brute.

Polly exhaled. 'I didn't feel I could, Jimmy. I felt as though I'd burnt all my bridges with Mags and Mrs O'Connell particularly after their kindness towards me, so I found myself wandering over to China and asked at the wash house if there were any jobs going there.'

Jimmy's eyes widened. 'So, they took you on there?'

'Yes, and I was given a small bed to sleep in. Some of the women doss down there, those of no fixed abode that is. I was desperate, Jimmy. I could think of nowhere else to go.'

'But if you've been working there, how come you're dressed so smartly?'

'I met a man,' she said, giving a wry chuckle. 'He asked me if I'd help him with his business and promised he'd pay me well and buy me some nice dresses.'

It was then it dawned on Jimmy that Polly was on the game. Though Mags had hinted at it to him, he'd thought maybe she was mistaken. The truth of it was, he didn't want to be reminded as it brought back a vision of what his own mother had got herself into. When she'd worked at that wash house, it put her in the path of some men who worked for the iron-works – managers and such. There had always been a rumour that the wash house was a front for a knocking shop of sorts. He remembered how quite suddenly, after living hand to mouth, the table was practically groaning with food, and there were new outfits and toys for him too. A widow on a washerwoman's wages alone wouldn't be able to afford such things. Of course, as a young lad, he didn't understand that.

Jimmy looked at Polly through new eyes. Whatever had happened to the young woman? Polly no longer seemed naïve or shy; there was now an alluring confidence about her that she'd not had before, and she seemed to be blossoming somehow. Who was he to judge though? He took a sip of his brandy and felt it warm him to the core. It was quite a pleasant sensation. Polly shifted around, straightening her posture as though holding court over him in some sort of regard. At this moment, she was the queen, and he, her royal subject. He watched hypnotically as Polly licked her lips. Her eyes seemed to be playing games with his and a stirring he'd not felt for her before came over him.

She removed her jacket, neatly folded it and placed it on the arm of the couch, making him become aware of her womanly curves.

She downed her drink. 'Any chance of another?' she asked, holding out her glass for him to fill.

'You are a naughty girl.' He laughed, but he did as told and then refilled his own glass, this time with a more generous measure.

For the following hour the conversation seemed to flow and so did the brandy. Polly patted the seat on the couch next to her. 'Why don't you come over here and sit beside me?' she said, her eyes sparkling.

Not wishing to be rude, he rose from his seat and sat beside her, inhaling that beautiful fragrance she was wearing. That was no cheap perfume common whores wore either; that was good stuff. He watched as her bosom seemed to swell before him as she took a deep breath in and exhaled as she closed her eyes, lost in her thoughts, and before he knew it his lips were hovering inches from hers.

Her eyes suddenly flicked open, and she pulled him towards her by the lapels of his shirt, their lips meeting as she parted them. He closed his eyes and groaned as he felt her take his hand and place it on top of her heaving bosom.

'Feels nice, doesn't it?'

'Yes,' he gasped.

'We could go upstairs to find the things I left behind, Jimmy...' she said breathlessly. 'That way we could make ourselves more comfortable.'

It was then Jimmy jolted back to his senses. What was he doing? And with Polly of all people. A little voice inside his head said, 'How could you do this to Enid? Shame on you, Jimmy Corcoran!'

Removing his hand from Polly's bosom as though it was too hot to handle like a glowing piece of coke from the embers of the fire, he pulled himself up to his feet and stood looming over her. 'We mustn't do this, Polly!' he said sharply.

Her face crumpled and her bottom lip quivered as though she was about to burst into tears. 'But why ever not, you liked me once?' she said croakily. 'And I've always fancied you, Jimmy. You knew that but you would never take any liberties with me, even though I longed for you to do so sometimes.' She shook her head.

'Is that why you came here tonight, Polly? To ply your trade with me? To lure me away from Enid?'

'No!' she yelled, standing now. 'It's because I love you, Jimmy!' she said, her features softening and her eyes shining. 'I always have. I only married Gethin as you didn't seem to want me. I thought at first you weren't that interested in girls but then that Enid came back into your life, and I saw the way you looked at her with such longing in your eyes as though she was someone so special to you. You never looked at me in that way, ever.' She began to sob uncontrollably and, quite naturally, he took her into his arms.

'There, there, Polly,' he said, patting her on the back. 'You really are an attractive young lady, especially now. But I can't have any sort of relationship in that sense with you as I plan to marry Enid. It's her I love not you. I've loved Enid since we were children.'

She looked up at him with glazed eyes. 'Then why did you start taking liberties with me on the couch then?' she yelled.

'No, I didn't!' he said firmly.

She stuck out her chin in defiance. 'Yes, you did! You touched my breast, and you kissed me on the lips too, and I bet if I hadn't mentioned taking things upstairs, you'd have gone further with me. I wish now I'd kept my mouth shut as then you'd have been mine. Once you'd tasted the fruits of my love, sampled their delights, you wouldn't want your virginal Enid any more!' She spat out the words as though they were poisonous grapes.

It was then Jimmy became aware of just how jealous Polly was of Enid, and of course, she had no idea that Enid was no longer a virgin either – she'd been violated though; she'd not given away her virginity to all and sundry. That was another reason he'd been prepared to wait for marriage as he realised that her being intimate with him, after what had occurred, might take some time.

'Go on, Jimmy! We could spend just one night together here, and no one need ever know,' pleaded Polly. 'In fact, I could call around here most nights for you to sample my wares and no one would be any the wiser. I won't tell your Enid.'

What might be an attractive proposition for some men sickened Jimmy. That Polly would give herself away so cheaply to him like that while expecting nothing whatsoever in return, save some attention in the moment of a sordid act, without any love or affection on his part. In some ways, in his book, that was worse than prostitution. At least his own mother had done it to survive, to put a roof over their heads, food in their bellies and clothing on their backs – that had been reason enough and he respected her for that.

A nerve twitched beneath his eye. 'Do you really value yourself so little that you'd come here every night for me to have carnal knowledge of you and I wouldn't even have to pay you a penny for it?'

She nodded slowly. 'I just want to make you happy, Jimmy. I know I could put a constant smile on your face.'

He'd no doubt in the moment of lust that she could but he wouldn't feel right about it. He'd be consumed by a deluge of guilt for doing something like that behind Enid's back. He pictured her face and how hurt she'd be. And even if Enid didn't exist, he wasn't the type to use someone like that for his own ends, giving nothing whatsoever in return.

'I think you'd better go now,' he said firmly, grabbing Polly's jacket from the arm of the couch and thrusting it towards her. 'I'll just fetch that clothing Mrs Baxter bundled up for you and then you can go on your way,' he said as he made to leave the room.

Polly accepted her jacket as though it was the ultimate rejection. Shaking her head as she blinked away tears. 'I'm sorry, Jimmy. Please forgive me,' she said softly, seeming contrite now.

'We'll never speak of this ever again,' he said. 'Now shall I walk you back to the wash house after I fetch your stuff? It's late and it's too dark for you to walk alone.'

'Yes, please walk me home but I'm no longer staying at the wash house; I'm living at the home of that man I told you about.'

He nodded, feeling unsurprised by it. The man was probably her pimp. 'Does he know you're here now? Did he send you to lure me?'

'Oh no, never! He doesn't even know anything about you, Jimmy. I swear. He's gone to the pub for a couple of hours, so I took the opportunity to nip over here.'

Jimmy swallowed hard. 'And during that time was he expecting you to solicit men?'

She nodded. 'Yes, but not in the way you expect. I don't go around hiding in the shadows or on street corners accosting them. He arranges for men to call to his house. There are a few of us girls working for him. He treats us well and buys us nice clothing in return. It's better than facing Gethin's fists any day...'

'I can see that, Polly. You do look smart, but that man isn't treating you well, is he? He's exploiting you,' he said, lifting her chin between his thumb and forefinger to peer into her eyes. He dropped his hands to his sides, awaiting her reply.

She nodded. 'I suppose so.' There was a wistful look in her eyes as though she realised it but thought she deserved nothing better for herself.

'Look, why don't I walk you back over to your parents' home in Georgetown? Your father called to see Mags at the stall the other day; he's very concerned about you.' He inclined his head to one side in a show of sympathy. All he wanted was for her to be happy and safe in life.

Polly's eyes widened. 'I can't go back home now. My parents would have a fit. I've besmirched the good family name. They'd never be able to hold their heads up in chapel ever again.'

Jimmy nodded with some understanding. 'At least think about things. You can't go on like this dodging your husband and living with a man who is literally living off what you're doing lying on your back. Sorry to be so crude, but that's how it is.' He watched with a sadness inside him as a tear coursed down Polly's cheek. She might have been his mother back in the day – a woman who saw no other option for herself in life – and he didn't want that for her, by damn he didn't. 'Put your jacket on as it'll be cold outside,' he said softly. 'I'll just get mine and your belongings and then I'll walk you home – wherever that is.'

'It's not too far from here; it's only Quarry Row. Leave me just before we get there, not for Spencer to see you should he come back from the pub before I arrive...'

He wondered if she'd even realised, she'd given the man's name away there. Who was this Spencer anyhow? But he just nodded and smiled at her. She did appear contrite now; he could see that. She'd humiliated herself tonight but in a way so had he.

As he locked the door behind them as they left the back of the property, both were unaware of someone hiding in the shadows.

20

The following morning, Jimmy was late rising from his bed. He supposed it was because he'd downed all that brandy last night with Polly; it had been such strong stuff that he was unused to. He had managed to get washed and dressed and a cup of tea and a piece of toast inside him before Harri came knocking on the front door.

Stifling a yawn as he allowed him access inside, he turned the CLOSED sign on the shop door to OPEN and, as he did so, Enid arrived. He smiled when he saw her and planted a kiss on her cheek, which caused Harri to flush with embarrassment. They weren't usually affectionate in front of the lad, but Jimmy was pensive this morning thinking of what he might have lost if he'd succumbed to Polly's demands on him. In the event, no real harm had been done as he'd seen Polly safely back to the house she was staying at in Quarry Row. He'd given her something to think about with regards to getting in touch with her parents again though.

He'd toyed with telling Enid what had occurred when they had a quiet moment together, but then he thought better of it in case she grew upset knowing that he'd kissed Polly like that. He did wonder if he hadn't had a couple of glasses of brandy whether that situation would even have occurred at all. But now in the hard, cold light of day he realised what a fool he'd been and how devastated Enid would be if she ever got to hear of it. Despite it all though, Polly had assured him she wouldn't be saying anything to anyone about the incident, and he believed her.

The morning seemed to fly by fast as the bell on the shop door kept tinkling until finally all quietened down, and he was just about to suggest they stop and close the shop for lunch when the bell tinkled yet again as the door flew open. Three sets of eyes were fixed on it as a man bounded in. No one had entered in such a manner before, apart from that time that so-called son of Mr Baxter's had threatened Jimmy with a knife, so understandably Jimmy was guarded.

Recognition dawned when he realised it was Gethin, who appeared to be stone-cold sober for once.

'All right then!' he shouted. 'What have you done with my wife?' He pushed past Enid and Jimmy, attempting to make his way through to the living quarters.

'You're wasting your time, man! No one's out there!' shouted Jimmy. 'Hey, come back here!' He honestly feared what the man might do as he appeared in such a temper, far angrier than he'd ever seen him before.

After a couple of minutes of Gethin shouting out Polly's name, thudding up and down the stairs and banging various doors, he returned to the shop floor. 'Right, where is she?' he demanded, glaring at Jimmy.

Jimmy shrugged his shoulders. 'How would I know?'

'Oh, you would know very well indeed, *Romeo*! I followed her here last night and saw you open the back door for her. I thought I'd bide my time and wait to see where she went afterwards. She was in here for over an hour and I followed you both to Quarry Row where I saw her step inside a house there. But I didn't knock as I realised who owns that house! A man who has his henchmen working for him!'

Jimmy's jaw slackened with shock as he caught Enid's baffled expression. What was he to say now? He decided to tell a part truth; he couldn't say she wasn't here if the man had seen her. 'S... she... er... that is, Polly did call here to see me, yes, you are correct.'

'But what did she want to see you for, Jimmy?' Enid drew nearer to him and blinked. 'You never told me about this.'

'I didn't want you to concern yourself, my sweet,' he said, looking at her while Harri stared in astonishment. 'She called here because she'd left her clothing and other personal items behind when she left here so abruptly that time he came knocking for her,' he growled at Gethin as he fixed his gaze on the man.

'He's lying! I'll tell you why Jimmy didn't tell you, lovely girl!' yelled Gethin. 'Because he's having a liaison with my wife, that's why! I peeped through the window and saw them together on the couch and from what I saw Jimmy was trying to get a leg over!'

Enid gasped.

'That's just not true, Enid,' said Jimmy, holding up the palms of his hands. 'It's true that she called here, and she asked me for some alcohol so we both had a drink together and then she...' he realised now how lame this would sound to Enid's ears but carried on regardless '...asked me to sit next to her on the couch...'

Enid's eyes enlarged and then she swallowed. 'Jimmy, please tell me the truth.' Then she glanced at Harri, as if realising this was too much for young ears to take in, and said to the boy, 'Harri, go and make us all a nice cup of tea; there's a good boy.' He nodded at her with a disconcerted look on his face, and then he left the three of them on the shop floor.

It was as if time stood still.

'Yes,' said Gethin, 'just what did you get up to with my wife on that couch back there?' He hiked a thumb in the direction of the living quarters.

Jimmy took a deep breath, then realised he had to come clean as it was evident that Gethin thought more had gone on than actually had. But he still needed to be careful as he didn't want the fact Polly was now a prostitute to come into the conversation. 'We, er, I admit we did share a kiss.' He felt his face flush.

'A kiss?' Enid's voice sounded croaky now. Her words seemed suspended in mid-air as though she couldn't believe quite what she was hearing from him.

Jimmy nodded and, swallowing, said, 'Yes, it was a kiss, nothing more than that.'

'You're not telling us the full truth though, are you?' yelled Gethin. 'I saw you fondling Polly's breast.'

Shamefaced, Jimmy nodded. 'I did, yes. But then I realised that what I was about to do was wrong and I thought of Enid and how it would hurt her, so I put an end to it.'

'You thought of me?' spat Enid as her eyes gleamed with anger. He'd never seen her so volatile. 'You thought of me? The only person you were thinking of there, Jimmy Corcoran, was yourself! I bet Polly was the one who put a stop to it!'

'No, you don't understand; it wasn't like that at all,' Jimmy protested.

'Oh yes, it was, lad,' said Gethin. 'You and she used to see one another until I came along and then she dropped you for me as she wanted a real man. You were a boy then but now you've matured so she's returned to see how you measure up against me!'

'That's not true,' said Jimmy. 'I never really thought of Polly in that way as my head was too full of Enid. I missed her so much.' He looked at Enid now with tears in his eyes to see she was shaking her head in disbelief.

'If Polly hadn't stopped you, you'd have taken her upstairs or on that couch!' shouted Gethin.

Enid, who was bubbling over with the build-up of anger, glared at Jimmy and threw something at him, which bounced off his chest, falling with a clink to the floor. He stooped to retrieve it to see it was the promise ring he'd bought for her.

'I'm returning that ring to you!' she yelled. 'You're no good, Jimmy Corcoran! And the ring is no good for me either as you can't keep your ruddy promises!' And then she turned, grabbed her jacket from the coat stand and headed for the shop door.

'Enid! Enid, come back! I can explain everything!' Jimmy shouted as he stood to make to go after her, but it was too late. The bell tinkled again as she slammed the door behind herself. He'd just have to speak to her tonight at Mrs O'Connell's. He couldn't chase after her, fearing leaving Harri alone in the shop with Gethin. No doubt the boy would be upset at all the shouting that had gone on; he was a sensitive sort.

Finally, and without another word, Gethin glared at Jimmy, shaking his head, and then he left the shop, leaving Jimmy feeling as though a whirlwind had suddenly entered his life, blowing over everything and everyone in its path.

* * *

'You've only got yourself to blame, Jimmy,' said Mags with little sympathy when Jimmy called around to the house later that evening.

'I know,' said Jimmy, shaking his head.

'But what came over you? You heard what Elgan said about Polly, so it's obvious she was going to be trouble what with her drinking an' all. And if anyone should know about that, I should as I had my problems with the demon drink for long enough.'

'I realise that,' said Jimmy, sighing. 'But in your case, you didn't solicit men for money!'

Mags's face reddened. Oh dear, had he touched a sore nerve?

'Well, no, granted I didn't get paid by men for any services offered but when I went off on a bender there were plenty of sorts who would have bought me drinks all night long and probably would have expected something in return, so what's the difference? Luckily for me, no one attacked me, and I was able to get away from them until Elgan found me again. I went off on a right bender after the twins were born and Gwendolyn and David had to take both mites into their care. I'm lucky to be reunited with them again. But I don't know if that was all drink. I think knowing what I know now that I might have had a sort of melancholia after pregnancy. Some women get that, you see. They feel they can't cope and end up feeling sad and crying. It seemed to go on for ages with me.' She shook her head sadly at the memory of it all, but then her eyes fixed on Jimmy. 'But we're not here to talk about me, are we? We're here to talk about you and what you're going to do about your relationship with Enid.'

'Is she upstairs in her bedroom?' Jimmy asked hopefully.

'No, she's not returned home as yet.'

'What?' Jimmy stood there open-mouthed.

'What's the matter? She might have gone shopping or something or is trying to scare you off after having a shock. Maybe she'll calm down and come home later on.'

Jimmy shook his head. 'No, Mags. Enid left the shop in a temper around lunchtime.' He glanced at the mantel clock. 'It's now a quarter past six. That means she's been missing for around six hours or so. Where can she have gone to?'

'Hang on, I've just thought of something,' said Mags, her voice having a note of alarm to it. He followed her as she left the living room and took the stairs to Enid's bedroom. With every step he took, a feeling of dread increased. Mags turned the doorknob then pushed open the door as Jimmy glanced at the neatly made bed, and then the woman flung the wardrobe door open.

She turned towards Jimmy. 'It's empty. Enid's wardrobe is empty,' she said in a trembling voice.

A sense of desolation filled Jimmy's heart. Then he slumped down on the bed. 'I've lost her again, Mags,' he said as he put his head in his hands and wept. He'd honestly thought, when she'd left the shop in a temper, he'd see her that evening to speak about things. He had no idea she'd have left the house too. Why didn't he use his head and leave Harri in charge so he could run after her? He could have caught up with her in minutes and maybe persuaded her to stay. He might have brought her back and spoken to her when Gethin had left the shop – for that man's presence, and what he had to say, made things sound far worse than they had been. What didn't help matters was the fact that he and Polly had once had a relationship of sorts, so it probably sounded to Enid as though Gethin had made a good point.

* * *

It was some time before Jimmy calmed down and was able to think clearly, realising that he had to find Enid at all costs or risk losing her yet again.

'First thing in the morning, I'm taking a trip to Cardiff, Mags. I'm guessing Enid must have gone back to Beechwood House to stay at her mother and father's apartment there.'

'But what about the shop, Jimmy? You can't just leave it, can you? You'd be letting Mrs Baxter down.'

'That may be so, Mags. But Enid is far more important to me.' He stroked his chin in contemplation. 'I could leave Harri there all day, I suppose. He can do minor repairs and take orders from people.'

'Oh, I don't know about that,' said Mags, shaking her head in disapproval. 'It might not be safe leaving a young lad unattended at the shop. The takings might get robbed or something if someone realises he's alone there all day. Now, I'll tell you what I'll do. I'll put off my sewing for the morning and open the shop for you until lunchtime; Harri can help me out. Then as Elgan has a quiet-ish day tomorrow, he can cover in the afternoon. That way no one is letting anyone down.'

Jimmy's heart swelled with love for Mags. She was such a stalwart person in his life. 'Thank you so much!' he said, hugging her to him and planting a kiss on her soft, powdered cheek. 'It'll only be for the day and, hopefully, if I can get Enid to listen, I'll bring her back home with me.'

'I know you will if you can get her to see sense. She's hurt right now.' She chewed on her bottom lip. 'Though...'

'Though what, Mags?'

'Though wouldn't it be better for you to wait a few days until Enid has calmed down?'

He shook his head vehemently. 'No, I don't reckon so. If I don't go after her, she won't realise how much I really love her.'

Mags nodded with understanding. 'Well, you take care now, Jimmy. What time do you want me at the shop in the morning?'

'Can you get here by half past seven so I can catch an early train to Cardiff?'

'Yes, of course. And you leave young Harri to me. I'll have him eating out of my hand. I'll ask Mrs O'Connell to make some jam tarts and scones for the lad; he'll love those. I'd make them myself, but she has a lighter touch than me.' She chuckled.

Jimmy smiled. It was well known that Mags, though not being the best baker in the world, was an adequate one, but Mrs O'Connell's baking was something else – it was in an entirely different realm!

* * *

The following morning, Jimmy arrived at Beechwood House and enquired if he might speak with Mr or Mrs Hardcastle. He figured he'd best not ask for Enid herself as she no longer worked there, and awkward questions might be asked of him. It was a good twenty minutes before he got to speak with Martha. Her husband had not been available as he'd taken the horse and cart to the marketplace to purchase some food supplies for the kitchen.

'And what on earth brings you here, Jimmy?' asked Martha, smiling, then her eyes took on a look of uncertainty. 'There's nothing wrong, is there? Is Mags all right?'

'Oh no, nothing like that. I, er, just wondered if Enid was here?'

They were both sitting at the kitchen table sharing a pot of tea that Betsy Appleton, the cook, had brewed up for them.

'Enid? But what would she be doing here? She's working with you at Baxter's the cobbler shop, isn't she?' Her forehead creased into a soft frown.

Jimmy inhaled, worrying now how best to explain the situation to the woman without discrediting himself or Polly, come to that.

Deciding to leave the girl out of it, blowing out a breath he said, 'It's something and nothing really. We had a little tiff over a silly disagreement yesterday and she walked out of the shop. I had expected her to return to Mrs O'Connell's place. She had told you she's now staying there, hadn't she?'

'Oh, yes,' said Martha, nodding. 'But didn't she arrive then?'

'No,' said Jimmy. 'Well, she did.'

'I don't understand?'

'What I mean is she walked out of the shop about lunchtime, and I expected her to be at home when I called after work, but she wasn't. Mags checked her room and discovered that all her clothing had gone from the wardrobe.'

'Oh, my goodness me!' Martha said, shaking her head. 'But where can she have got to, Jimmy?'

He felt panic-stricken now. 'I honestly don't know, as I hoped she'd be here with you. What about her friend, Connie? Is she still working here?'

Martha nodded. 'Yes, she's taken on the role of housekeeper these days...'

A shard of guilt coursed through Jimmy's veins at the thought – the reason Connie now held that position was because Enid had refused it, choosing to be close to him in Merthyr, but now he'd ruined all of that.

'Could you ask Connie if she's seen her then?' he asked hopefully.

'Yes, I'll go and find her right away. You stay here and finish your cuppa,' said Martha kindly as she rose from the table.

He watched her leave the kitchen, which was empty of staff right now, and he was glad of that as he felt dreadful that he didn't much feel like making small talk with folk. His eyes wandered around the large, empty whitewashed room with its plethora of oak cupboards and clear counter space with copper pots and pans suspended on hooks from a large wooden overhead hanger. He imagined how busy it might get at various times of the day as Cook stood over the old black stove and maids walked back and forth carrying serving dishes for the master of the house whenever he was entertaining guests.

Then a vision came to mind of what it must have been like for Enid working here. She had her family close by, and Betsy Appleton seemed a good sort and Connie had been a close friend for her, whom she'd shared a lot with both at the workhouse and here at the house. Now he felt guilty for tempting her away from the one place she'd felt safe.

Martha returned ten minutes later with a disconcerted expression on her face. 'No, Jimmy,' she said as she sat down. 'Enid's not been in touch with Connie either and she has no idea where she might have gone to.'

A wave of unease washed over him.

* * *

It seemed an age until Jimmy collected his thoughts. 'Are there any places around here that Enid was fond of?' he asked.

Martha placed her index finger on her chin as she gazed at the ceiling. 'Let me think now. She liked going shopping, of course, just browsing really. Sometimes she visited the library – that's not too far from here, but she enjoyed walking around the public gardens most of all – the official name is "Sophia Gardens"; they're named after Sophia Crichton-Stuart, Marchioness of Bute, who wanted to provide a public space for people. They're ever so pretty. You might try those for a start.'

'Thanks, Mrs Hardcastle. If you can write down some directions of how to get to these places, I'd be grateful.'

'Of course,' said Martha, nodding. 'I'll just fetch a pencil and some paper.'

As Jimmy waited for Martha to return, he noticed an attractive young woman approaching. She didn't look like the usual sort of staff one would expect to see working in the kitchen as she wore a long navy high-necked dress with a white collar with a silver chatelaine of keys dangling from her waist. Then he realised it must be the housekeeper, Connie.

'Hello, Jimmy.' She smiled, the set of keys clinking as she approached. 'I'm Connie O'Mara.' Her violet eyes twinkled warmly, and Jimmy felt comforted by hearing her sing-song Irish accent.

'Hello, Connie. I've heard a lot about you!'

'All good, I hope?' She chuckled.

'Oh, yes.' He nodded enthusiastically, then he frowned. 'You've heard why I'm here?'

'Yes, Mrs Hardcastle explained. But I can't understand Enid going off like that; it's just not in her nature. Now if it 'twere me, folk would under-stand that, as I've behaved like that myself a time or two, but Enid, never!' She shook her head.

'I'm afraid it's all my fault.' Jimmy explained to Connie what had happened between them.

'Aw, now then, don't be too hard on yerself, Jimmy,' she said, lightly touching his forearm. 'She's had a nasty shock 'tis all. She'll calm down.'

Jimmy nodded, hoping he wouldn't break down in front of the young woman. To focus his thoughts he said, 'Hopefully. Mrs Hardcastle has thought of a few places she might have gone to if she's come to Cardiff, that is – she's just gone to get something to write directions with.'

'Well, that's a start then,' said Connie in a reassuring tone of voice. 'Though there is one place you might call at that might have given her a bed for the night – she'd have had to sleep somewhere overnight even if it was on a park bench!'

Jimmy's heart slumped. He hadn't considered that. There was nowhere else in Merthyr she could have gone to as all her family were now in Cardiff. 'Where else were you thinking of?'

'The workhouse! It's where I ended up returning to at one point when I went missing from here. There's safety there, you see. Even though workhouses aren't exactly like home, it's the routine thing. I've even known of girls who have left there with good jobs to go to, but they've ended up returning as they couldn't settle to normal everyday life.'

'You don't think...'

'Good heavens no!' Connie shook her head. 'I don't think for a minute that Enid would want to sign herself back into that place for good, just as a stopgap maybe.'

'Well, I know all about what the workhouse regime is like,' said Jimmy. 'I was there for a spell myself as a young lad, but unfortunately, my experience of the place wasn't all that good.'

'The Merthyr spike?'

'Aye. The master and matron weren't the best there.'

'Yes, Enid did say. Master and Matron Finchley at the Cardiff one run a tight ship; they're firm but fair to the inmates so she'll have no bother if she's gone back there.'

'Thank you. I'll check it out after I've visited those other places Mrs Hardcastle mentioned.'

'Good,' said Connie, smiling again now.

Jimmy hoped the young woman was right as he couldn't bear losing Enid again.

* * *

After visiting the library and the gardens and seeing no sign of Enid whatsoever, he asked someone to direct him to the workhouse. The Cardiff workhouse, which was about a mile from the centre of Cardiff, had an imposing entrance block with a central clock tower. He gulped.

Even though this workhouse didn't look the same as the Merthyr one, it still evoked some memories for him and not all good ones at that.

He enquired with a porter at the gate if he might speak with Matron Finchley. He was in luck as the man directed him inside the building where he led him down a low, dark corridor, and then knocked on a door.

'Please enter!' came the clipped female voice on the other side.

The porter opened the door and popped his head into the room, briefly summarising the situation to Matron, giving Jimmy's full name and explaining he was after the whereabouts of Enid Hardcastle. Excusing himself, he looked at Jimmy and winked. 'I hope you find the young lady in question!'

Jimmy smiled at him, appreciating the man's concern and allowing him on to the premises to speak with Matron herself.

On hearing Enid's name, Matron was quick to allow Jimmy access inside the room and told him to sit the other side of her desk.

'So, you think Enid might have called here, do you, Mr Corcoran?'

Jimmy fixed his gaze on the woman. 'It's the only other place anyone can think of in this area where she might have headed for.'

Matron looked at him with some sympathy shining from her hazel-brown eyes. She shook her head. 'I'm afraid it's been a wasted journey for you. She hasn't shown up here at all. Indeed, I was under the impression she was settled now in Merthyr. She came to visit me before leaving Cardiff,' Matron said in an appreciative manner, making it obvious to Jimmy just how much the woman respected Enid and how highly she thought of her.

Jimmy let out a long, shuddering breath. 'I don't know what to do next,' he said in desperation, hoping the woman could think of somewhere Enid might have gone. Anywhere that gave him a lead to work on.

'You know,' said Matron kindly, 'we've had people go missing from here and they almost always show up somewhere at some point. How long has Enid been missing for?' Her forehead creased into a soft frown.

'Only since yesterday lunchtime.'

'That's not long at all.' Matron smiled. 'But if I were you, and she doesn't show up by this evening, then I would contact the police.'

'I suppose I could,' he said thoughtfully, though the mention of the police made his stomach lurch. Although he had a good relationship with Sergeant Cranbourne, in his experience any dealings with the police led to bad news. He thought of the night the sergeant had brought the news of his father's death to their door. His mother had been devastated. Then there had been her death too where the sergeant had woken him out of his sleep, and he'd been sent to stay with Thelma and Elgan while his mother's lifeless body had been pulled out of the River Taff. Then there were Elgan's dealings with the police himself and his gaol sentence. And more recently, that no-good imposter pretending to be Mr Baxter's son who had robbed the couple blind. No, any dealings with the police were most definitely not good news.

The rustling of paper caught his attention.

'Would you like a peppermint?' offered Matron as she held a pink candy-striped paper bag in front of his nose.

He nodded and smiled appreciatively as he took one. 'Thank you.'

Matron took one herself and they both sat in silence for a minute as they sucked their peppermints. How he had missed these; they were his favourite treats and he'd been saving up his money lately with a view to treating Enid to something special. Jimmy couldn't have ever imagined the matron at Merthyr offering him a peppermint.

Then finally, Matron Finchley said softly and with great warmth, 'You know Enid was very kind to me. She used to bring me a bag of these whenever she visited here.'

'She said the same thing about you being kind to her, Mrs Finchley,' said Jimmy. 'She thought highly of you.'

The woman blushed. 'That's good to know indeed. If I were you, I'd also contact the police in this area as well as the Merthyr ones, Jimmy.' She lifted her silver fountain pen from the table and scribbled down an address, then ripping the leaf she'd written on from her notepad, handed it to him. 'Here's the address of the police station. It's not too far away from here.'

'Thank you, Mrs Finchley,' he said, standing, and he slipped the piece of paper into his jacket pocket. 'You've been most helpful.'

The woman nodded approvingly, then stood to open the door for him. 'I wish you luck, Jimmy.' She smiled. Then touching him lightly on the forearm said, 'Please keep me informed if Enid shows up, won't you? And I'll do the same for you if Enid shows up here. How might I contact you if she does?'

'Thank you. You can write to Mr Baxter's Cobbler Shop on Merthyr high street, and it will get to me as I'm currently residing over the shop there,' he said.

As Jimmy walked away from the workhouse, he wondered if he'd ever set eyes on Enid again. He'd built up his hopes of finding out something from Matron even if Enid hadn't set foot in the place, but it was evident that she was just as baffled as he was.

At the front desk of the police station, he reported everything he'd told Mrs Finchley to a policeman. The constable didn't appear to be all that interested, especially when he explained that Enid had been a former inmate at the workhouse. Her working at Beechwood House and rising up the ranks held no interest for the man whatsoever. It seemed to Jimmy as though the constable thought it an everyday occurrence for young women to go missing in that area and maybe it was compared to Merthyr. In Cardiff there was a railway station, road and a seaport. It seemed to be a cosmopolitan sort of place where people went hither and thither. But he figured if that young man lost his girlfriend or wife in that manner then he'd feel desperate too.

21

When Jimmy arrived in Merthyr, tired and exhausted from his search for Enid, he thought he'd pop into Mrs O'Connell's house for something to eat before calling to the Merthyr Police Station.

'Any luck?' asked Mags as he came barrelling through the front door. She was stood halfway down the stairs as though she was just descending them as he entered.

Glancing up at her, he shook his head. "Fraid not.'

'You called to Beechwood House though?'

'Of course I did, and I searched around some places her mother said she liked to visit. That friend of hers, Connie, suggested I try the workhouse too in case she'd been looking for a bed for the night, but no luck there either. Though Matron told me to inform the Cardiff police about Enid's disappearance, which I did, and the Merthyr police, of course. I just came here for something to eat before calling to see Sergeant Cranbourne. That's if you don't mind, Mags?'

'That's a good idea,' she sympathised. 'You need to keep a sharp mind as you go about it all. When did you last eat anything?'

'Not since breakfast this morning. I was given a cup of tea at the big house but to be truthful, I've hardly had any appetite all day.'

'Well, you go and relax in the living room. The twins won't disturb

you as I've just put them to bed. There's a bowl of lamb cawl on the hob
I've kept for you. I'll slice some bread and bring it through for you on a
tray.'

It was most unusual for Mags to allow him to eat in the living room.
She usually insisted everyone ate at the kitchen table or the large dining
room table if they had guests, so he guessed the woman must be
concerned about him.

'Thanks, I'd appreciate that. Where's Elgan?'

'He's chatting to Mrs O'Connell in her living room. Seems that pair
have a lot in common since he's started doing the garden for her. If she
was my age and not old enough to be my mother, I'd be right jealous of
them getting their heads together!' She chuckled and then made her way
to the kitchen to dish up the stew for Jimmy.

He removed his jacket and threw it on the arm of the fireside chair,
then slumped down in it as he closed his eyes, inhaling a deep breath and
letting it out again. It was most odd that Enid hadn't turned up by now.
He'd really hoped she'd be with her family in Cardiff. She had no one
else in Merthyr to turn to... except! He'd forgotten all about Betsan, who
had recently moved back into her old house. Her father had been sent
home, declared fit and well by the workhouse doctor, reunited with his
young wife and new baby too.

Leaping out of the armchair, he ran to the kitchen where Mags was
busy stirring the cawl on the hob. As tempting as that delicious aroma
was there was somewhere else he needed to be.

'Better hang fire on that,' he said. 'I've got to go out for a moment!'

'What on earth!' yelled Mags as he slammed the door behind himself
and ran down the passageway to the front door.

* * *

Betsan wasn't at home when he knocked on her front door in Plymouth
Street.

'Oh, she'll be so sorry to have missed you, Jimmy,' said Elinor. 'Won't
you come inside and wait?'

He shook his head. 'Where might I find her?'

'She's working overtime tonight with Francis Bradbury at the factory. They're working on a new collection together,' she said with some pride in her voice. It seemed amusing to Jimmy that Elinor was now being a proper stepmother to Betsan instead of them being at loggerheads with one another. Previously the pair had seemed in competition for David Morgan's attention and affection. The man being admitted to the workhouse, and the birth of a baby, seemed to have finally cemented them all as a family.

'Thank you!' he yelled, and then he ran up the street in the direction of the factory.

When he arrived, all was in darkness except for a light on in one of the downstairs windows. Of course, most if not all of the staff would have gone home by now. It was the end of their working day unless they were toiling over a big order, and then, Betsan had told him, the workers would receive 'overtime payments'. It sounded to him from all she said that the Arden Brothers were firm but fair bosses.

He raised the door knocker and rapped loudly. Then, hearing muffled voices from inside, he waited patiently for the door to be opened to him.

There, on the other side, was a young man with shoulder-length hair, dressed up in a long brocade coat with a velvet collar. He had one of those tweaked-looking curled-up moustaches, a right dandy if ever there was one. That Bradbury fella!

'Hello?' He smiled warmly at Jimmy as if to ask, *Who are you and what is your business here?*

Jimmy cleared his throat. He'd made up his mind long since he wasn't going to like the fellow even though Betsan appeared to be in awe and think highly of him.

'I'm looking for Betsan Morgan and I've been told by a family member she's working here this evening.'

James Bradbury nodded, and he rubbed his chin thoughtfully. 'I suppose you'd better come in then. We're working on some new designs together. Who shall I say wants her?'

'It's Jimmy. Jimmy Corcoran.'

'Oh!' James Bradbury raised his brow. What was going on here? Had Betsan mentioned him to the man?

'You seem surprised?'

'Oh, it's not that at all!' Bradbury chuckled. 'It's just when Betsan used to describe you to me I always imagined some young barefoot urchin in an oversized flat cap!'

Jimmy stiffened. He didn't like the way that fellow was poking fun at him. 'Well, as you can see, I'm most definitely not that!' The throwaway remark offended his senses and caused his hackles to rise, putting him on his guard against the fellow.

'I can see that – of course that's what made me chuckle. It's just you're so grown up and manly looking, your appearance took me by surprise.'

Jimmy, understanding and relaxing now, grinned at the man. 'I suppose I have grown up a lot this past couple of years and, to tell you the truth, your initial description of me would have been correct a few years ago.'

'Please step inside,' said Bradbury, gesturing with a sweep of his hand.

Jimmy watched as the man closed the door behind him and then he followed him down a long corridor to an office, which must have been the room that he'd seen lit up from outside. As the man pushed the door open, the first thing that Jimmy noticed was Betsan seated on a stool at a large desk intently sketching a design on a large piece of white paper. She looked up as they entered.

'Jimmy!' she cried. 'What on earth are you doing here?' Then her forehead creased into a frown. 'There's nothing wrong, is there?'

'Oh, no!' He waved a hand of dismissal. 'Well, not in the sense you probably mean,' he said, drawing closer now as James excused himself from the room as if to allow the pair some privacy, and Jimmy was grateful for that.

She angled her head to one side before speaking softly. 'What is it, then?'

He huffed out a short breath. 'It's Enid. I was wondering if you've seen her lately. We had a bit of a falling-out. More an exchange of words really but she was upset by something I'd done. I haven't seen her since. She's been missing since around midday yesterday.' His voice sounded croaky now. 'I've even been to Cardiff to see if she went to stay with her parents, but she's not there.'

Betsan pursed her lips and nodded. 'I have seen her, actually.'

Jimmy felt as though his heart had stopped suddenly. 'You have?'

'Yes, she called to see me all upset yesterday afternoon but didn't tell me why she was so emotional; at least she didn't indicate it had anything to do with you.'

Mystified, Jimmy frowned. 'What did she tell you?'

'That she intended going to see Mr Clarkson.'

'Mr Clarkson?' Jimmy gulped. 'You mean actually returning to Hillside House after all that happened to her there?'

'Yes.' Betsan nodded slowly. 'Though why I have no idea. The reason she came to me was because she had no money on her and needed a cab to get to the house. So, I paid her cab fare and gave her a little extra.'

Jimmy shook his head. 'This isn't making any sense whatsoever. In the first place I can't understand why she would want to go anywhere near that house as it holds so many bad memories for her. And why would she be seeking Donald Clarkson? Our disagreement, if you can call it that, has nothing to do with the man!' He was feeling angry now that Enid would involve him in their business.

'Look, Jimmy,' said Betsan, 'the man has helped her in the past. Maybe she was desperate for some reason. It's hard for me to comment without knowing what has gone on.'

Jimmy nodded with understanding and then he explained what had occurred. 'I know I do share some of the blame there, but honestly, Betsan, Polly made a real play for me. It became evident after a while that she's on the game.'

'The game?' Betsan's eyes enlarged and then she swallowed hard. 'You mean she's involved in prostitution?'

Jimmy nodded. 'I really feel for the girl as the same thing happened to my own mother and I believe it's an occupation that led to her death.'

'So, you think Enid didn't believe you when you explained what happened that night?'

Jimmy shook his head. 'I don't think so – she threw that promise ring I bought her back at me.'

'No doubt she was very hurt to think you'd had that kiss with Polly

and the woman's husband turning up out of the blue accusing you probably made things twice as bad for you!'

'Yes, exactly. He made it sound as if far more had happened than actually had. I finally came to my senses and stopped what was happening as
Polly wanted me to take her to bed.'

Betsan bit her bottom lip. 'That isn't good, is it? I can't believe she'd be
behaving that way.'

'Nor can I, to be honest, but the behaviour of that brute of a husband
of hers probably forced her out on to the street, and she was too proud to
return to us or her parents' home. She's also drinking alcohol.'

Betsan nodded at him. 'It all fits, doesn't it?' She sighed deeply. 'I'm
sorry to hear what happened to you and Enid though, Jimmy. I realise
how much you care for her.'

With tears in his eyes, he swallowed a large lump in his throat. 'I do. I
always have...'

'Well, if I were you, I'd pay Mr Clarkson a visit to see if he knows of
her whereabouts.'

He blinked away the tears that were threatening to fall. Not wanting
to break down in front of the young woman, he nodded and forced a
smile. Then he turned and left the room where James Bradbury was
waiting outside in the corridor. As if realising Jimmy needed no small
talk, he led him back down the corridor and bid him a simple 'Good-
night!' before closing the door behind him.

22

Early the following morning, Jimmy donned his Sunday best and paid to take a hansom cab to the Clarkson residence, not intending to turn up on the horse and cart in his working gear like he'd done previously when he'd had dealings at the house – this time he wanted to make a good impression on one person only and that was Donald Clarkson himself. He was the one he most needed on his side to discover Enid's whereabouts.

Enid had explained to Jimmy how kind the man had been, securing a job for her in Cardiff and finally arranging for her to spend time at his sister's home in West Wales after her ordeal of giving evidence in that awful trial against Cornelius Sharpe and his associates. That's the sort of man he was, having Enid's best interests at heart, and that was good enough for Jimmy.

He thought the sensible thing to do as he had no prearranged appointment with the man was to knock on the kitchen door and ask Cook or one of the kitchen staff to fetch the housekeeper, Mrs Webster, so he might ask if it was possible to speak with Mr Clarkson on a matter of great importance. If the man was unavailable or did not wish to speak with him, then he could at least ask Cook if she knew of Enid's whereabouts as the woman had been very fond of her. He trusted Mrs Shrimpton as she'd spoken to him in the past.

Luck was on his side as, to his surprise, the housekeeper ushered him in quickly to speak with Mr Clarkson. 'I know he'll want to speak with you, Jimmy,' she said as she led him along the corridor in the direction of Mr Clarkson's study. Jimmy was taken aback by this; it was almost as though he were expected at the house. Surely questions needed to be asked first as to why he was there, but they were not, so he said nothing, just carried on following her past the rather imposing portraits that stared down at him from the walls.

One caught his eye. It was of a good-looking young man with dark hair that appeared to be slicked down with pomade. He wore a smart black jacket, white shirt and breeches, and a silver-grey cravat was neatly pinned at his throat. In his hand he held a black, shiny top hat and the other hand he had placed against a solid-looking chair. Behind him was a large French window with a view of a green mountain in the distance – no doubt the portrait had been painted here at this house. There was something about the man's eyes though that the artist had somehow caught with his brushwork. Although smart in appearance and dapper at that, his eyes told a different story. Those were steely, determined eyes. There was a feeling to Jimmy as though he was a man not to be messed with; it was then he realised as he'd stopped to stare at the portrait that it could only be one person.

The housekeeper suddenly stopped in her tracks and turned towards Jimmy as though realising he was no longer trailing behind her. 'That's the master's son, Anthony Clarkson. Now deceased,' she said curtly.

'I did wonder if it was him,' replied Jimmy as a shiver ran the length of his spine.

Although both were now silent, there was an understanding between them about the man and then the silence was broken as the housekeeper smiled at him and said, 'Not much further now; the master's study is through here!' She gestured with a sweep of her hand and then she opened a door that led into another corridor. She knocked on the first door they approached.

'Enter!' shouted the male voice inside.

The housekeeper turned the doorknob and, from the corridor, Jimmy could see a middle-aged, distinguished-looking man standing near the fireplace staring at him.

'Do come in,' he said warmly as the housekeeper sidestepped to allow Jimmy over the threshold. Then Mr Clarkson called over Jimmy's shoulder, 'Please fetch us both a pot of coffee, Mrs Webster.'

Mrs Webster nodded. No doubt the woman herself would summon one of the kitchen maids to do that as she'd have important work to see to elsewhere.

'Please take a seat,' said Mr Clarkson, gesturing to a leather sedan high-backed chair near the fireplace while he took an identical one opposite.

Jimmy smiled tentatively as he did the man's bidding. 'Thank you, Mr Clarkson.'

'Now then,' said the man, his blue eyes twinkling as he spoke, 'you're Jimmy Corcoran, Enid Hardcastle's young fellow?'

'That's correct,' said Jimmy, nodding, surprised that the man knew so much about him and Enid. 'I apologise for calling here unannounced, but Enid has gone missing. I've even been to Beechwood House in search of her...' Jimmy held his breath in the hope that what Betsan had said was correct and that he at least knew of her whereabouts.

'You won't find her there as she's here!' said Mr Clarkson.

Jimmy released a breath of relief. 'Actually staying here at this house?' His eyebrows shot up in surprise. 'But I can't see Enid staying here after everything...'

'You mean after everything that went on?'

'Well, yes. And what about Mrs Clarkson? She never took to Enid, did she?' He was beginning to feel this might be some kind of trick and maybe the man was lying to him for some reason. He watched as Mr Clarkson steepled his fingers over the small paunch on his stomach.

'Admittedly, some might find it hard to believe but my wife has changed so much since the death of our son. We both wish to make amends to Miss Hardcastle and other young women in the town...'

'Other young women?' Jimmy screwed up his features. What on earth did the man mean by that? 'I'm sorry, I'm not following you, Mr Clarkson.'

'There are women in Merthyr Tydfil, who – how shall I put this – have fallen from grace one way or another. It was after the trial of Cornelius Sharpe and his association with my son that made me think about this. Young and even middle-aged women in this town who fall upon hard times often drift into prostitution and, as a result, become used by men of a certain class...'

'You mean how someone like your son might have used them?'

Mr Clarkson sucked in what looked like a painful breath through his teeth and nodded, then he let it out again. He had a sad look in his eyes now, the colour seeming to have changed from blue to grey. 'Exactly that. So, recently I set up a foundation called "Friends of the Fallen" to help such women and girls.' Jimmy nodded. 'My wife, Dorothea, became involved recently as she wishes to make amends to such women, particularly after what happened to Enid as it was our own son who violated her so savagely.'

'That's all well and good,' said Jimmy, 'but it sounds to me as if you're saying Enid is no more than a prostitute herself!'

'No, you've got it all wrong, Jimmy!' Mr Clarkson had another look in his eyes now, one that spelled determination. 'We just wish to make amends to the women and girls who have no voices of their own. I've asked Enid to help as she was also involved in that big trial at Cardiff when her friend Connie had been forced into prostitution, as had a number of women and girls in that area.'

'Oh, I see,' said Jimmy, feeling calmer now. Things were finally making sense. He remembered what young Harri had said that time about a gentleman and a lady visiting the wash house in China in a fancy carriage. It must have been Mr Clarkson and his wife.

'I think Enid will be an asset to the foundation,' said Mr Clarkson, breaking into Jimmy's thoughts.

'So, Enid's agreed?' He quirked a surprised brow.

'Yes, she has. She called here on another matter yesterday to ask if I could help her find a hotel for the night as, the following morning, she intended catching the train to Cardiff to return to her parents and to stay at the apartment at Beechwood House, so I asked her then. I managed to talk her out of leaving Merthyr. Later, at her request, I took her in my coach to retrieve her property from Mrs O'Connell's house. I thought it in her best interests to keep her in Merthyr. When she stayed over here, I spoke to her about my idea for "Friends of the Fallen" and she's very keen to help out. I even persuaded her to speak to Dorothea and the women are now on acceptable terms with one another. It will take both of them time to trust the other though, which is under-standable.'

'But where is Enid now?' asked Jimmy as he made to stand.

'Please sit yourself down,' Mr Clarkson said, showing the palm of his hand. 'She won't be back for a while. She's gone with my wife in the coach to collect Polly from Quarry Row.'

'Polly?' Jimmy blinked. 'But how did you know about her?'

Mr Clarkson smiled. 'Enid told me what happened between you and why you had that disagreement, causing her to storm off like that.'

A hot flush swept over Jimmy's face, and he hoped the man wouldn't notice, but then a young maid knocked on the door and entered with a silver tray containing a coffee pot and cups, diverting his attention.

'Can you please pour, Milly?' said Mr Clarkson.

The young maid who looked no more than thirteen years old set down the tray on a small table between both men, dipped her knee and then poured the coffee. Then she excused herself and left the room, closing the door behind her.

Mr Clarkson studied Jimmy's face. 'You didn't think Enid would tell me such a thing, did you?'

'Well, no!' said Jimmy, mortified that Enid had told the man what had gone on with Polly. 'So, what are her plans? Do you think she'll return to the shop?'

'No! Definitely not!' said the man, raising his voice.

Jimmy blinked. 'Pardon?'

'It's not that she wants to leave you in the lurch, but she's fired up now to work for the foundation. Several churches and the local temperance movement are getting involved to help fallen and destitute females in the area. You must understand that this is very important and necessary work, Jimmy. We will be finding the women a safe haven and helping them to stay on the straight and narrow in life. It's worthwhile work.'

Jimmy nodded with understanding, relieved at least that Enid was safe, but whether she'd fully forgiven him was another matter.

Jimmy stayed for a while longer chatting to the man who explained to him that once Polly and some other women whom he described as 'The Unfortunates' were collected by Enid and his wife they would be taken to the safe haven he spoke of where he and several local businessmen would be paying for their upkeep. He did not give the address of the premises away as it was explained that it was a large house in the Merthyr area, the address of which would only be given out to those who needed to know. The idea behind it was that certain menfolk would not know where these women had disappeared to as the aim was to get the women back on the straight and narrow. Some were heavily into alcohol, as well as prostitution and thieving. Religious instruction from chapel ministers would be provided daily with the hope that most would give their lives to the Lord and turn away from the destructive path they'd been set upon.

Finally, Mr Clarkson spoke. 'Return home, Jimmy. I'm sure when the time is right Enid will come in search of you. For the time being, she is safe staying here and working for the foundation.'

Jimmy, though, did wonder whether Enid would be safe as surely some of those men, including people like Polly's husband and her pimp, could cause problems.

* * *

It was late that night when Enid came knocking on Mrs O'Connell's door, and Jimmy was awakened from his fitful sleep. There, stood on the doorstep with Mr Clarkson's coach and driver parked outside, was Enid.

'I'm so sorry,' she said breathlessly. 'May I come inside?'

'Of course,' said Jimmy, smiling tentatively as he led her into the house and into the living room where he turned on an oil lamp.

Enid removed her bonnet and took a seat near the fire, which was now only embers. Jimmy sat opposite her. 'I'm so sorry. I should never have doubted you, Jimmy.'

He nodded. Any woman might have doubted him the way things had transpired when Polly's husband had shown up at the shop making all sorts of accusations towards him. 'What changed your mind though?'

She drew in a deep, composing breath and let it go again. 'Believe it or not, it was Polly herself who convinced me of your innocence. When I delivered her to that safe house... I understand Mr Clarkson has told you about that?'

'Yes, he has.'

'She began to cry at my kindness towards her saying she didn't deserve my help after how she'd tried to seduce you that night. She explained how she'd arrived out of the blue at the shop as you were ready for bed and were only going to allow her in for a short while, but she'd insisted you pour her a drink of brandy.' It was evident that the words were painful for her, as now her voice seemed shaky. She paused for a moment. 'She said she'd kissed you and placed your hand on her breast and for a moment you responded but then you came to your senses and told her to leave, telling her that it was me you loved not her!' Tears streamed down both of Enid's cheeks now.

'Here,' said Jimmy, standing as he held out both his hands to help her from her seat. And before he knew it, she had risen and was in his arms once again and he was crying too. 'I never want anyone to come between us ever again,' he said as he placed a kiss on the top of her head.

She looked up at him through glazed eyes and nodded. 'No one ever will.'

'Enid,' he said breathlessly. 'We must get married and soon. I don't care what anyone says. Mags or anyone. Though I would like to seek your parents' permission first, particularly your father's.'

She nodded eagerly. 'Shall we go to see them about it on Sunday?'

'Yes,' he said brightly, feeling elated now. 'Hang on a moment...'

She looked baffled at him as he left the room and then a couple of minutes later returned.

'Close your eyes and hold out your left hand,' he instructed.

She did as told and then he slipped the promise ring he'd bought for her back on it.

'Oh, Jimmy!' And she was crying again.

'I don't have enough money to buy you that engagement ring I promised but, by next month, I hope to slip a wedding ring on that finger,' he said, drawing her close to him. 'I'll ask Mrs Baxter if we can move into the living quarters over the shop after the wedding like she'd suggested we do,' he said, smiling.

'But what about my work with those unfortunate women? I can't stop that just because I'm marrying you?' she asked as her forehead creased into a soft frown as though the matter had only just occurred to her.

Jimmy lifted her chin with his thumb and forefinger to gaze into her eyes as he smiled at her. 'And you shan't have to, Enid. I realise that your work with those poor women must continue as it means so much to you.' Then he hugged her tightly to his chest, relieved that before long they would be united in marriage as two would become one at long last.

EPILOGUE
ONE MONTH LATER

Jimmy gazed adoringly at his new wife as they both stood before the altar. He had never seen Enid look as breathtakingly beautiful as she did right now. A feeling of love and extreme pride that she was his new bride swept over him. It was as if the congregation did not exist for that moment in time. All he saw was himself placing a gold band on her finger and he was aware of the minister saying, 'I now pronounce you man and wife!'

In the distance, he heard several gasps and someone saying, 'At long last!' Jimmy had no idea who had uttered the words, but the way Enid turned to look behind her, he guessed they were spoken by her mother. Then his new bride turned back towards him and smiled.

The organist struck up the strains of Mendelssohn's 'Wedding March' and, before he knew it, they were gliding back up the aisle in the direction of the chapel's double doors as people either side of the aisle nodded and smiled at the pair. Of course, Jimmy realised, most had their eyes fixed on Enid in that beautiful gown she wore, not him. The groom rarely got that kind of attention. Mrs Baxter had insisted on paying for the materials for it, which was a mix of light pink taffeta silk and white Belgian lace. Mags and Betsan had both worked on the gown for hours together until its completion. Betsan had designed it and cut out the pattern and

Mags had sewn it on the Singer treadle sewing machine that had made so many gowns by her sister Gwendolyn's hand over the years.

Mags, Elgan and Mrs O'Connell sat in the front pew as representatives of 'Jimmy's family' and as he and his bride passed them, Mags winked at him. He could imagine her thinking, *Haven't you done well for yourself, lad?*

Jimmy noticed Enid give a little wave to someone on the bride's side of the congregation and by the young woman's dark hair, eyes and swarthy complexion, he guessed it was Maria, whom she had once shared a room with at Hillside House. He was so pleased that both had reunited. Mr and Mrs Clarkson were guests of honour at the wedding, and they'd insisted on paying for the reception at a fine local hotel afterwards.

Arthur Hardcastle had proudly not so long since walked Enid down the aisle with his head held high. Before leaving Merthyr for Cardiff, he'd been a broken man. He'd regained his pride at last, forgoing his love of alcohol and gambling, and now worked hard at Beechwood House to provide for his family. Alys had been a flower girl and Aled a page boy and both walked either side of Betsan as she was their bridesmaid along with Enid's sister, Iris. It was good to see David Morgan and Elinor in the congregation with young Isobelle too. And seated behind them, with big beaming smiles on their faces, were Connie and Mrs Finchley who had travelled all the way from Cardiff.

As they emerged through the double doors of the chapel, Jimmy became aware of Mrs Baxter and her sister-in-law headed towards them, obviously having slipped outside to speak with them first.

'I wanted to catch you both before everyone comes out and showers you with rice!' Mrs Baxter smiled. 'I just want you to have this,' she said, pushing a brown envelope into Jimmy's hand. He exchanged baffled glances with Enid and then fixed his gaze back on the woman. 'But what is this?'

'Open it,' urged Mrs Baxter with her hands clasped together as though in prayer.

Jimmy opened the envelope carefully to see some sort of document, which read 'Cobbler Shop, High Street Merthyr Tydfil' on it in neat copperplate handwriting.

His forehead creased into a soft frown as he shook his head. 'I don't understand, Mrs Baxter?'

Mrs Baxter was beaming now. 'They're the deeds to the shop. I've been to see a solicitor and I'm giving the shop and the living accommodation that goes with it to you now, Jimmy. For you and your beautiful bride.'

'But don't you want to make a living from it any more?' asked Jimmy incredulously.

The woman shook her head. Then looking at her sister-in-law said, 'I'm quite happy living with Cissie at her home in Aberdare. We're good company for one another. My Josiah has left me well provided for financially as he earned a decent living from the shop over the years and also rented out properties to folk. It's what he'd want for you; I know that.'

'I don't know what to say,' said Jimmy as he gasped.

'You could try saying "thank you"!' murmured Enid.

Jimmy nodded approvingly. 'Of course.' Then he looked at Mrs Baxter and, stepping forward, pecked a kiss on the elderly lady's soft cheek. 'Thank you, Mrs Baxter.' He glanced at the sky. 'And you too, Mr Baxter!'

'You've been so good to us both.' The woman smiled.

There was no time to say anything else as the next thing Jimmy and Enid knew they were surrounded by wedding guests and being showered with handfuls of rice. They were about to step into an exciting future together, knowing that all that really mattered was their love for one another. And as Jimmy lowered his head to plant a kiss on Enid's lips, he realised to love her and be loved by the woman he'd just married was what he desired most of all in life.

* * *

MORE FROM LYNETTE REES

Another beautifully emotional historical saga from Lynette Rees, *The Workhouse Girl*, is available to order now here:

https://mybook.to/TheWorkhouseGirlBackAd

ABOUT THE AUTHOR

Lynette Rees lives in Wales and has been writing since she was a child. She enjoys the freedom of writing in a variety of genres including: crime fiction and contemporary romance, though her first love is historical fiction. When she's not writing, or even when she is writing, Lynette enjoys a glass of wine and the odd piece of chocolate as she creates stories where the characters guide her hand. She honestly has no idea how a story will turn out until the characters tell their own tales in their own unique ways.

Sign up to Lynette Rees' mailing list here for news, competitions and updates on future books.

Visit Lynette's website: www.lynetterees.wordpress.com

Follow Lynette on social media:

facebook.com/authorlynetterees
x.com/LynetteReeso
instagram.com/booksbylynetterees7
bookbub.com/authors/lynette-rees

ALSO BY LYNETTE REES

Sixpence Stories

Introducing Sixpence Stories!

Discover page-turning historical novels from your favourite authors, meet new friends and be transported back in time.

Join our book club
Facebook group

https://bit.ly/SixpenceGroup

Sign up to our
newsletter

https://bit.ly/SixpenceNews

Boldwood

Boldwood Books is an award-winning fiction publishing company seeking out the best stories from around the world.

Find out more at www.boldwoodbooks.com

Join our reader community for brilliant books, competitions and offers!

Follow us
@BoldwoodBooks
@TheBoldBookClub

Sign up to our weekly deals newsletter

https://bit.ly/BoldwoodBNewsletter

www.ingramcontent.com/pod-product-compliance
Ingram Content Group UK Ltd.
Pitfield, Milton Keynes, MK11 3LW, UK
UKHW020322040225
454637UK00001B/10

9 781805 490197